New York Times and *USA TODAY* Bestselling Author

MAGGIE SHAYNE

USA TODAY Bestselling Authors
LINDA WINSTEAD JONES
DAY LECLAIRE

The HEART of
WINTER

HARLEQUIN®

TORONTO • NEW YORK • LONDON
AMSTERDAM • PARIS • SYDNEY • HAMBURG
STOCKHOLM • ATHENS • TOKYO • MILAN • MADRID
PRAGUE • WARSAW • BUDAPEST • AUCKLAND

ISBN-13: 978-0-373-83758-8

THE HEART OF WINTER

Copyright © 2011 by Harlequin Books S.A.

The publisher acknowledges the copyright holders of the individual works as follows:

THE TOUGHEST GIRL IN TOWN
Copyright © 2011 by Margaret Benson

RESOLUTION
Copyright © 2011 by Linda Winstead Jones

MYSTERY LOVER
Copyright © 2011 by Day Totton Smith

CONTENTS

THE TOUGHEST GIRL IN TOWN

New York Times and *USA TODAY*
bestselling author Maggie Shayne

Dear Reader,

There's nothing colder than a heart without love, and that's the way I approached the theme of this anthology, *The Heart of Winter*.

In my story, I play with my theory that in life, it is what we believe about ourselves that determines who we are. I give a lot of advice— I actually write an advice column on the side. And often the words I offer are the same ones I'll offer here, and the truth I try to depict in this story.

You know that woman you're always thinking you wish you could be? (She's slender; I wish I could be like that. She's so smart; I wish I could be like that. She's so successful, happy, beautiful, bubbly, enthusiastic, energized...fill in the blank.) You know all those things you're always regretting not being? Well, stop regretting and just be those things.

Just be the person you wish you were. You might be faking it when you begin, but keep at it. A belief is just a thought you keep on thinking, and what you believe about yourself really does become what you are. So improve those beliefs. And then live them. And you, too, could be "The Toughest Girl in Town."

Maggie Shayne

CHAPTER ONE

"My walk home from the train after work at night *always* takes me past groups of those slathering dogs, but this was the first time one broke away from the pack to follow me."

Rodney Foster, Melinda Terwilliger's best friend and part-time therapist, nodded. He was always nodding during their "sessions." He was only a grad student, but his father was one of the most brilliant minds in psychotherapy, and Rodney was planning to follow in his father's footsteps.

Melinda didn't mind being his lab rat, really. Their sessions were informal, helpful and free. And, most important, she trusted him.

"When did you first become aware the thug was following you?" he asked.

Melinda's muscles tensed as she felt transported back to the events of a few days earlier. "I felt his eyes on me. I know he turned his head to watch me as I walked quickly past, and there was some kind of warning bell going off in my head, telling me something was up. But I didn't know what to do, or whether to trust it." She felt like an idiot now for having ignored what, in hindsight, seemed so obvious.

"Not surprising," Rodney said. "You know, the instinctive awareness of danger is something animals have, particularly in the wild. There's no reason to assume we humans don't have similar senses. I happen to believe we do, but we bury them in things like reason and logic and even good manners. Often, to our own detriment."

"That's exactly what I did." She nodded slowly as she recalled the incident. "I didn't turn around, didn't look back, but I heard his footsteps behind me, and I *knew* he was following me. A cold shiver rushed up my spine, just like people always say it does. I felt it so palpably that I wanted to slap it away. No, no, that's not what I wanted to do. I wanted to break into a dead run. Everything in me told me to run. I had to fight *not to*."

"At least you know your instincts were working. You just weren't listening to them."

"I will next time, that's for sure."

"There you go, something positive came from this."

"You and your positive thinking," she muttered.

Rodney shrugged his skinny shoulders in a distinctly feminine way. "It works for me. But back to you. Why do you think you didn't want to let yourself run, Melinda?"

She shrugged. "I guess I thought I'd look like an idiot."

"To whom? The thug? Why did you care?"

"I don't know."

"And yet, you didn't run. You basically put your chronic worry about what other people think of you, your constant need to please others, to be liked and approved of by them, ahead of your own well-being."

She pursed her lips as he touched on her most sensitive issue. "I—I quickened my pace, though."

He sighed, but didn't press her on what he called her Doormat Tendencies. "And then what happened?"

She drew in a nasal breath and caught a whiff of her own perfume, tender-scented sweat pea. It gave her little comfort. She even smelled like a 'fraidy cat, she thought miserably. Why couldn't she be strong and tough and self-assured the way some women were?

"He quickened his pace, too," she said. "And there was a dark alley up ahead, the last one before my duplex. The one that always gives me the worst case of goose bumps when I walk past it after dark. I just knew he was going to yank me into that alley when I got close enough. So I started to cross the street. That's when he grabbed me."

"Stop right there," Rodney interrupted. "Answer quickly, without thinking first. What did you *feel* when he grabbed you?"

"Panic, of course."

"Surprise? Now try to answer honestly."

She frowned. "No. No, I was expecting it by then."

He nodded. "I think you've been expecting it for months. Ever since those thugs moved into that house on the corner."

"They're ruining the neighborhood. It used to be so nice, but now...you just see those four who live there, lurking around all the time. Looking like gang members or something. The fat one, the skinny one and the heroin twins."

He smiled a little. "That's a great nickname for the two females. It fits them."

"I just know they're dealing drugs out of that house, what with the lowlife scumbags that are in and out of there at all hours of the night. More and more of them are hanging around longer. They don't seem to have jobs or lives or, God forbid, bathtubs. They just stand around, taking up space in the streets and making the neighbors nervous. You know Mr. Peabody's coffee shop was robbed last week?"

"I know."

"Broad daylight, guy in a stocking mask, waving a gun around. Got away with eighty-seven bucks. Probably went straight to that drug den and spent it, too."

"Did your guy have a gun? Your mugger?"

She shook her head, refocusing. "He had a knife. I felt it pressing into my side. He said not to make a sound, and I didn't. I just stood there and let him take my purse. I already had my keys in my hand, but he got everything else. And I just let him take it."

"Given the circumstances, that was probably the smartest thing to do, Melinda."

She shook her head. "After it was all over—after I unfroze enough to look around me and he was gone and I was alone—I realized there was a tear in my coat. From that knife. He'd pressed it hard enough to tear my coat, and he could have torn my flesh just as easily. It was like my body suddenly snapped back to life. I broke into a run and didn't stop again until I was behind my own door."

"That's the fight-or-flight response."

"Well, why was it so slow in coming?"

Rodney frowned.

"Why does *my* fight-or-flight response only kick in *after* my 'deer caught in headlights' response gets finished? Why couldn't I have broken into a run *before* I passively handed over my credit cards?"

"Because that's what you expected yourself to do. Look, hon, we've been having these sessions for almost a year now, and all your problems are just new versions of the same basic story. You're a doormat. You're a victim. This is just the blown-up version of the same tale."

"Oh, come on, getting mugged isn't the same as—"

"As what? Doing your colleagues' work for them without pay? Letting your sister drive your car while you take the train and make the payments? Loaning money to every ex-boyfriend who asks even though you know you'll never get it back? How is this different? Tell me? This guy didn't know it, but he didn't even need that knife. All he had to do was tell you he needed your purse and you'd have handed it over."

"I would not!" she denied.

"You're a sucker, Melinda. You are taken advantage of constantly because you expect to be. And, I believe, because you think people won't like you if you say no to them."

"I don't—" She drew a breath, sighed. "I do. You're right, I do that. Maybe not to the degree you say, but yeah. Why, though? Why am I so weak?"

"Because you believe you are."

She rolled her eyes and sat up. She'd been lying on her own sofa, as if she were in some clichéd shrink's office, telling Rodney about her latest drama. And instead of helping her, or telling her how to get stronger or at least how to feel better about being the victim of a violent crime, he'd gone off on his usual tangent about her creating her own experiences. *If she really wanted to change, she would do so. She must be getting some kind of gratification from being used, or she would put a stop to it.* If she let him keep going, he'd get onto the flimsiness of reality as we believe it to be and quantum physics and dead cats in boxes.

That was where he usually lost her. "I'm going to make some more herbal tea," she said, to distract him. "You want some?"

Rodney sighed loudly. "Sure." Then he was quiet for a long moment as she padded past him in her socked feet and headed to the tiny kitchen to put a kettle on the four-burner range. When he spoke again, he was on an entirely new track. "How are things going with the new math teacher?"

"Going?" She didn't know what he meant. There was nothing going whatsoever. Just because she got goose bumps and a little queasy feeling in her belly every time

Matt MacGuire flashed his to-die-for dimples in her direction, didn't mean anything. She never should have mentioned the new math teacher to her busybody, well-meaning friend. "I haven't even met the man yet. Why on earth do you ask?"

"Because you're attracted to him."

"So?"

"So, I suggested you go up and introduce yourself, ask him out to lunch. Have you done that?"

She was very glad he couldn't see her face just then. It heated at the very thought. "I'm not one of those aggressive, make-the-first-move types, and you know it. If he has any interest in me, he'll let me know when he's ready."

"Shoot, how's he supposed to know there's anything to be interested in? You make yourself practically invisible."

She rolled her eyes as she took cups from the cupboard. "I like being invisible."

"No, you don't. You're miserable. Constantly asking me to tell you how to change your life, and then never listening to the advice I give. What good can I do if you won't even listen to me?"

He stayed where he was, in the easy chair by the window. She leaned back away from the range, so she could see him through the doorway. It was snowing again, big fat flakes falling past the window at his back. "I thought the shrink was supposed to listen to the patient," she said.

"I'm more than a shrink. I'm your friend."

"Best friend." She said it softly, glancing back at him through the doorway. "Fine, I'm listening. Talk."

Rodney shrugged. "You keep telling me you want to stop being a doormat."

"I do."

"Then here's your answer. Stop being a doormat."

She paused with cups in her hands, waiting for the

punch line, but he was finished. "Geez, Rodney, if you're ever going to be a great shrink, you're going to have to do better than that. I am what I am."

"You are what you believe yourself to be."

"Bull." She broke eye contact, opened a cupboard, took down the glass dish that held a selection of organic, herbal teas, each in their own little compartment.

"How about if I prove it to you? How about that, huh?" Rodney asked.

She frowned, backing away from the cupboard again and turning to stare into the living room at him. "What do you mean?"

He drew a deep, nasal breath, then blew it out slowly. Finally, he got to his feet. He was tall. Way over six feet, probably six-three or -four. And he was scrawny as a scarecrow. His nose and Adam's apple were the two most prominent features one noticed on him, and as a result, his high school nickname had been Turkey. Turkey Foster. Go figure. No one called him Turkey now. He was a bona fide genius. She tended to forget that because they were such old friends.

"What are you thinking, Rodney?" she asked.

"Okay, it's drastic. But it could work. It could make you feel like a whole new woman, give you confidence, change your life entirely. Depending, of course, on how badly you really want to change. And how susceptible you are to hypnosis, of course."

"Hypnosis?" She felt her mouth split into a smile, but when he didn't return it, she knew he wasn't kidding. Not at all. He was dead serious. She poured hot water into the cups, set them on a tray with the tea bags, creamer and sugar bowl, and started for the living room with the lot of it.

Rodney kept talking the whole time, apparently on a

roll. "If I can make you believe that you are a woman who never lets anyone walk all over her, then you won't be. It's that simple. It's what I'm basing my thesis on. Will you let me try?"

Tilting her head to one side, she studied him. "You're going to turn me from a doormat into a barracuda, just by…what, dangling a pocket watch in front of my face?"

He shrugged. "Something like that. If you're game."

"You really believe in this stuff?"

"Doesn't matter if I do or not. It's what *you* believe that's going to matter here. If you believe it'll work, it'll work. If you believe what I tell you while you're under, you'll become it. Are you game?"

She lowered the tea tray onto her coffee table, considering things as she went. "You won't make me…mean or snotty, will you?"

"I promise."

"Are there any…you know, side effects?"

"Definitely. The people who are used to taking advantage of you are going to be damned disappointed to find they can't do it anymore. They might stop coming around. Or, they'll respect you as an equal, remain as a friend and go find a new doormat to take your place as their favorite enabler."

"I'm not an enabler."

"Yeah, you are. But you won't believe that until you see what happens when you stop."

She drew a deep breath. "I guess—I guess it wouldn't hurt to try."

"Great. How about tomorrow?"

"How about right now?"

He smiled at her, shaking his head. "First she's hesitant, then she's in a big, fat, hairy hurry," he said.

She shrugged. "If I don't get over being a big coward,

I'm going to have to move. This neighborhood is no place for weaklings. Annabelle, next door, chased that same herd of thugs down the sidewalk with a broom a week ago. Accused them of trying to steal her cat, Percy. And she's seventy-something."

"You could learn a lot from Annabelle." Rodney leaned forward to choose a tea bag and dropped it into his cup. "Tomorrow night, after work. My place, okay? Around seven?"

"Okay." She fixed her own tea, took a sip and burned her tongue.

"So what did the police say about your purse?"

"That I shouldn't walk home alone from the train station anymore."

"*That's* helpful." Rodney rolled his eyes. "You'll have to drive."

"I would, except that would mean leaving my car there all day, and God only knows who'd get after it. I'd come home to find it stripped."

"And your sister has it anyway," Rodney added. "Love the positive attitude, by the way. Just assume the worst-case scenario will always come to be. If you leave the car there, it'll get stripped. Why not assume it won't?"

"Because I'm not an idiot?" she tried.

"Because you're a pessimist," he corrected her.

"So maybe you can tweak that a bit tomorrow night, too."

He nodded and sipped and looked thoughtful. "Don't think you're going to emerge with a new personality. You won't. You'll just be a little more…confident. Sure of your-self. A little more aware of your own value and that of your time. A little less of a doormat and a little more positive. Okay?"

"Hell, what have I got to lose? Not a purse, that's for sure."

"You're just a ray of sunshine, aren't you, Melinda Terwilliger?"

"Indeed, I am. As you would be, after a day of teaching ninth-grade English."

"I'd like to be a fly on the wall in that classroom," he muttered.

She closed her eyes, already dreading the next day, the kids she had landed this semester were all but impossible to handle, much less teach. It was all she could do to keep them from destroying the classroom most days. Oh, she had one or two who really wanted to learn, and the rest were just…impossible.

"I have a headache," she said with a sigh. She leaned on the windowsill and looked at the sidewalks outside, and remembered when her neighborhood had been beautiful and safe and fun. Rosewood, New Jersey, was just far enough from Newark to be considered "outside" the city. It used to have all the pluses of big city life with none of the downsides. Now, it seemed that situation had reversed itself.

The snow on the sidewalk was dirty, the slush along the edges of the street, even dirtier. But it was that house on the corner that seemed, to Melinda, to have cast a dark shadow over the entire neighborhood. It used to be just an eyesore. Now it was a detriment to the entire community.

"Drink your tea," Rodney said. "I'm going to help. One more day of wimpdom, Miss Terwilliger. And after that, I can almost guarantee you, you'll feel like a whole new woman."

"Would your father approve of this little…experiment?"

"My father would probably call it practicing without a

license and have me banned from psychiatry forever," he said, shaking his head. "'A little bit of knowledge in the hands of a novice doctor is the most dangerous thing a patient can face.'" He quoted his father's words, mimicking his father's distinctive voice, which Rodney had down to perfection. It made Melinda laugh.

Dr. Foster was a by-the-book, straightlaced, ultraconservative psychiatrist and would probably disapprove strongly of the use of hypnosis at all, much less by an amateur.

But Rodney was brilliant, and besides, Melinda was sure he wouldn't be able to put her under anyway.

She couldn't have known just how wrong she was.

CHAPTER TWO

MELINDA WAS STANDING at the blackboard, writing down the homework assignment, when the spit-wad hit her right between the shoulder blades. She spun around fast, but the ninth graders gave nothing away. They sniggered and snorted and hid their faces, but there wasn't any one in particular who looked guiltier than the others.

"Who did that?" she asked.

They looked at each other. Several asked, "Did what?" innocently and nearly in unison.

"You know perfectly well what." She watched their faces, but they gave nothing away. And then the bell rang. They surged to their feet and stampeded toward the door as if it had been a fire alarm. "Wait!" she called. "The assignment's on the board. It's due tomorrow! If you didn't copy it down yet, then—"

They were gone. Just like that. The room was empty. She took a look around and saw a plastic straw on Danny O'Brian's desk. That little monster was the shooter, then. She should have known. He was usually the instigator of any trouble that erupted in her class, and in several other classes, as well. In fact, the only teacher who hadn't had trouble with him yet, according to the chatter in the teachers' lounge, was the gorgeous new math teacher, Mr. MacGuire, and she suspected young Danny was just trying to feel him out first.

Going to the principal would do no good whatsoever

because Danny's father golfed with the man and was on the school board besides. Which was, she imagined, the real source of the problem.

Oh, well. Only another month to go until the end of the semester. Not that the next semester was likely to be any better. Melinda sighed and went to the closet for her jacket and purse, and then she left her classroom, stopping by the office to grab the mail from her in-box on the way.

There was a large yellow envelope that shouldn't have been there, and when she peered inside, she saw a stack of essays. It was the stack the other ninth grade English teacher, Mary Blesser, was supposed to grade. There was a note on top, no doubt full of reasons why Mary couldn't get to them. It would include an insincere apology and an even more phony thank you. Mary probably didn't doubt Melinda would do her share of the work because she'd pulled this before—repeatedly. And Melinda *always* did Mary's share of the work. It was one of the things Rodney was constantly riding her about.

Sighing, Melinda tucked the envelope into her bag and headed for the exit. But she was waylaid by a tall male body stepping right into her path.

"Ms. Terwilliger?"

She looked up, and into the rich brown eyes of the handsomest male ever to hold sway over a classroom. Matthew MacGuire—the new guy. He taught algebra and had the female members of the staff acting more like their own students. Giggling and gossiping in the teachers' lounge, talking about how "hot" he was. While the male teachers sniped and found fault with his teaching style, his obvious lack of experience and, they claimed, skill.

He certainly had set the local grapevine alight. But why was he talking to *her?*

"You *are* Melinda Terwilliger, right? I didn't get the name wrong or—"

"No. I mean, yes. I'm her. Me. Ms. Terwilliger. Melinda." She bit her lip and lowered her eyes. Great. Impress the hot guy by chattering like a poorly trained spider monkey. Here he was, finally talking to her, and she was—

"I, um—I heard you were mugged last week," he said, cutting off her self-deprecating thoughts. "Are you all right?"

She had to give his words a moment to sink in, for her brain to translate them. He'd heard about the mugging. He was showing concern. Polite of him. But that was all. Just a colleague doing what he probably figured was expected of him. "I'm fine," she said. "Thank you for asking."

"I'm glad to hear that. Did they…get away with much?"

"No, not really. I had thirty or forty in cash, but aside from that, and losing my favorite bag, no harm done. I mean, other than having to spend an entire afternoon canceling credit cards, closing out accounts and opening new ones and retelling the tale to the local police—" She stopped herself there. "But I don't need to bore you with all of that."

"You're not boring me at all. I just thought maybe I could be of some help."

She lifted her brows. "I don't know how you could, but thank you for the thought." She started walking again, but to her surprise, he fell into step beside her.

"I could drive you home," he offered.

She looked up fast, then looked away just as quickly. Why would he want to drive her home? He was gorgeous and built like an athlete. And she was… Well, Annabelle, next door, called her "Twiggy" instead of Melinda. And it fit. She was skinny and she was plain. Her thick brown hair was usually in a ponytail, and her clothes consisted mostly of knee-length skirts and pastel cardigans. There was nothing special about her at all. Why would he—?

"Melinda?" he prompted.

He called her by her first name, and she felt as if he'd touched her instead. Her blood pressure kicked up several notches and her palms grew damp. "Oh. Sorry, I was... um, no. Actually, I'm meeting my best friend, Rodney, at the train station, so—"

"Oh. Okay. Well, if you'd like a ride tomorrow night, or anytime, just let me know. You live out in Rosewood, don't you?"

She was stunned. Tongue-tied. He knew where she lived. "Yes." When he waited for her to elaborate, she tried. "It's nowhere as nice a neighborhood as this one, but living here costs more than teaching here pays, so—"

"I don't know, I think Rosewood's pretty nice."

He not only knew where she lived, he knew her neighborhood. "It used to be," she said.

He nodded. "Well, anytime you want a ride home, just say the word, okay?"

She tipped her head to one side, frowning deeply. "Thanks. That's really nice of you."

He shrugged, flashing those delicious dimples with his smile. It made her knees go weak. "It's a chance to get to know you better. I've been waiting for one of those. See you tomorrow, Melinda."

"Uh...yeah. See you." He was gone by the time she completed her rapier-sharp reply. God, she was a lost cause, wasn't she? Why would he want to get to know *her*? Was he *blind*?

Sighing, she puzzled over this odd turn of events all the way to the train. She spotted an empty seat and headed for it. She was just about to sit down when an overweight college kid with a serious acne problem beat her to the spot.

He slid into the seat so suddenly that Melinda nearly sat on his lap. Then he smiled at her when she shot him a look of surprise.

Creep.

The ride went on and on. He got off two stops before she did, and she was able, finally, to get off her feet. Her legs hadn't even had a chance to stop aching, though, when her stop was announced. She hefted the heavy shoulder bag once more, and wondered if she would be brave enough to walk home alone ever again.

Maybe she would take Mr. MacGuire up on his offer. Tonight, at least, it wasn't necessary. Rodney was waiting at her stop.

She smiled her relief at the sight of him. "You didn't have to do this," she said. "But I'm really glad you did. Did you bring your car, or are we walking back to my place?"

"We're going to *my* place," he said. "We have a date, remember?"

"For you to tinker with my brain, right?"

"For me to help you get in touch with your own inner strength," he said. "You'll thank me later. Come on, my car's in the parking lot."

An hour later, Melinda was ensconced in Rodney's comfortable duplex, five blocks from her own place. His neighborhood was a hotbed of liberal-minded, starving artists, most of whom were gay, bi, transgendered or experimenting. She loved it there, but found it slightly too urban feeling. Her own little community had an ever so slightly more suburban feel. Or at least, it used to.

"Are you comfortable?" Rodney asked.

"Very." She was sitting on a giant-sized pillow on the floor. It was stuffed with rice and lavender, he'd told her, and it felt as good as it smelled. Her eyes were closed, and her mind, very relaxed. The tea he'd given her had helped with that. And so had the Xanax she'd taken just before. Her doctor had given her a very small supply, to help her deal with post-traumatic stress right after the mugging. But she wasn't going to tell Rodney that. Let him think *he* was responsible for the mellow state of mind.

"Good. Are you relaxed?"

"Utterly."

He moved, and she felt something on her shoulders. Oh, it was heavy and warm, a pillow stuffed with more herbs that he must have heated up in the microwave.

"Now listen," he said softly. "Here's how this is going to work. I'm going to talk you into a deeper and deeper state of relaxation. And then I'm going to help you to realize what a strong, powerful woman you are. You're going to go back in your mind, and you're going to remember why and when you let your power be taken from you. You'll remember exactly when you started letting people take advantage of you and, more important, you'll know why it happened. While you're under, we're going to take that power back, and when you wake up, you'll feel amazing."

"But different, right?" She thinned her lips, unsure how comfortable she was letting him play around with her mind.

"Not different so much as better. This won't change your personality, honey, it'll just restore the part you lost along the way. You'll see. It'll be fine."

She nodded slowly. "Okay. Okay."

"Good. Then let's begin."

And Rodney began talking. She didn't really recall all of what he said, because the Xanax was kicking in and she was *really* relaxed. But soon she felt just as if she were floating on a soft, dark cloud, and she followed her friend's voice back, back into her past, to find the confident, sure-of-herself Melinda she used to be, according to Rodney, although she personally didn't ever remember being more than just a doormat. After a while, she wasn't aware of much of anything. She knew he was still talking to her, and that she was responding, but she felt as if someone else was speaking for her, while the real her had retreated so far away that she could barely hear the conversation anymore.

After a while, Rodney said, "Perfect."

"Perfect," she repeated softly.

Then there was a loud ringing sound that jarred her, and Rodney moved quickly into another room to make it stop. Vaguely she knew it was a phone. From far, far away she knew he had bolted to get it, so it wouldn't interrupt their session. Her ears heard him knock something to the floor in his haste, and then she felt that she was utterly alone.

Only, she wasn't. There were voices. And those voices were telling her about her past. The past she had forgotten. Sinking deeper once again, she listened.

"It's all true," a man was telling her. "Your memory of your work, your true calling, was erased when you left our organization—we couldn't let you quit, knowing the things you knew. You understand, don't you?"

"No," she whispered.

"You were a spy, a deep-cover Federal agent. You knew twenty-five ways to kill a man without a weapon."

"I *did?*"

"You were one of the best we ever trained. A black belt in five of the martial arts. An expert with any firearm we put in your hands. You know how to kill a man with a ballpoint pen, baby. You are the toughest, most fearless woman I've ever known. I was devastated when you decided to resign. But it was what you wanted to do. So…we did what *we* needed to do. We erased your past."

"Erased my past," she repeated softly.

"We took away your memory of your work for us. And since no one else ever knew your true identity anyway, no one thought too much about it. You stepped into the role that was originally just your cover. That of a docile, soft-spoken, mild-mannered journalist."

"A schoolteacher, you mean." Was her speech slightly slurred?

"You've lived that life for so long by now that it's easy for you to believe it's your real life, your real personality. Not just a cover anymore. But now—well, now you need to know the truth."

"Why?" She wanted to know.

"Why now?" someone else, not her, asked.

"Because now there's trouble, and you're the only one who can stop it. We need you to remember who you really are again. But you must tell no one. *No one.* Do you understand?"

"No," she said. "I don't understand at all."

"Don't understand what?" Rodney asked. She felt him leaning close to her. "Melinda?" He paused, and then he spoke softly to her. "Melinda, I need you to return now. You're climbing up a staircase, and with each step you take, you become more grounded in your own body, more awake, more alert. Take the first step and feel your head clearing. Take the second step and a deep breath with it."

He kept going, coaching her up seven steps, and then telling her to open her eyes.

She blinked, looked past him, saw a car commercial on the television screen and frowned hard at it.

Rodney turned, following her gaze. "Who turned that on?" Then he saw the remote, bent to pick it up off the floor. "Hell, I must have knocked it down when I ran to get the phone." He picked up the remote, clicked it and turned off the TV. Then he turned to her again. "I'm sorry, hon. It was my mother. She's really hard to get off the phone with. Do you want to start over?"

She blinked and looked at him. "What?"

"Do you want to start over?" He frowned. "Are you okay? You still look dazed. I would have thought between the phone ringing and the TV blaring you'd have lost your relaxed state entirely, but I think you're still a little blissed out."

She gave her head a shake. "I took a Xanax before we started. That's all. I'm fine."

He tipped his head to one side. "You sure?"

"Uh-uh."

"Well, we were about finished anyway."

"We were?"

"Yeah. You should be finding yourself feeling more confident in no time. But don't push it. Just wait, feel your way, see what happens."

She nodded again. "All right. I—um—I have to go home, though. I have—a lot of work to do."

"Yeah." He was still studying her. "I think you should have a bite to eat with me first. It'll ground you back in the real world faster than anything. How about a turkey on rye?"

She met his eyes as she got to her feet. "I want ham. On wheat. You have that?"

He frowned a little. "Hey, see that? Usually you'd have said whatever I was having was fine, whether it was what you wanted or not. That's good, Melinda!"

It was good. She rolled her eyes. "I must be a pretty lost cause if ordering a sandwich is some kind of a breakthrough."

"You are where you are." He went to the kitchen, leaving her alone again, and she stood there, reeling over what had just happened. Not that she'd managed to state her preference in sandwich meat. But what she had heard in her mind while she was under. God, could she *really* have a secret past she'd known nothing about? Still knew nothing about? Or almost nothing.

"Rodney?" she called.

"Mmm?" He remained in the kitchen. She heard him moving around, rattling plates and pouring something fizzy.

"When someone is hypnotized, is it possible for…repressed memories to come flooding back?"

Dead silence was her reply. And then he was in the doorway, staring at her. "Sure." He moved closer to her, stood in front of her. "People come out of hypnosis and suddenly know where they left their car keys. Crime victims sometimes recall details about the—hey, is that what happened? Did you remember something about the mugger?"

She lifted her eyes, met his. "Yeah. Yeah, that's what happened."

He nodded. "Then you should call the cops, that lieutenant who came out and investigated. He left you his card, didn't he? What was his name?"

"Conlan. And yeah, I have his number somewhere."

"You should call, let him know right away."

"So you think I should trust the memory, then? It couldn't be a false one?"

"No reason to think it would be," he told her, seemingly relieved. He moved back into the kitchen, still talking. "There was no one feeding you anything, so whatever rose to the surface came from within your mind. I'd trust it."

He returned a second later, bearing a tray with sandwiches and soft drinks on ice. She smiled and thanked him and did all the right things, but inside, her mind was whirling. She was some kind of covert operative. She was some kind of kick-ass chick—the kind she'd always so admired and secretly believed she could never, ever be.

But now that the doors of her memory had opened, even just that little crack, it seemed a whole lot more was flooding into her. No details, no memories. But feelings. Feelings she'd seldom had. She felt her chest expand and her spine straighten as it occurred to her that she probably could have put that mugger into the hospital, had she wanted to. She probably could have killed him.

He was very lucky she hadn't realized it at the time, then, wasn't he?

"You're awfully quiet," Rodney said softly. "Are you okay?"

"It's the Xanax. I'm fine. I just need to get home and get a good night's sleep, that's all."

"I'll drive you as soon as we finish our snack."

She tilted her head to one side as it hit her that she would prefer to walk. Odd, wasn't it? Only a few hours ago the thought of walking home in the dark would have terrified her. Now she felt almost…eager to test herself and find out if this new thing bubbling up inside of her was real. Like trying on a new outfit to see how it fit. She wanted to try this on. This person she had been.

Really? Was she really believing this?

Yes, she realized. Yes, she was. It was real. She had lived it. She felt it right to her toes. "Thank you, Rodney," she whispered. "God, I think you were right. I think this session is going to change my life."

He smiled, but behind it, she thought he looked just the slightest bit worried.

CHAPTER THREE

MELINDA WENT TO SLEEP with the words she'd heard being spoken to her playing over and over again in her mind. And she awoke to the sound of the alarm clock's gentle chimes. Their volume increased incrementally. It was the most pleasant an alarm clock could possibly be.

In between, she'd slept oddly. Her night had swung between wild dreams and deep, heavy slumber. No wonder, she thought, because the dreams had been exhausting. She'd relived the mugging over and over, and each time, she had reacted differently. Once she had flipped the mugger over her shoulder and stomped on his throat. Once she had elbowed him in the rib cage, spun around and kicked him in the chin. Once she had fought off ten of him all at once, armed with a ballpoint pen that she wielded like a sword. And every single time, she had held on to her purse and walked away unscathed. And empowered. Damn, she'd felt a full foot taller in those dreams.

Smiling a little, she got out of bed and went through her ordinary morning rituals of showering and shaving her legs—but she stopped short afterward, as she eyed her reflection in the steamy bathroom mirror. "I *look* like a wimp," she whispered. "I need a change. A drastic one." There were scissors in the cup on the back of the sink. She trimmed her plain brown hair every six weeks, without fail, to get any split ends that might have shown up since the last time.

But today, she thought, a little more was in order.

She knew how to cut hair. She'd cut her kid sister, Tracy's, their entire lives. Besides, what she had in mind wasn't all that difficult. She wiped the mirror with a towel, then picked up the comb and the scissors. As she snipped, and snipped and snipped, she wondered if she had any clothes that would suit her new look. She hoped so. Because she felt different, and the old things were no longer suitable. They wouldn't *fit* anymore.

By the time she finished, she had a short, spunky new haircut, with spikey bangs that made her eyes look bluer than they had ever looked before. She had forgotten the coppery highlights in her hair. They'd been hidden by the heavy, thick weight of her locks, but now they showed through as vividly as if she had added highlights.

She found a pair of leggings she'd bought on a whim and never worn, paired them with a long sweater and tall, fur-trimmed boots that she'd received as a Christmas gift two years ago and never even put on. She thought about trying her hand at some makeup, but the only stuff she had was years old, and besides, she had so little practice applying it that she didn't dare.

She was nearly out of time, anyway.

Sighing and taking a last look in the mirror, she decided she liked what she saw. It wasn't so much that she was changing back into this woman she had allegedly been before—the female superspy. It was more that, now that she knew what she had been, she wanted to test it a little. See how it felt to try on a little bit of that former persona. She still wasn't convinced that the newfound knowledge came from anyplace other than her own imagination. But unless she stretched a little bit, saw how it felt, she would never know.

And if this new look was the only change that her session

with Rodney ever brought about, she decided, then it had been worth the effort. She liked her new look.

She walked to the station to catch the train, and she watched for the man who'd taken her purse. She hadn't been able to identify him for Lieutenant Conlan—but she knew perfectly well who he was. It had been one of the thugs from the house on the corner, the fat one, and if she saw him, she intended to...to look him in the eye and let him know she knew what he had done.

Oooh, boy, that'll fix him, a sarcastic little voice within her said. But hey, for her, that was a big step!

Still, she didn't see him. Too early for his kind to be up and around, she supposed. Breathing a sigh of relief, she got on the train, headed for the only remaining empty seat, and spotted that same fellow who'd stolen her seat the night before. He stood an equal distance from the seat, in the opposite direction, and he was eyeing it, too. He started toward it.

Something inside of Melinda tensed up, like a cat preparing to pounce on an unsuspecting mouse. Did she dare put her newfound self-knowledge to the test?

What would it hurt to try?

She lunged forward and slid into the seat before the rude passenger could do so, even though it made her stomach tie itself in knots. She didn't want anyone to see her as rude or pushy or obnoxious or—

The pimply faced young man scowled at her and she felt herself begin to shrink like a delicate violet in the path of scorching sunlight. But then an older woman in the seat beside her leaned closer and said, loud enough for the jerk to hear, "Good for you! That brute almost knocked me off my walker last week, to take my seat. It's about time someone was woman enough to stand up to him."

The punk looked away, ashamed perhaps. And Melinda

felt herself grow, somehow. As though she was getting taller, only she knew it wasn't on the outside. It was on the inside. She felt a foreign sense of strength unfolding its iron petals over those of her shrinking violet. And it felt good.

She was eager to push herself just a little further as she walked from her train stop in the very suburban village of Sentinel, to the school building and into the office where she opened her satchel and took out the stack of still ungraded essays. Guilt tried to assault her, but from somewhere down deep inside her, a little voice asked her why she should feel guilty for not doing someone else's job.

It was a smooth, female voice, very much like her own, only more confident, firmer, louder, stronger. It didn't waver and was pitched a bit lower. She thought of it as the voice of her former self. Her inner kick-ass chick. "You're right," she whispered.

She slid the stack of essays into Mary Blesser's in-box, snapped her bag closed and turned to the secretary, who was just settling in at her desk. Melinda smiled and said, "Good morning, Sally," though again, her stomach was still churning at the notion of bucking the current that had carried her for so long.

Yet, she realized, that current had been tumbling her around at will, dashing her against rocks or rushing past her and eroding her spirit. Now, she thought, it was time to ride its waves instead of letting them ride her.

The secretary said, "Good morn—" and stopped mid-greeting as her head came up. Her eyes met Melinda's, then widened. "Wow! You look fantastic!"

Melinda lifted her brows. "Really? Thanks. I just...I decided it was time for a change."

"You're right, it was. I love it." Then she tipped her head to one side. "Did you do something to your eyes, too?"

"No. Not even makeup. I figured I'd take baby steps."

"Funny, I could have sworn. There's something different, Melinda. More than just the hair." She shrugged. "Anyway, it's a good change, whatever it is."

Odd. Did the burgeoning change in her actually *show?* How could that be? "Thanks," she said. "Who does Danny O'Brian have for homeroom?"

"MacGuire."

Melinda tried to school her features and not show her powerful reaction to his name. What was *he* going to think of the new her? He'd liked her just fine the way she was, if yesterday was any indication.

She swallowed hard, reminding herself that always acting based on what other people might think was one of the doormat tendencies she was trying to leave behind. Certainly her superspy alter ego wouldn't be worrying about what some math teacher thought of her new haircut, would she?

"Oh, the new guy?" she said, trying to sound as if she was only barely interested.

"Yeah, 221," Sally said. "Have you met him yet?"

"Yes, yes I have."

"Then you know. God, what a hunk, huh? If I were single…"

She pictured him in her mind's eye, his brown eyes, those Cary Grant dimples that etched deep into his face when he smiled. She heard herself whisper, "Fortunately, I am."

It was a cocky, confident thing to say, and for a moment, she was shocked to hear the words spill from her own lips. And a little embarrassed, too, but Sally seemed pleased as punch.

"You *go, girl!*" she said with a broad smile.

As Melinda turned to leave the office, Mary Blesser walked in and went straight to her in-box. She spotted the fat envelope there, called, "Thanks, Melinda. You're a gem."

And by *gem,* Melinda thought, she meant *sucker.* "Not anymore," Melinda replied. She felt the truth of those words right to her soul. Wow. The other woman frowned, clearly not understanding at all, but Mary didn't bother continuing the conversation. Instead, she opened the envelope, pulled out the stack of essays and started flipping through them while humming to herself.

The hum stopped abruptly, and she looked up fast. "These aren't graded."

"No. No, they're not." Melinda felt a surge of guilt rising up in her chest. Mary was going to be furious and would probably hate her for this.

The other woman was still blinking at Melinda in shock, noticing, Melinda thought, her changed appearance for the first time, when Sally, from the desk, said, "Gee, Mary. It looks like you're going to have to actually do the work you're paid for around here, doesn't it?"

Mary huffed loudly and then strode out of the office, clearly angry. But Sally let loose a snort of laughter as soon as the woman was out of earshot. Melinda looked at her, a question in her own eyes, and the secretary said, "You're finally learning to stand up for yourself. It's about time."

Melinda smiled wide. For once, it wasn't the weak, forced, false smile she'd grown used to bestowing. She really felt it this time. Apparently, everyone around her had seen her more clearly than she had seen herself. She'd been a victim long before that mugging. Rodney had been right about that. And she'd done it to herself. But maybe now that she was aware of who she *really* was, all of that would change.

She was still smiling when she got to room 221, and came face-to-face with Matthew MacGuire, who nearly mowed her down on his way out, then apologized as profusely as if he'd committed a crime. "Whoa, sorry!" He backed off, smiling down at her, but then his smile froze in place and he went as still as stone.

She forced herself to hold his gaze, wondering if he would approve of the change in her appearance or hate it.

His eyes flashed with something potent, then slid down to her boots and up to her newly sassy haircut again. "You look…wow. Amazing. Gorgeous. I mean—not that you didn't before, but this is…wow."

She didn't think he was pretending. She smiled, felt her face get warm, knew she was probably blushing. She wasn't used to compliments from men. Hell, she didn't think she'd ever received one before.

"Thanks. I wasn't sure what kind of reaction I would get. But so far, it's been fairly positive."

"You're not going to get anything else. Damn, lady."

She almost lowered her eyes and her head shyly, but that, she reminded herself, wasn't who she was anymore. So she lifted her head, looking him right in the eyes. "Thanks," she said.

The late bell rang, and students dashed around. Then, like magic, the halls were empty and just as silent as the space between the two of them.

"It's more than the hair. It's something about the bearing, the attitude. Hard to put a finger on."

"I suppose that makes sense."

"Does it?" He smiled. "I'd love to hear why."

She looked past him, leaning sideways to do so, and saw

that his classroom was full of students who were watching them curiously. He followed her gaze. "Oh. Right. Is there something I can do for you?"

"I need to speak to Danny O'Brian. Just for a moment."

He lifted his brows, then turned toward the students in the room at his back. "Daniel, could you come out here please?"

The kid took his time, but he came out. Cocky and smirking until he caught sight of her, and then he looked surprised and maybe a little bit uneasy. Melinda crooked a finger until he came closer, then she leaned in and said, "Do you know who I am?"

He frowned, and looked a little less confident. "Yeah. Why, did you forget?"

"No. As a matter of fact, I just remembered. Among other things, Mr. O'Brian, I'm the person who decides whether you end up taking my class all over again next year. And whether you spend your summer vacation sitting in a classroom instead of doing...whatever asinine garbage you generally do. I don't think that would be any more pleasant for you than it would be for me."

He blinked, maybe a little shaken, but not enough. Not yet. "My grades are good. You can't fail me if my grades are good." He turned to Matthew. "She can't do that, can she, Mr. MacGuire?"

"What? I'm sorry, I didn't hear a thing." He sent Melinda a wink, then went back to studying the attendance book in his hands.

Melinda snapped her fingers in front of the kid's face, bringing his eyes back to hers. "I'm the one who *gives* you the grades, Danny, and if you act up in my class one more time, your grades will drop and they'll drop *radically*. Do you understand?"

He stared at her. "You can't do that."

"Watch me."

She held his eyes, and she made hers deadly serious. Finally, he lowered his head, looking at his shoes.

"I'm done with your bullshit, Danny. If you plan to go running to your father, you go right ahead and do so. I have tenure. He has no power over me. I'll expect you to sit still and shut up for the forty-five minutes a day I am forced to bear your presence from now on. No more warnings, no more chances."

She waited, but he didn't reply. So she waited some more. Finally he nodded and said, "Okay."

"Good. You can go now," she told him.

He scurried away, just the way she usually did from any sort of confrontation. The voice inside her whispered, *Congratulations. You intimidated a fifteen-year-old.*

She sighed, feeling a little bit mean. He was just a kid. Then again, she'd needed to do something. Her entire class was following his lead and sliding out of control. As he turned and slunk back to his desk, she heard a low, slow whistle from Matthew MacGuire. She looked up quickly. "I was too hard on him, wasn't I?"

"You were brilliant."

Her brows rose. "I was?"

"Sure. Hell, it's prison logic. Pick the biggest bully, kick his ass and no one bothers you for the rest of your stay."

"You're an expert on prison logic?"

He shot her a quick look, then averted his eyes. "All I know is what I see in the movies. But it seems to be a widely held belief. I just never thought of applying it to freshmen before."

"Unfortunately, no one saw me, er, kick his ass, as you put it. So it won't do much good."

"No one needs to see. Kids talk, and even if they didn't,

they'll notice his attitude toward you has undergone a radical change. I predict any problems you've been having with Danny and his cohorts will vanish in short order."

"I hope you're right." She nodded toward his room. "You'd better get in there or you won't even have time to take attendance."

"Yeah." He started to turn away, but turned back. "Do you mind if I pick your brain a little more? I could use some advice from someone who really knows this job."

She lifted her brows. "I wouldn't mind at all."

"Good. Um, lunch?"

She smiled. "I usually eat out by the fountain."

"Good. I'll see you there." He held her eyes for a moment longer than normal. As if he was stuck in her gaze or something. It was like a physical touch, and it sent a shiver of awareness right down her spine.

Then he tore his eyes away and ducked back into his classroom. She turned to hurry away toward her own. But the entire time she hustled through the hallways, she was fighting a sense of amazement. She'd only known about her past for a single night, and already her life was changing radically.

What a difference a little bit of knowledge could make. She smiled more widely as she entered her classroom, where wadded-up papers were sailing through the air and students were raising hell. Sweeping the room with her eyes, she said nothing, simply walked up to the chalkboard and wrote in giant letters, "ANY DISRUPTION OF MY CLASS BY ANYONE TODAY RESULTS IN A ZERO IN THE GRADEBOOK FOR THE ENTIRE QUARTER."

The classroom quieted as students read her message, frowning and whispering to one another.

"You have five minutes left of homeroom, and six hours left in your day. Unless you'd like to spend those six hours in detention, you will sit down and *shut up* for the remaining five minutes. Fair trade?"

They quieted. They sat. She moved behind her desk, flipped open her book, began taking attendance. Midway through, she caught her own reflection in the mirrorlike surface of the computer screen on her desk. It brought her up short.

She really *did* look different today, and it really was more than just the new hair or the different clothes.

She looked sure of herself. She looked confident. She looked…tough. And she liked it.

CHAPTER FOUR

THERE WAS SOMETHING FAMILIAR, she thought, about the man who walked beside her to the benches near the big fountain. Right now, that fountain was little more than a dry sculpture of a rearing Pegasus, wings outstretched, standing in the center of a frozen pool. The water was turned off for the winter. The park lay just across the street from the high school, beneath a blanket of snow, and, aside from the handful of skaters who took to the ice most weekends, it was usually abandoned this time of year.

Matthew paused near the bench, bending to brush the snow off so they could sit. "You like the outdoors, I take it."

She nodded. "Desperately. And I like being in a place where it's safe to *be* outdoors. My neighborhood just isn't that way anymore."

"That's really sad," he said. "I'm sorry to hear that."

"It won't be that way forever." She could see her breath, but the sun was warm on her face and she loved it. She was smiling as she sat, and Matthew seemed to get his eyes stuck on her face for a moment. But then he turned to sit down beside her.

He unzipped the insulated lunch bag he'd been carrying, and removed a sandwich from a plastic bag. "So tell me about yourself, Melinda Terwilliger," he said, after taking a big bite of the delicious-looking roast beef.

She had packed her usual lunch of yogurt and fruit—an

apple today—but she was regretting it now. It seemed as though a tough, kick-ass chick such as she ought to be eating something a little more substantial. His question was making its way into her brain and she found herself searching longer than usual for an answer.

Eventually, he said, "Interesting."

"What is?" she asked.

"That you're having trouble answering. It's a pretty straightforward question."

"Normally, it would be. But today, telling you about myself is harder to do than you can probably imagine," she said.

"Why's that?"

She studied his face, searching his eyes, wondering why she wanted to talk to him about it. She ought to be cautious. She didn't know this man, after all. Just because she was attracted to him didn't mean he could be trusted. "I recently learned some things about my past that I had…suppressed, I guess. It seems to be changing everything about me."

"Really? That's fascinating." He looked at her as if he meant it.

He thought she was fascinating. Imagine that. But he was waiting for her to elaborate and she really couldn't. After all, it was a secret, one she needed to keep.

So she hedged. "The most I can tell you is that I'm currently in a state of flux. A transitional phase, of sorts."

"Like a caterpillar turning into a butterfly?" he asked.

"More like a chickadee turning into a red-tailed hawk, I think."

He lifted his brows, looking surprised, but he covered it quickly. "I guess that would explain a lot."

"Such as?"

"Well, the way you were with Danny O'Brian this morning, for example." He seemed to be choosing his words with care. "I had come to think of you as…timid. Quiet. But you were one hard-ass with him outside my room today."

"I've been letting him walk all over me," she said. "Been letting a lot of people do that. I'm done with that."

"Part of your…transformation?"

"Yeah. I'm still a little nervous about trying out my newfound toughness on those who *really* have it coming, though."

He frowned, tipping his head to one side. "Like who?"

She smiled. "Oh, I have a list."

He smiled back. "Do you now?"

"Yes. There's an ex-boyfriend who still owes me money."

"Excellent."

"My sister, who borrowed my car six months ago and hasn't so much as offered to make a payment."

"Good for you!"

"The thug who stole my purse."

He opened his mouth, closed it again and blinked at her. "What do you intend to do to him, exactly?"

She nodded. "I don't know. But I'm livid that I let him rob me. That I complied without even putting up a fight."

"That's what you're supposed to do, isn't it?"

Melinda shrugged. "No, I don't think so. I mean, I don't think it's what *I'm* supposed to do."

"Now, listen, Melinda, you know, learning to stand up for yourself, becoming strong and confident and deciding not to let yourself be taken advantage of, that's really good. I applaud it. But *strong* and *confident* are not synonymous with *reckless*."

She nodded. "It's not reckless if there's no risk."

He frowned. "So this thing you've discovered about yourself—is it that you're invulnerable?"

She averted her eyes from his dark, probing ones. "This mugging triggered something inside me. I think I have that thug to blame—or to thank—for these changes I'm undergoing right now. I think I'm figuring out who I am for the first time in my life." She lowered her head, smiled self-consciously. "Listen to me going on about all this. I'm sorry."

"No. You're on some kind of a journey, I can see that, and I find it fascinating. You're nothing like what I thought you were, Melinda."

"In what way?" she asked, wondering whether her new-found inner strength made her more appealing to hunky members of the opposite sex.

"You're deep, complex. You have layers to you that aren't apparent at first."

She tilted her head. She liked the way he was looking at her. But she'd given away enough about herself. She wanted him to reciprocate. "Tell me about you, Matthew," she said, using his first name even though it seemed like a bold thing to do. It felt good when she did it. "I take it you're new to teaching."

"Is it that obvious?"

She shook her head. "Not at all. I just assumed when you asked for advice—"

"Oh, right. Yeah, I'm new. This is my first job, as a matter of fact."

"So what did you do before this?"

He shrugged. "Lots of things. Nothing nearly as interesting as sitting here talking to you today."

"Now you're just flattering me."

"No, I'm not. And you didn't answer my question. What, exactly, do you intend to do to this…thug who took your purse?"

She shrugged. "I don't know. But I'm definitely going to do something."

"Are you sure that's a good idea?"

She lifted her brows, tipped her head and searched her heart. "It *feels* like a good idea. Someone's got to stand up to jerks like him. Otherwise, they just keep doing what they're doing. Right?"

"I guess. But shouldn't that someone be the police?"

"Probably. Sadly, they're not doing their jobs at all where my neighborhood is concerned. So…"

He frowned at her, but she switched her focus to her meal and the notions spinning around inside her mind. Could she really stand up to the jerk who'd mugged her? Maybe it was just a fantasy, but it sure was a pleasant one.

MATT HADN'T EXPECTED the docile, wallflower Melinda Terwilliger to be any problem at all. He'd thought he could handle her. Keep her out of the way and keep her alive. But now that he was getting to know her a bit, he realized she wasn't going to just roll over. There was a lot more to the soft-spoken schoolteacher than met the eye.

A lot more. Enough to intrigue him. Yeah, he was dying now to know more about her. But he had to keep his focus. He couldn't afford to lose focus right now.

How could he have known what a thorough distraction the pretty, quiet woman everyone described as a mouse would be? She was no mouse. She might just be a lioness in disguise.

MELINDA GOT OFF THE TRAIN at her usual stop, but nothing about tonight felt usual. She'd stood up to the rude little bastard on the train. She'd stood up to her colleague Mary Blesser, who had been taking advantage of her for the better part of three years now. And she had stood up to the most disruptive kid in her English class.

Amazingly, Danny O'Brian sat quietly through her class today, although the brooding and dark expression he wore told her the lull was likely only temporary. He was probably plotting ways to test her—see if she really meant what she'd said.

Oddly, she wasn't worried about it. She was finished letting him disrupt her class. It wasn't fair to the other students—the handful who wanted to learn.

She was feeling something else tonight, too. She was feeling...pretty. Attractive. Fascinating, even. All because of her lunch with Matthew MacGuire. His attention had been something new to her. No man had ever seemed so intrigued by her, so interested in what she had to say, so attentive. She found she liked that kind of attention. She liked it a lot.

He'd offered her a ride home again, but she'd turned him down. She wanted to test her wings a little bit more.

He would ask her again. The way he looked at her, she was certain of it. And when they walked back to the school after sharing that lunch in the snowy, pristine park, she'd felt the eyes of her colleagues on her. The women were jealous, and the men—admiring, at the least. All of them were surprised. All of them looked at Melinda with a new curiosity in their eyes, as if they had never truly seen her before.

And maybe they hadn't, because maybe she had never seen herself before.

Walking home from the train, her mind was on Matthew, more than it was on the nerve-racking gauntlet she had to run to reach her duplex. In fact, the mugging and the thugs who hung out in packs around her neighborhood were so far from her mind that when she saw her neighbor

Annabelle Johnson clinging to her big quilted handbag while an overweight jerk yanked on the other end, it took Melinda a second to realize what was happening. When she did, something rose up inside her. Something she'd never felt before—or maybe she'd felt it in that other life, the one she'd forgotten.

The fat punk yanked Annabelle's purse free, ripping its strap and probably yanking the poor old woman's shoulder out of its socket in the process. Then he spun around, running full bore toward Melinda.

She did not dive to the side to avoid being flattened. Her knee-jerk reaction was to find a weapon. She looked left, looked right, spotted a wastebasket on the sidewalk—a big wire mesh one, meant for the depositing of doggy droppings. There was no time to question her decision. She ran around the basket, kicked it over onto its side and then, with another well-placed push from her high-heeled boot, sent it rolling toward the man. He was running headlong, but looking over his shoulder at Annabelle, who was screaming at him to stop. Perfect. He faced front again, but couldn't stop in time. The rolling trash can hit him in the shins and blew his legs right out from under him. He flew over the top of it and hit the sidewalk face-first. The handbag arched through the air, landing several feet ahead of him.

Melinda walked past him to the handbag and picked it up. She looked behind her at the man as he pushed himself off the sidewalk. His chin and one cheek were scraped raw—sidewalk burn. She hoped that wasn't the only damage she'd done to the bastard.

He looked her right in the eyes. "You're gonna pay for that, lady."

"Oh, I paid in advance, last week, when you mugged me. Remember?" She shrugged. "I know how to kill a man with a ballpoint pen, pal. And I'm not going to let you get away with any more of your bullshit. Not in *my* neighborhood. It ends today. You and your friends in the drug den might as well pack up and leave. You're finished here."

She turned away, striding toward Annabelle, holding out the woman's bag and trying to ignore the powerful tremors that were making their way through her body. It was like an earthquake down deep, with shock waves radiating into her limbs. She fought not to let them show, even while wondering who the hell had just said those brave words to the criminal on the sidewalk. Not her, surely. They'd come from someone else—someone inside her. Someone she didn't even know.

Annabelle took the bag, blinking in stunned surprise. "Th-thanks, Twiggy. What the hell brought *that* on?"

Melinda shrugged. "I'm sick of being a victim, I guess. Are you okay?"

"Uh-huh. But you might not be." She nodded toward something.

Melinda turned to see that the fat guy had got up, brushed himself off and was striding toward her, his fists clenched at his sides. He was humiliated, and dangerous. Melinda held up her cell phone, pushed a button, then another, then another.

"I just took your picture, pal, and then I sent it to the cops. You want to see?"

She turned the phone toward him. "Camera adds ten pounds, they say."

"You're going to die, you scrawny little—"

But he stopped there, because several other people were gathering now on the sidewalk behind Melinda and Annabelle. Neighborhood people. There was Mr. Peabody waving his glossy, wooden walking stick menacingly. And

Olive Sparks, waddling her five-foot, two-hundred-pound way closer, a baseball bat in her hand. And several other residents of the block stood around, too. None young or buff or rugged. Most were retirement age or older. But they were all fed up.

Melinda smiled as the twenty-something fatso backed off and finally turned and ran, vanishing around a corner.

The neighbors broke into a smattering of halfhearted applause, and several clapped her on the shoulder or patted her on the head as they dispersed.

Annabelle wasn't so cheerful. She was scowling, in fact. "Are you out of your gourd, Twiggy? Do you know what those punks are gonna do to you now?"

Melinda shrugged. "What they'll *try* to do, you mean."

"Try, my wrinkly ass! You just painted a big old bull's-eye right on your forehead, Twiggy. Just make sure you ain't standin' near me when they show up."

With that, Annabelle turned and stomped away, muttering about the torn strap on her handbag and having to sew it and hoping they didn't firebomb the duplex or God only knew what else.

Sighing, Melinda followed, but kept her distance. She headed into her half of the two-family house, and Annabelle went into hers, slamming the door behind her. The last words Melinda heard were "Damn fool girl!"

Okay, Melinda thought as she yanked the mail from her box and entered her own living space. She tossed her bag onto the sofa and sank down beside it. Maybe Annabelle was right. Maybe she was teasing a killer dog, and setting herself up to be eaten by it.

She glanced down, wondering if she had made a terrible mistake and saw, right on top of her pile of mail, a tri-fold flyer advertising martial arts lessons at the gym right down the street.

Slowly, her lips pulled into a smile. Maybe, she thought, she ought to find some other ways to test her mettle. And to prepare, too. Just in case.

CHAPTER FIVE

TWO WEEKS LATER, MR. PEABODY had her coffee waiting when she stopped in on her way to the train, just as he had done every morning since "the incident," as her neighbors had begun calling it.

To her surprise, Matthew MacGuire sat at a booth in the diner, lifting a cup in greeting when she walked in.

"Morning, Melinda."

She felt warm inside at the sight of him. They'd been having lunch together every day at school for the past two weeks. And she'd eagerly, and somewhat proudly, told him about tripping the would-be mugger with a trash can.

Still, they hadn't yet seen each other outside school. Their lunches on the snowy park bench seemed to be the extent of their…relationship. And while he seemed attentive and eager for more, he never asked.

"Morning," she replied, pleased right to her toes to see him. She'd been wondering if he was truly interested in anything beyond friendship.

This, she thought, was definitely progress.

She slid into the booth opposite him. "What are you doing in my neighborhood this morning, Matthew?"

"I heard Delaney made bail."

The spark of attraction petered out. She went cold inside and felt her eyes widen before she reminded herself that she wasn't a frightened little thing anymore. She was tough. And she'd been feeling more and more as if that were true.

The fat mugger, Marvin Delaney, had been arrested and left to cool his heels in the city jail. Apparently, that was no longer the case.

Then she frowned. "When did he get out?" she asked, and then another thought occurred to her. "And who told you?"

"He was released last night," he said, answering one question and not the other. "Have you had any trouble?"

"No." Then she blinked. "But there was a strange car parked a few yards from my house last night. I don't know how long it remained. Every time I looked it was still there, but when I got up this morning, it was gone."

He lowered his head. "That was me."

She lifted her brows, sucking in a sharp breath.

"I just figured… I just wanted to make sure you were safe."

Blinking in shock, she had to avert her eyes. Wow. Okay, so maybe he was after more than just friendship. But she never would have guessed he was harboring feelings that… protective. Wow.

"Th-thanks. You didn't have to do that, Matthew, but… why didn't you just come to the door, for Pete's sake?"

He shrugged. "So you haven't had trouble so far?"

"You're changing the subject. And confusing the hell out of me, to be honest."

"That's not my intention."

She studied him. It went way beyond the limits of their friendship for him to be this protective. He hadn't shown that depth of feeling until now, and while she welcomed it, it didn't fit with his behavior toward her in every other way.

She'd been waiting for him to make a move. For a touch. For a kiss.…

"Has he given you any trouble so far?" Matthew asked, distracting her from her swirling thoughts.

"No. No, and the other thugs have been keeping a low profile, but they haven't disappeared entirely."

"No? So you've seen them around, then?"

She nodded, not adding that she felt their hostile eyes on her every time she left her home. Lieutenant Conlan had told her to let him know if they made any threats. But the thugs knew how to threaten her without saying a word.

"I've seen them around," she said. "And believe me, I'm under no illusions that I've frightened them into submission. I think they're just biding their time."

"Waiting for what?" he asked.

"For my neighbors' newfound vigilance to die down a bit. Everyone on the block has been keeping an extra eye out for me. Even grouchy old Annabelle, though she would rather undergo torture than admit it."

"They're grateful," he suggested.

"They're terrified."

"The question is, why aren't you?"

She shook off the little chill that danced up her spine at his words and lifted her chin the way she imagined her alter ego, the kick-ass undercover secret agent, would have done. "I know something they don't. I've been taking Tae Kwon Do lessons. Working out at the gym, too. I'm sore as hell, but I'm stronger than I realized. And I'm thinking about buying a gun."

He'd been smiling softly until she got to that last part. His good looks were marred by what appeared to be pure horror. "A gun?"

She pressed a finger to her lips. "Don't let it get around. Lieutenant Conlan would have a fit. Besides, if I do, it'll be totally illegal. They won't give you a pistol permit if you live in this neighborhood. I tried. It's a high crime district, they said. That's why I need one, for crying out loud."

"Melinda, I think you're letting this newfound confidence of yours go to your head."

She frowned. "No. I'm getting in touch with who I really am. And I'm not a victim. That's all." She leaned closer. "In fact, I think I'm getting sick of waiting for them to make a move against me. I'm considering going on the offensive." And even as she said it, it hit her that she might have to take a similar tactic with him. Maybe he was waiting for her to make the first move.

Matthew lifted his brows. "In what way?"

She smiled slowly, but looked left and right, and then shook her head. "Not here. In fact, I shouldn't say more than I already have. I don't want to get you involved."

"You're protecting *me,* now?"

Her smile grew. "Yeah. I am."

She got to her feet. He got to his, as well. "I'm taking you to school."

"You don't have to."

"I want to," he said, putting a hand on her shoulder.

She turned and stared into his eyes. "Do you?"

He held her steady gaze and seemed to know what she was asking. "Yeah, I do. There's been a lot going on lately, Melinda. A lot more than you know. And I've been busy. But I...I really want to spend time with you. More than just on the way to and from work."

She couldn't seem to look away from him, and she felt his hand on her shoulder as if her skin were suddenly hypersensitive. He pulled her a little closer. She let him, and in a moment, her body touched his and her eyes closed. He leaned down and kissed her, long and slow, on the mouth, right there in the middle of Peabody's Coffee House, with most of her neighbors nearby, watching with far more interest than was called for.

She heard Mr. Peabody snort or choke or something, and then all she could hear was her heartbeat pounding in her ears. Deep down, she was thinking that it was about time, and hoping Matthew would follow up with an invitation for a real, full-blown date.

MATTHEW SPENT THE DAY trying to pretend that it was ordinary. Just another part of the game he was playing. Pretending to be a teacher, pretending to be a peaceful, law-abiding citizen and pretending to be mildly interested in an ordinary, plain, everyday girl like Melinda.

The problem was, she wasn't ordinary or plain, and he really was interested. So he spent the day with a little knot of nerves in his belly because he knew he was pushing his luck.

When they shared their lunch hour in the park, and she said, "Remember when you offered to drive me home anytime I wanted?"

He nodded. He'd known this was coming.

"I'd like to take you up on it. Tonight. And I'd like you to stay, let me make you dinner."

He swallowed hard. He wasn't supposed to get involved. But, he was human. A man. And she was truly intriguing. "I'd love to," he said.

CHAPTER SIX

THEY SAT ON OPPOSITE SIDES of her tiny kitchen table. The meal was over. She'd made steaks, baked potatoes and a tossed salad. He'd helped, and it had seemed...intimate. They'd laughed and talked and cooked and eaten together, and now...well, now, she guessed, they were both waiting to see what was going to happen next.

Since he wasn't making excuses and hurrying the hell out, she assumed he was open to...more. But if she was going to wait around for him to make the first move, she figured she might be waiting all night.

So she took her courage in an iron grip, and she got to her feet, held out a hand. "Come to the living room?"

He took her hand, let her tug him up from his chair. But when she started to pull, he stood still, held on, didn't move. Puzzled, she turned and stared up at him.

His eyes were glued to hers. "I like your place," he said.

"Me, too."

He nodded. "I understand why you want to fight to get your neighborhood back. It's your home. I can see it's important to you."

"It is. And so is standing up for myself."

"Since when?" he asked softly. "According to everyone you work with, you're the most mild-mannered thing around. What changed, Melinda? Will you tell me that?"

She held his gaze. Then she pressed a palm to his chest,

closing her eyes. "My friend Rodney—I've told you about him—he put me under hypnosis to help me with my confidence and self-esteem. And I…I remembered some things about myself that…I can't talk about. But suffice it to say, I'm not the doormat I've been pretending to be, and you don't have to worry about me taking on more than I can handle. I can handle way more than you know. Way more. That's all I can say."

He frowned at her. "I wish you'd say more."

"And I wish you would," she told him. When he looked up again, frowning, she went on. "You're sending me so many mixed signals, I hardly know what to do here," she confessed. "What are you doing with me, Matthew? Are you really into me, or are you just—"

Before she could say more, he pulled her against him and kissed her as if he'd been holding himself back for days on end. She melted against him, let her mouth relax beneath his and kissed him right back.

Oh, it was so good. Her entire body went into a state of superheightened awareness. She felt everything, every brush of his clothing against hers, the heat of his skin beneath it, his breath on her lips, his hands on her back and in her hair.

The next thing she knew, he was turning with her in his arms. They were walking and kissing, nearly falling down and still walking. Clothes came loose as they moved, scuffing their feet over dropped shirt, blouse, skirt and jeans, until they reached her bedroom. They fell onto the bed, limbs entangled, mouths melding, mating. Then their bodies were doing the same. He was sliding inside her. She was moving beneath him, holding him, eager and aroused and amazed that this much passion had been between them, bubbling just beneath the surface. She'd felt it, but she'd almost been too afraid to believe it was real, much less to believe that he'd been feeling it, too.

It was amazing. Hot, exhausting, passionate, exciting, sweaty, breathless sex. She'd never done anything like that before.

And after falling asleep in his arms, she wondered if she ever would again. Because when she opened her eyes a few hours later, it was to find herself alone. He'd slipped away while she slept.

And he hadn't even left a note.

"THE HANDS-OFF ORDER remains in effect," the new boss said to the members of his loosely organized gang.

"Aw, come on, man. That skinny bitch split my chin open," Marvin Delaney, the fat-ass who called himself D-Man, whined. "I been waitin' to make her hurt, man, and I'm *sick* of waitin'."

The others muttered, swore, complained, but under their breaths.

"Look, we've got a good thing going. We stir things up with this woman, and it's going to bring trouble to our enterprise. You do that, and Big Dog is going to be furious. You shouldn't have messed with the neighbors in the first place. You broke the rules. You're lucky you're still employed. And if you want to keep it that way, you damned well better do your jobs, collect your cuts and keep your damn heads down. Got it?"

Reluctantly, the others, two men and two women, nodded. They dispersed, to go about their business, but they didn't like it. And Matthew wasn't sure how much longer he could hold them off. He had to try to control Melinda, and soon.

But right then, he had to leave. He had a busy night. As much as he would have loved to have fallen asleep in

Melinda's arms, in her bed, in her apartment, he had to keep her alive. And, if possible, keep her from screwing up the thing he had going. The thing that was going to make his career.

He had an appointment for a long talk with Melinda's best friend, Rodney Foster. Maybe that fellow could shed some light on the radical changes in her behavior. Those changes were threatening what he had going, and could end up getting her killed, too.

CHAPTER SEVEN

"YOU'VE CHANGED," RODNEY said softly.

He sat in Melinda's half of the house. It had been an entire day since she'd seen Matthew. He hadn't phoned since they'd made love. He'd taken a sick day from school, and now it was Friday night and she didn't know what to think.

There was big band music coming from next door, barely muffled by the thin walls. The TV was on, but the volume was low. She and Rodney were sipping tea and eating blueberry muffins provided by Olive Sparks, down the road.

"Is that a compliment or a complaint?" she asked.

Rodney tipped his head to one side. "Well, I definitely like the hair. It's short, kind of sporty and without that ponytail, your natural highlights show through."

She nodded. "I know. I didn't realize how much red I had."

"I'm not so fond of the wardrobe changes, though. I liked your knee-length skirts and pastel cardigans and ballerina flats."

"Jeans and leather boots are a lot more practical, though. Someone tries to mug you in these babies, you have a shot at fighting them off."

He studied her face. "I'm worried you're making too many changes based on that one incident, honey. You're letting that mugger dictate your entire outlook on life."

"Why? Because I decided not to be a victim anymore? I thought that was what you wanted."

"I wanted you confident and happy. But you've become—hostile. Angry."

"I have reason to be." More than he knew, she thought miserably. "Rodney, do you know why Annabelle's house is so uncharacteristically loud tonight?" Before he could answer, she rushed on. "Because Percy has gone missing. She's so lonely and worried she can barely stand it. You know how much she thinks of that cat. She could have a heart attack over something like this."

"I fail to see the connection between a missing cat and your altered personality."

"Do you?" She got up, paced to the window and yanked the curtain wide, staring outside at the dirty slush along the edges of the sidewalk. "She's had that cat for fifteen years and he never wandered away before. Do you really think he just up and left on his own? I don't. I think those thugs are behind it."

Rodney gaped at her. "Drug dealers who kidnap felines on the side?"

"And Olive—Olive who baked that muffin you're eating. Her car tire was flat this morning. You don't think that was just a coincidence, do you?"

"Yes, as a matter of fact, I do."

"Well, I don't. I think those thugs are trying to deliver a message. To intimidate us. The streetlights in front of that house on the corner are all broken out. Tell me *that* wasn't deliberate."

"Okay, that might have been them. But as for the rest—"

"Someone has to stand up to them."

He disagreed with her. "I think you want them to pick

a fight with you. I think you're looking for excuses to confront them."

She let the curtain fall closed. "Maybe I am."

He nodded. "You can't relive that mugging, you know. It's over and done with. You don't get do-overs in life. You need to let it go and move on."

"I'll let it go and move on as soon as those animals move out of my neighborhood." She shrugged and turned to face him again. "I don't know why you're complaining, anyway, Rodney, these changes are all your fault."

He set his teacup down on the china saucer with a clinking sound. "My fault?"

"Yeah. Look, I've been meaning to…thank you."

"For what? We barely did anything during your session. I told you you were stronger than you knew, I suggested you go back in time to find that strength and reclaim it."

"And it worked. Something…happened to me while I was…under. I remembered something."

He frowned harder at her. "Yeah, something about the mugging."

"No. It was about me. Who I am. But I can't tell you more than that."

He blinked. "What's that supposed to mean?"

"Just that the mild-mannered, mousy schoolteacher you knew wasn't the real me. She was just who I was pretending to be. And for a while, I thought she was real, but she wasn't. The woman you see emerging, that's the real me. And I like her a lot better."

"That's just a bizarre thing to say, and I'm going to have to insist you elaborate."

"Sorry. No can do."

He lowered his head. "Look, I want you to do something for me."

"What?"

"I want you to see my father."

She paused with her teacup halfway to her lips and stared at him. "Your father? The most prominent psychiatrist in the state? Are you telling me you think I need his professional services?"

"I'm telling you that I never should have messed around with your psyche. I thought I knew what I was doing, but I didn't, and now I'm afraid you're going to get yourself killed because of it."

"Oh, don't be ridiculous."

"I'm not. Even your new boyfriend is worried about you."

"My new—you mean Matthew?" She averted her eyes, felt her cheeks getting red-hot. "What do you know about him?"

"You've talked about him so much I feel like I know him as well as you do. Although I can see from your expression that isn't quite true. Did you two—"

"How do you know he's worried about me?" she asked, cutting Rodney off.

He smiled. "You *did,* didn't you?"

"Rodney."

"Okay, okay." He shook his head and contained his smirk. "He came to see me last night."

Last night? After he slipped away from her? "Why?" she asked.

"I told you, he's worried. He said you had told him about our…sessions and he seemed really interested in the details of our last one. The one where you…changed."

"Oh, for Pete's sake. What did you tell him?"

"Nothing you don't already know. But dammit, Melinda, his questions made me wonder if I really did go too far with you. You're acting like…well, like some masked avenger, and I don't like it."

She smiled, relieved. Rodney was just feeling guilty, not seriously concerned. "Don't be ridiculous. Look, I know you're only worried because you care about me. And… well, I guess Matthew does, too." She smiled softly as a warmth suffused her chest. "More than I thought he did, as a matter of fact. But I promise you, I'm not going to get myself killed. I'm fine. I've just found my confidence, my inner strength. There's nothing wrong with that. You helped me, Rodney. You really helped me."

"I wish I knew that for sure."

She shrugged. "Did you notice that my car was in the driveway tonight?"

He nodded. "Yes, I did. How did you manage that? Last I heard, you were sure your sister's life would be over if she couldn't keep using it while you made the payments and kept it insured."

"I phoned her a couple of days after our session, told her she had two weeks to get the car back to me. I figured that would be long enough for her to find alternate means of transportation."

"And?"

"She actually qualified for a loan and bought herself a halfway decent used car. And you know what? She was proud of herself for doing it. She felt good. She thanked me for making her try."

"Amazing." Rodney nodded slowly, rubbing his chin as if he had a goatee, only he didn't. "My father says people tend to live up to our expectations of them. Maybe he's right."

"I think he is." Melinda shrugged. "And I think maybe the real me would have come to the surface sooner or later either way. Maybe you putting me under only hurried things along a little bit. Maybe not even all that much."

He pursed his lips. "Just take it slow, okay? Don't go crazy on me with this tough-bitch routine."

"Okay," she promised. But it was a lie. Hell, she shouldn't feel so guilty about the deception, or even uncomfortable. She must have told lots of lies in her former profession. It was justified—she'd had to do whatever it took to get the goods on the bad guys.

Just as she had to do now.

Tonight.

She felt itchy and eager as Rodney finished his tea. She thought he was going to stay all night, but eventually, he said he had to go and headed out.

She cupped his cheek. "I love you, you know," she told him. "You're my best friend."

He smiled. "Thanks. I'd marry you and get you the hell out of this neighborhood if you were a guy."

"Gee, thanks." She patted his cheek instead of cupping it. "Go home."

"Night, Melinda."

"Night, pal."

Rodney headed out, and Melinda rushed to her bedroom, took out the black spandex outfit she'd bought and put it on. She'd been slender before, but two solid weeks of twice daily workouts at the gym, and Tae Kwon Do lessons to boot, had her looking much more taut and firm than she had before. She felt stronger, too.

She got out the tiny camera she'd bought at a pawn shop—digital and as small as her forefinger.

Tonight, she was going to sneak over to that drug den on the corner. She had already checked it out, cased it, as it were, and there were plenty of places where she could hide while taking pictures. Several overflowing trash cans near one side, some long-neglected shrubs and snowdrifts near the rear windows. She was going to get photos of the illegal goings-on and take them to the cops. She would get that place shut down once and for all.

She'd been planning this for days now. It was time. The cops were not moving fast enough, so she was going to do it herself.

It took her about a half hour to get ready. Then she headed out her front door and down the steps to the sidewalk below. That was when a low moan caught her attention. Frowning, she turned to see someone lying on the sidewalk a few yards away.

"Hey. Hey, are you all right?" She ran closer, looking around, half expecting it to be some kind of a trap set by those animals on the corner. But no, it was no trap. It was a man, and he was badly hurt. Leaning closer, she saw his face. It was broken and bloody. Eyes swollen shut. Nose broken. Lips split. She yanked out her phone to dial 911.

As she did, the man on the ground said, "They said this was a warning to you, Melinda. They said to tell you—"

He stopped there, but his voice…and his clothes…were familiar. Her fists clenched as realization dawned. It was Rodney! So battered she hadn't even recognized him. All because of her.

She felt her stomach lurch and had to fight against waves of nausea. The operator came on the line and Melinda said, "A man has been badly beaten. I need an ambulance immediately."

When she closed the phone and dropped it into her pocket, she tore her eyes from Rodney and stared down the street at the drug house. The lights were on. There was noise and movement coming from within.

There was going to be a lot more before this night was out. A *lot* more.

CHAPTER EIGHT

RODNEY WAS SWEPT THROUGH the E.R.'s double doors, and Melinda, running along in his wake, was stopped short before she could catch up. She could go no farther, she would have to bide her time in the waiting room.

That was where she had been for a half hour now. There were elevator banks nearby. There were chairs lining two walls. There were vending machines and magazine racks. There was a tiny room marked Chapel, with nothing remotely religious inside.

Melinda made use of none of it. Mostly, she paced. Periodically, she stood on tiptoe to peer through the glass of those double doors, but she never once caught a glimpse of Rodney. Just as often, she pulled out her cell phone and started to call Matthew, only to stop herself from hitting the buttons. Their relationship was so new, so fragile—calling him in an emergency seemed to stretch its boundaries a bit. Or maybe not. She was too new at this kind of thing to be sure.

All she knew was that she would have loved to have him there with her while she paced the waiting room and worried about her best friend. She would have loved to have someone there who cared, someone to lean on, someone to tell her that everything was going to be all right.

Hardly the attitude of a kick-ass chick, she thought.

Maybe it wouldn't bother Matthew too much if she called. She wouldn't ask him to come. Just hearing his voice on the phone would be comforting. Yes. That made sense. They'd had sex, after all. Mind-blowing sex that felt like a soul-deep connection more than a physical one. At least in her mind it did. But even if that was just her, it was still sex, and sex was personal and intimate, and surely if she could have sex with the man, she could call him in a time of trouble. Right?

She pulled the phone out again, flipped it open, scrolled to his name and as her finger hovered over the call button, the phone chirped at her.

She was so startled she almost dropped it, and then she saw the name of the caller. It was Matthew.

"Are we that connected? No, no, that's just coincidence."

The phone rang again. She drew a breath and answered the call. "I'm so glad it's you," she said.

"I heard what happened to Rodney. Are you at the hospital?"

"Yes."

"Good. I'm on my way there. How is he?"

"I don't know yet. They haven't…but how did you know?"

"I have a friend at the police department. Are you okay, Melinda?"

"I…I'm angry. I'm furious, and I'm heartbroken, and I'm…I don't even know." Emotions were boiling up. She'd been doing fine until she heard his voice, the sympathy and caring it seemed to hold. The connection she'd told herself she was imagining felt very real. It was hard to doubt something that palpable.

"Hold on," he told her. "I'll be there soon. Five minutes, okay?"

She nodded because her throat was too tight to allow

words through. Forcing her voice to operate, she managed to say, "Okay," but the word emerged pinched and tight.

Matthew was true to his word. Only minutes later, the elevator doors whooshed open and he stepped out, swept the waiting room with his eyes and then, spotting her, hurried forward. Melinda stood still where she was, uncertain, and fighting her own impulse to rush into his arms…and then he was there, and those arms were around her. One hand cupped the back of her head, and he held her close against him. His mouth near her ear, he whispered, "It's okay. It's going to be okay. I swear, it is."

His embrace was warm, strong, and it infused her with feelings she hadn't felt before. Not ever. Not only was this connection between them real, she realized, it was powerful. It wasn't weak or fragile or new. It felt potent and strong and as old as time. It hummed at a far higher voltage than it had up to now. And the look on his face when he finally drew back enough to meet her eyes told her that he felt it, too.

"How is Rodney?" Matt asked.

"I still don't know. They rushed him through those doors, told me to stay here and that's the last I—" She broke off as the double doors swung open and a doctor came through. He was a barrel-shaped man with silver hair and a face like a favorite baseball mitt.

He paused in front of the two of them. Matthew kept one arm around Melinda's shoulders, holding her close beside him, as if they were a real couple. As if he would support her, should she waver. As if it were his job to stand beside her and hold her that way. That was yet another new feeling for her.

It seemed like a fantasy. It seemed too good to be true.

She was still trying to process this new reality—if

indeed that's what it was—when the doctor said, "He's going to be all right."

Her knees went weak, and she thought she would have sunk to the floor if Matthew hadn't been there to hold her upright.

He seemed to sense it, holding her even harder, and she let herself lean on him as the relief surged through her.

"He has three broken ribs," the doctor went on. "And some pretty serious damage to the right eye. We can't say yet whether he'll have full use of it. We have a specialist on the way. But he's stable."

"Can I see him?" Melinda asked.

"You're going to have to wait in line. There's a police officer in with him now. As soon as he leaves, though, if he's still up to it, I'll come for you. I will warn you, he's heavily medicated. He'd be in a lot of pain otherwise."

"I understand," Melinda said. "How long does he have to stay?"

"Overnight, at least. We'll reevaluate him tomorrow."

"Thank you, Doctor."

He nodded and left them alone in the hospital waiting room. Melinda turned to Matthew. He wrapped her in his arms, held her firmly, then led her back to the chairs. They sat down together.

"Now that we know Rodney's going to be okay," he said, "do you want to tell me why you're dressed like a cat burglar?"

She lifted her gaze, met his eyes and saw in them a look she'd seen before, one that indicated a lot more going on than what was apparent on the surface. "What do you mean?" she asked.

He nodded at her legs, and she looked down at the black spandex leggings. The turtleneck shirt that matched was visible beneath her unzipped black jogging jacket. Even the gloves and the knit cap sticking out of one pocket were black.

"You mean my workout clothes?" she asked in as innocent a tone as she could manage.

"Workout clothes," he repeated. "That's what you wear to the gym?"

"Yeah."

"And you were going to the gym at this hour?"

"It's open till midnight every night. Really convenient for a working girl."

He stared at her, his eyes caring, but a little too knowing. "You were going over there tonight, weren't you, Melinda? To that drug house? What exactly did you think that would accomplish? What were you going to do, threaten them? Tell them to get out of town like some Old West lawman?"

She lowered her head. "I was planning to take some photos. Get some evidence the police could use to put them out of business. That's all."

He studied her. "And if you'd been caught? What do you think they would have done to you, Melinda?"

She narrowed her eyes and her voice emerged deeper than before. "What they would have *tried* to do to me, you mean."

He frowned. "I don't want you to get mad over this, Melinda, but...I've been talking to people about you."

"Yes, I know. Rodney told me about your conversation. And I'm not mad, just irritated. If there's anything you wanted to know about me, you could have just asked *me*."

"I have asked you. But you hedge every time."

She shrugged.

"Everyone around school says that you've always been extremely mild-mannered, shy, quiet and even..."

"Even what? Go on, say it. A doormat, right? A sucker."

He sighed, squeezing her shoulders. "Selfless. Giving. Pacifistic and nonconfrontational, and yes, often to your own detriment."

She nodded. "Same thing."

"Not really. But still, they all feel this change in you has been very sudden. It doesn't seem organic, like a natural evolution, but more like a reaction to some trauma. The consensus seems to be that it was the mugging that changed you."

"It wasn't."

"Then what was it, Melinda? Because you've gone from a shy and softspoken wallflower to an overconfident risk taker."

"And which one of those got your attention? Which version of me were you attracted to, Matthew?"

"The real one. The one I sense is lurking somewhere in between the two. That's the woman I've been getting to know intimately, Melinda. And I've seen her, when you're not on a tear about these brutes taking over your neighborhood. I've seen her when we tumbled into your bed together. But I'm worried. I'm worried you're going to get yourself hurt or worse, before I ever get the chance to really know that part of you."

She met his eyes and tried to keep her tears from surfacing. "Rodney didn't do *anything* to them. And *he* got himself hurt. How can I be any worse off by at least trying to stand up to them?"

A man in a tan overcoat with a badge clipped to the breast came out through the double doors. Lieutenant Conlan, the same cop she'd been working with on her mugging case. He met Matthew's eyes, started to nod as if in greeting, then stopped himself and focused on her instead. "Ms. Terwilliger. We meet again."

"I wish it were under better circumstances."

"I wish I'd quit finding you all wrapped up in every case that happens in your neighborhood."

"Someone has to try to get rid of the scumbags," she said. "They're going to take over and drive us all out, unless we beat them to the punch, Lieutenant."

"If you'd just be patient…" He shook his head. "It's like talking to a stone with this one," he muttered to Matthew. Then he flipped open a notepad. "So you're the one who found Mr. Foster?"

"Yes. He'd visited me earlier. They must have jumped him when he left my place."

"And how long was it after he left that you found him?"

"I can't be sure. A half hour, maybe." She lowered her head.

"I don't suppose you saw any of the attackers."

Her head came up fast. "Didn't *Rodney?*" she asked.

"No. He said they hit him from behind, and from then on things happened too fast. Said they ran off a few minutes before you found him."

She lifted her brows and decided that if there was ever a good time to lie, this was it. "He's confused. Probably traumatized. The fact is that the beating was still in progress when I stepped out onto the sidewalk."

Conlan lifted his head, narrowed his eyes on her. "You just said you found him about a half hour after he left your place?"

"Did I? I misspoke. I went outside and saw the act in progress. And I saw them, all of them. I can identify them. I know every face by heart. In fact, I can take you to them right now, if you want."

Lieutenant Conlan looked more than stunned. He

looked…worried. He met Matthew's eyes again. Matthew shrugged helplessly, shaking his head.

"What are we waiting for?" she asked. "Are you going to arrest them—or should I tell all my neighbors and maybe the press that the local cops don't care about our safety?"

"We'll need to get a statement from you first, ma'am."

She frowned even harder. "Are you…stalling? What is this?" She shot looks from Matthew to the cop and back again. "Do you two *know* each other?"

She took several steps backward, as the timing of Matthew's phone call suddenly seemed dark—sinister, even. What if he knew what had happened because he was somehow…involved? And this cop, as well? Was that even possible?

A tiny voice deep within her whispered that she was sabotaging herself—that for some reason it was easier for her to believe in wild conspiracy theories, and even in her own alternate history, than it was to believe that a man like Matthew MacGuire could actually care for her.

She silenced that voice with a stern hand and tried to paste a placid expression over her face. She didn't want to look as shocked and mortified as she felt.

"I've met Lieutenant Conlan before, yes," Matthew said. "I told you I had a friend on the police force. But, Melinda, I don't think he's stalling. There's just a protocol to be followed here. You wouldn't want the thugs to get off on a technicality just because the lieutenant didn't follow protocol, would you?"

She blinked and nodded as if that made perfect sense. "I guess I'm just…riled up. They beat my best friend, maybe did permanent damage to his eye. They could have killed him. It's…it's overwhelming, that's all." Shaking her head, she said, "I'm not up to giving that statement tonight, Lieutenant. And there's really no hurry, is there? Those four criminals will still be squatting in my neighborhood tomorrow, won't they?"

"Yeah, you're right," the lieutenant replied. "It's late. We can do it tomorrow morning, if that's convenient for you."

She nodded. "I want to see Rodney now, then just go home and try to get some sleep. You're finished talking to him, I take it?"

"Yeah," Lieutenant Conlan said. "But he was pretty much out cold. Pain meds kicked in."

She nodded, turned to go.

"I'll wait for you, give you a ride home," Matthew said.

"No, no, that's okay. I brought my car." She walked away, not looking at him, not trusting him entirely. And still unsure she could believe in what she had begun to feel for him. What if she was just being a sucker all over again?

She didn't want that to be true. She really didn't want it to be true. Damn. Okay, she wouldn't think about that right now.

Besides, she needed him to leave. Because she was going to pay those bastards on the corner a visit tonight. And it would be a visit they would not soon forget.

CHAPTER NINE

"YOU'RE RUNNING OUT OF TIME, MacGuire," Conlan said after Melinda left them alone in the hospital waiting room. "That woman is going to do something to screw things up thoroughly, and soon."

"I know," Matthew said. "Believe me, I know."

"So what are you gonna do about it?"

"Follow her home. Watch her. Try to keep her alive until this is over with. What else *can* I do?"

MELINDA PULLED HER CAR into her driveway, popped the trunk and got out. She went around to the back where she'd put the can of gasoline she'd bought on the way home. It was a three-gallon container. She'd had to buy it at the gas station, but she'd paid cash and kept her face averted from the security cameras. That she'd even thought of those things seemed to prove to her that her history as a crime fighter was real. They were things that would not have occurred to her before.

She set the can down and went into her house for a lighter and the bag full of fabric she'd used as drop cloths when she'd repainted her bathroom six months ago. For once, she was glad she never threw anything away.

Slinging the bag of old sheets over her shoulder, she headed back outside, picking up the gas can on the way. Tonight, she was going to get those animals out of her neighborhood once and for all. Yes, the actions she planned were drastic. But the sight of her best friend lying beaten half to death on the sidewalk fueled her. They were sending her a message? Well, they'd better be ready to deal with her reply.

When she got close to the drug house, she crouched in the snow-dusted bushes and waited. Watching and listening. It was nearly midnight, but the place was still busy. People coming and going. Deals going down all night long. She didn't care. She waited, and she waited some more. It was cold outside. She could see her breath. But she didn't shiver. Anger kept her warm.

When the place quieted a bit, she got up and crept closer, and then, slowly, she moved around the house. She tore fabric and poured gasoline as she went, stuffing wadded-up, gas-soaked rags against the house, sloshing more gas onto the walls and the bushes, which would make great kindling once the snow melted off, she thought. She drenched the front steps and the windowsills. She didn't want a stick of this place left standing when she finished.

Finally, she tossed the gas can into the bushes. Now, all she needed to do was get everyone out. Because as angry as she was, she didn't want a half-dozen dead thugs on her conscience. She just wanted them to go away.

Was that odd? In her memory, her former boss—or the voice she thought of as that of her former boss—had told her she had killed many criminals. She was trained to do so. Why would it bother her to do the same to these criminals? Wasn't that the whole point of getting her memory back?

But she hadn't really got it back, had she? Aside from that one conversation, she didn't remember a thing about that former life. Not one detail had surfaced in her mind.

She stomped down her misgivings and kept on working. She was leaving footprints in the snow here and there, and she didn't like that. But she hoped the firefighters would stomp all over them when they arrived later, obliterating any sign that she had been there. Oh, they'd know it was arson. But they wouldn't know who'd done it. She imagined thugs like these had lots of enemies.

Finally, when all was ready, she marched to the front of the house. She faced the door. Her plan sort of faltered at that point. She wasn't at all sure this final part would work, but she hoped so. Hefting a suitably heavy rock she'd found around back, she hurled it with all her might.

It smashed straight through a window.

Commotion from inside came fast, and she stood there just long enough to be seen.

"It's that damn schoolteacher!" the fat one, Delaney, shouted.

"That's it," his scrawny cohort replied. "I don't care what the boss says, I've had it."

"Let's get her."

"I don't want any part of this!" That was a female voice, but Melinda didn't have time to figure out which of the heroin twins it was. The big guy who'd tried to steal Annabelle's bag came surging out of the house, pausing on the front porch to stare at her as if stunned to find her still standing there.

"Yeah, right, you're going to come after me," Melinda shouted, though her throat was tight with fear. "Who are you trying to fool, Delaney? We both know you're nothing but a coward. Stealing purses from little old ladies. Kidnapping geriatric cats."

"Cats? What the fu—"

"Come on. Come see what you can do with someone as strong as you are. Stronger. Come on! I dare you!"

The other man came outside, tapped the fat boy on the back, and then the two of them surged toward her. With no more time to wait, she ran. She weaved and dodged through the entire neighborhood. And they gave chase. There were still two more inside, that she knew of. The women. She needed them to leave, as well.

But first, to outrun the pair on her tail. She got far enough ahead for her hastily formed plan to work and then ducked into an alley and through the back door of an empty duplex down the street from her own. She closed the door behind her, went to lock it, but found the lock broken, which explained why she'd been able to get inside so easily. She'd expected it to be more of a challenge. Maybe things were finally going her way.

Quickly, she went to a window, crouched and waited, watching the alley.

As soon as the two men ran past, she headed to the front of the house and out that door. Then, she pulled the lighter from her pocket, held it in her hand and returned to the drug house, just in time to see the two women leaving in the rust-bucket of a car that had been parked in the driveway. They spun their tires as they vanished into the night.

So the house was empty. She hoped.

She threw another rock through another window, hoping to draw out anyone who might still be inside, then she dashed around back and flicked her lighter. If there was anyone still in there, they would move toward the front, drawn there by the sounds of shattering glass. They'd be near the exit, and on the opposite side of the house from where the fire began. It was the best she could do, and better than they probably deserved.

Crouching in the bushes, she flicked the lighter.

That was when a hand came around her face from behind and clapped over her mouth, while another hand wrested the lighter from her grasp.

She struggled, got her lighter back and shoved it into a

pocket, but he still held her and his grip was unbreakable. Backing into the bushes, he crouched with her, and when she strained her neck to turn around and see him, he held her even harder.

"Stay quiet and be still! I mean it!" he whispered harshly.

Familiar. That voice. The feel of those arms. The subtle scent of him. Blinking in stunned disappointment, she whispered, "Matthew? What are you doing here?"

He didn't answer, just stared at her, apparently searching for words. Then someone else spoke. "Huh. So *that's* why you wouldn't let us take care of her."

This voice came from the darkness, and then slowly, the fat guy and the skinny one stepped into sight. The skinny one said, "We kept telling you this broad would be trouble, Boss, but you wouldn't listen. Now here she is trying to burn us out." He kicked her empty gasoline can as he said it. "And here you are, trying to protect her."

Matthew's grip went slack in surprise, and Melinda took the opportunity to yank herself free. She spun around and smacked him hard across the face.

Panting, she faced him while the other men laughed.

"Boss?" she asked. *"You?"*

Matthew held her gaze, and there was something that looked a lot like regret in his. "Yeah, me. You're alive because of me, though, so don't act quite so arrogant about it, okay?"

She narrowed her eyes. His voice was different. Altered. Gruff and unpolished. "Why?"

He had to look away. "Why does anyone do anything? There's money in the drug trade, Melinda. Lots and lots of money."

"I know that," she whispered. "I meant why did you tell them to leave me alone?"

"Why do you think?" the fat one said. "Pesky bitch that you are, you're still a prime piece of tail."

She didn't look at the jerk, only kept her eyes on Matthew and wondered, too, what the old Melinda would do in a situation like this. Fight now? Or wait and bide her time? Would she even *have* any more time? What was she supposed to do with the bitter hurt that was, even now, trying to cripple her. He'd been using her. Using her, the whole time!

"Come with me," Matthew told her.

The other men looked at each other and then at him. "Are you effin' kidding, Boss?"

"I'm taking her. Stay out of it."

"No. No way, I don't like this one bit, man. This don't seem right. This seem right to you, J?"

"J" shook his head slowly, left then right. "Hadn't seem right in a while now," he said, and his pronunciation made the English teacher in Melinda wince, despite the direness of her predicament.

"To me, neither," said the fat ass. "I think we ought to call the Big Dog."

Matthew sent them a wide-eyed look. "There's no need to do that—"

"You just proved there was, just by the fear in your eyes, Boss." The fat guy pulled a gun, nodded at the others. "Tie 'em both up. We'll talk to the Dog, let him decide what to do with 'em."

"Toss 'em in the basement with the old lady's cat."

"I knew it!" Melinda said. But she didn't struggle as the men bound her hands and escorted her and Matthew down into the house's dank basement. She was slammed into a wooden chair, quite unceremoniously. Matthew was shoved inside as well, his hands tied behind his back. The two men bound their feet, too. She thought about kicking their teeth in, but decided to wait it out. Then the door was closed and bolted from the outside.

A plaintive yowl drew her attention, and Melinda looked down to see Percy curling around her legs. "Looks like they've been feeding him, at least."

"He wandered in and one of the girls took a liking to him, decided to keep him," Matt said softly.

"Yeah, that figures. Their kind take what they want. They don't care who they hurt in the process. And what about you, Matthew?"

"What about me?"

She shrugged. "You're the boss."

"Yeah. Only now, thanks to you, my own gang is turning on me."

"Because of me? Or because you're not who you say you are at all?"

He frowned, but averted his eyes.

"You couldn't have been more obvious. The minute they said they were going to call this Big Dog, your panic was clear on your face."

He smiled slowly. "Yeah. Because that was what I wanted them to see."

Her brows went up.

He leaned closer. "I'm not a teacher, Melinda, and I'm not a drug dealer, either. I'm a cop. I'm undercover. Conlan and I are working on this together. They put me at the school to get a close-up view of the kids and their buying habits, which led me to this neighborhood. Then I got inside with them—I was the new boss sent by the Big Dog to manage things here. Only the real guy he sent is cooling his heels in jail."

"And no one knows what he looks like?"

"This Big Dog is cagey. Never sees anyone face-to-face. No phone numbers, no email addresses, nothing that can be traced. The only reason this drug house has been allowed to stay open is because we've been trying to find out who this mysterious leader is. He's the money behind a dozen drug dens like this one—and those are just the ones we know of. Your impatience might have screwed up the case I've been working on for six months."

She wanted to sigh, or maybe cry, in relief. She'd known he couldn't be one of them. And yet, he was using her all the same, wasn't he? Maybe she shouldn't be relieved at all.

"My impatience," she said at length, "seems to be the impetus behind finally getting this head honcho to come into the open. You should be thanking me."

He smirked. "I'll thank you if we live through this."

"Oh, we will."

"You sound pretty confident."

It was her turn to smirk. "That's because there's something you don't know about me, Matthew." She frowned. "Is that even your real name?"

Matthew nodded. "First name, at least."

She went silent, then, lowering her head as the reality of all of this finally settled over her. "So you aren't really a teacher at all. Or a dealer. Or a MacGuire."

"No."

"And all of this attention you were paying to me. That was just part of the case, too, wasn't it?"

He lifted his brows as if surprised by her assumption.

"You don't have to answer," she said. "I knew. I knew from the beginning that it was too good to be true. I was believing in a fantasy. Something that I only wished was real." Tears welled up. She lowered her head and tried to blink them away, but they spilled over. Some tough chick she was turning out to be.

"Yes, Melinda, you have been believing in a fantasy. But

you're all wrong about the rest of it. The stuff that's real and the stuff that's make-believe—you've really mixed them up."

She sniffed, shook her head. "Don't try to spare my feelings. I'm tougher than you think. There's a lot you don't know about me, Matthew."

"What don't I know?" he asked.

She fought past the pain, clinging to her alter ego, drawing from the depths of *her* strength, *her* confidence, because Melinda didn't have any of her own left. "I used to work undercover, too. On a far higher level than you. I know twenty-five ways to kill a man with my bare hands. I've taken down terrorists and assassins. I'm one of the best there ever was."

He blinked at her. "So that's what you…remembered while you were under hypnosis?"

"Yes. That's what I remembered."

"Yeah, I figured it was something like that after I talked to Rodney."

She nodded, then lifted her head, met his eyes. "And ran a background check, no doubt."

"I admit it, I did."

"But my true history didn't show up, did it? Just my cover as a mild-mannered schoolteacher."

He nodded again. "So tell me, how is it you only remembered this past of yours now?" he asked.

"When I decided to retire, they had to erase my memory. It's standard with agents with clearances as high as mine. I was privy to some supersensitive info." It was easier to ignore the pain of his rejection when she delved more deeply into the life she'd lived before.

"Sensitive information, huh? Such as?"

She frowned. "I wouldn't tell you if I could."

"But you can't."

Pursing her lips, she shook her head left and right. "No. No, I haven't remembered many details yet."

"Many details? Or *any* details?"

She shrugged. "You sound like you're doubting me."

He looked up quickly. "I talked to Rodney at length. We went over and over that session you had with him, and I keep getting hung up on one little detail."

"What little detail would that be?"

"You were under. The telephone rang, and he got up and left the room to answer it. Correct?"

"Yes."

"When he came back, the television was on. Correct?"

"Yes, that's right."

"And this was on Tuesday night, sometime between 8:00 and 9:00 p.m."

She blinked. "That's right."

He shrugged. "I phoned Rodney's father, asked him if it were possible for you to hear something on TV and interpret it as a real memory in your ultrarelaxed state. He said it was more than possible. It was likely. He said a person with a natural eagerness to please others makes for a person who is extremely vulnerable to the power of suggestion."

She frowned, tipping her head to one side.

"So you think...I heard a TV show and interpreted it as my history?" It was ridiculous. It was almost... laughable.

"That's what I think," he said.

She pursed her lips, closed her eyes and shook her head no. "That's not possible. I'm sorry. It's a great theory, but this...feels real to me."

"I checked the listings, Melinda. There was a rerun of a spy movie on, right at the time you were at Rodney's. A movie where a female superspy whose memory has been erased is called back into service. There's a scene in the first fifteen minutes where her former boss tells her who she really is and that her life as a mild-mannered journalist is just a cover."

She blinked. "Journalist?" That voice in her mind *had* said journalist, she recalled. She remembered correcting her own memory—hearing *journalist* and thinking, *No. Teacher.*

"But…I stood up to a guy three times my size. I took him out when he tried to steal Annabelle's purse. I tricked them all into chasing me, and then I eluded them."

"Because you believed you could."

"I stood up to the bully on the train, and my colleagues at work and the troublemakers in my class. I even got my car back from my sister."

"Yes, you did. You did all of that."

"So it had to be real! Don't you see, I could never have done any of those things before. Not until I remembered—"

"Not until you believed you could. According to Rodney, when you believe your memories are real, they basically are. Your brain doesn't know the difference. So you were able to do all those things simply because you believed you could."

She blinked slowly and shook her head. She felt, very clearly, as if she were shrinking into herself. Her mind turned inward, in search of the woman she had, temporarily, believed herself to be. But all she found waiting there was the frightened, shy victim she had always been.

"I should have known it was too good to be true," she whispered. "I'm…I'm the same little nobody I've always been. It was all just a fantasy."

Tears bubbled up from somewhere deep, and her eyes burned as she fought not to let them spill over. Her hands were tied behind her, so she couldn't even dash them away, and within a moment, she felt them burning their salty trails down her cheeks. "I feel like such an idiot."

"No. Melinda, that's not what—"

"Oh, God!" She realized suddenly just what a mess she had got herself into. She was the captive of a gang of murderous drug dealers. "They're going to kill us, aren't they? We're done for." Her eyes widened, and her entire body began to shake and tremble. It was no longer the toughest chick in town sitting there, bound and plotting her revenge on the thugs who dared to best her. It was Melinda, the shrinking violet, the weak, scared doormat who would walk a mile out of the way to avoid confrontation.

And *she* didn't stand a chance.

CHAPTER TEN

"MELINDA."

He'd said her name several times now, waiting a minute or two between each effort to see if she could stop crying long enough to form a response. This was the first time his voice was tinged with impatience, however. And it got her attention. She lifted her head, blinking through her hot tears to see Matthew sitting on the floor. His knees were drawn up in front of him, his back was against the corner and his hands were in front of him now.

She frowned, wondering how he'd managed that when a moment ago his hands had been tied behind his back like hers were.

"Melinda, I'm very sorry I told you all of that. I just don't want you getting yourself killed in some ill-advised act of heroism while we're getting ourselves out of this mess. I wanted you to return to being a normal human being with a healthy sense of self-preservation, not to turn into a bowl of jelly."

She blinked back a rush of fresh tears. "You must be very disappointed in me. I'm not the woman you thought I was at all, am I?" Then she shook her head hard. "Hell, it doesn't matter to you either way, does it?"

"You're not the woman *you* thought you were, Melinda."

"I know. I know. I'm not tough or smart or confident or strong or—"

"Yes, you are. You're all those things. What you are

not is a meek mouse who's afraid of her own shadow. You thought you were. Then, with one line of dialogue from an old made-for-TV movie, the strong woman you really are was unleashed. You couldn't have done any of the things you did, if there wasn't a part of you who really was tough and confident and strong. Don't you get that?"

He pulled his hands up, tugging on the rope with his teeth. Then he paused to look at her. "Pull your arms down the backs of your legs and over your feet. It'll tug at your shoulders, hurt a little, maybe, but you can do it."

She got off the chair, onto the floor, and did as he said. The motion did stretch and pull at her shoulder sockets, but it didn't hurt all that much. Probably all the stretching and working out she'd been doing at the gym and in Tae Kwon Do class.

As she worked, she mulled over what he had said. "But if there really was this tough, confident woman inside me, where has she been all these years?"

"What difference does that make?" he asked.

"A lot! I mean, it's the whole crux of the matter, really. Is she real, or just a figment of my imagination?" Melinda was ignoring, deliberately, the topic she really wanted to address—which was whether he'd ever felt any attraction toward her at all. She was afraid to ask that question.

He sighed as if nearly out of patience, but then he met her eyes and his seemed to gleam with a new thought. "Do you know the story of Dumbo, the little elephant with the great big ears?"

She blinked. "I seem to recall something about it from my childhood, yes."

He nodded. "Okay, then, let's review. Dumbo was given a magic feather and told that as long as he held on to it, he could fly. And it worked. Later, he learned that the feather wasn't magic at all. It was just a feather. And he thought he could no longer fly, because the magic that had made it happen wasn't real."

She closed her eyes and nodded.

"So Dumbo was only able to fly because he believed in a lie. But the point is, he *could* fly. That ability was in him all along."

She stared at him as if he were a moron. "We're trapped in the basement of a drug den and you're trying to inspire me with fairy tales?"

"I'm trying to make a point. We can fight our way out of this, Melinda, but I need your help to do it. I can't get us out alive if you're going to cower and weep and shake like a leaf. I need you to have my back. I need you to be that woman you've been for the past few weeks. But I need you to be her with full disclosure, eyes wide-open, all the intel. Not with a false sense of indestructibility, but with the whole, real truth in hand. You understand?"

She lifted her chin. "I understand." The whole truth. God, why didn't she just ask him? Why didn't he just *tell her?*

"Will you try? Try to channel that tough chick for me, just for one more night?"

"Yes. Yes, I'll—I'll try." And as soon as she said it, her hands slid over her feet and were in front of her. She brought her hands to her mouth, bit the knots in the rope, and within a few more seconds, her wrists were free and she was bending to untie her ankles.

"You did that faster than I did," he said.

She nodded. "My Tae Kwon Do instructor says I'm very flexible."

He met her eyes, and there was a spark in his. "I could have told him that."

She had to look away. That spark, it had looked like

desire. Was it real? Or was he just pumping her up for what was to come?

He gave one last tug on the ropes around his wrists. They fell away, and he bent to untie his feet. "Gather up the ropes. We might need them."

"Right." She picked up the lengths of rope that had bound her and wound them into a tight bundle, tucking it into the side pocket of her black jogging jacket. "Now what?"

She was shaking, but she was trying to be strong.

"It's okay to be scared," he told her. "You'd be nuts not to be. Fear is healthy. It keeps you sharp, and it'll keep you alive. I'm scared, too."

"You are?"

He nodded.

"It was easier to be brave when I thought I knew twenty-five ways to kill a man with my bare hands."

He actually laughed very softly, and the sound of it sent shivers of longing up her spine. "It only takes one, Melinda. It only takes one."

She blinked, swallowed, nodded.

"Take a look around, see if there's anything we can use in this room."

She began to look, while Matthew went to the closed door, pressed his ear against the wood and listened. She moved around the entire square room. It had cinder block walls, a dirt floor and barely enough light to see by. She found her lighter in her pocket and flicked it, using its flame to guide her, gathering up every item she found that seemed as if it might be useful. A length of lead pipe. A broken chunk of cinder block. She lifted the lighter up high to see above her as well, but it only illuminated thick cobwebs and floor joists. She paused when she spotted something significantly better.

"Matthew," she whispered. She held her lighter higher. A tiny casement window was set high in the wall above them, right at ground level.

He hurried toward her, grabbing her wobbly wooden chair on the way. She let the flame go out, worried someone would see it from outside.

"If I stand on this chair, it'll break. You'll have to do it, Melinda."

"All right." She bent at the waist, feeling the chair as he set it against the wall. Then she stood on it. She brushed cobwebs away by sweeping her hands over the glass, and then she pressed her face close, bracketing her eyes with her palms and trying to see outside.

"Bushes. Shrubs. Snow."

"Can you tell which side of the house it's—"

"The back," she replied without hesitation.

"You sure?"

"They're rosebushes. Out of control, untrimmed, thorny rosebushes. They were only at the back of the house, right side, if you're standing on the road looking at the front. There were no ground level windows above them."

There was a brief hesitation, before he said, "How do you know all that?"

"I cased the place, looking for spots I could hide while trying to get photos of them doing something illegal. It seemed like the sort of thing a former superspy would do."

"That's good. That's really good," he said, and his praise warmed her.

"I was glad this wasn't a good spot, because I didn't relish the thought of hiding among all those thorns."

"How do you feel about crawling out through them now? 'Cause there's no way I'm gonna fit out that window."

She blinked. "You...want me to leave you behind?"

"You have to. You've got to go get help."

She got down off the chair and stood close to him in the darkness. "But what if they come down here and find out I'm gone? They'll move you, or worse."

He put his hands on her shoulders. "I don't see any other way, Melinda. It's your best chance to survive this, and maybe *my* only chance. Do this. Please."

Swallowing hard, she lifted her chin and said, "Okay. I'll try."

"Okay. All right, good. Now I want you to call Lieutenant Conlan. He's my contact, all right?"

"Yes."

"You still have his number?"

"He gave me his card. I…" She thought for a moment, gnawing her lower lip. "I left it in my car. My cell phone's in there, too."

"All right. All we have to do is get you out that window. I'm glad you wore gloves, but I'm not sure what to do about protecting your face."

She zipped up her jacket and pulled the collar up high. It came to the bridge of her nose, covered most of her ears. There was a thin hood that rolled up into the collar and was held there by a zipper. So she unzipped it and put the hood up. The drawstrings would secure both in place. "Feel," she said, reaching for his hands. She found them and drew them to her head.

He pressed his palms to either side of her face, feeling the way it was covered, the hood, the collar. His hands stilled, and he was quiet, but close. Very close. She felt his breath on her face and everything in her longed for more.

Slowly, his hands moved again, pushing the hood down, moving the collar away from her chin and lowering his head, all in one motion. Then his lips touched hers. They were gentle, tender and almost hesitant. As if he were waiting for her to turn away or tell him no.

But she didn't. She wanted him to kiss her. She was gratified to know that this time, he was kissing *her*. The real Melinda. Not some kick-ass secret agent. But the *real* her.

And even as she thought that, she wondered if she truly knew who the real Melinda was. She was confused. She felt almost as if she had several Melindas running around inside her brain, at war for dominance in her mind.

"This part was never a fantasy," he whispered. "I want you to know that, just in case."

"I was afraid to ask," she confessed.

"I know. Listen to me, Melinda. You can do this," he told her. "Protect your eyes, okay? You don't have them covered, and they're too damned pretty to ruin."

She smiled. "Okay."

Turning, he reached up over his head and gripped the edges of the casement window. It was set amid the cinder blocks, but they were old and crumbling and so was the caulk that had held the window in place. He shook and wriggled and worked it until the entire window came free, and then he drew it inward and set it on the floor.

"Straight out of here. No messing around. Your objectives are the car and the phone and Conlan. You wait for him before you come back here. Be sure he knows the ringleader is on the way. I'm pretty sure they won't do anything to me until he gets here."

She nodded. "I will." She turned toward the window, then turned back again and snapped her arms around his neck. "I really care about you, Matthew. Please don't die."

"I care about you, too, Melinda. Please don't get caught."

"I won't."

Leaning down, he kissed her again, then gripping her shoulders, turned her to face the window and slapped her on the rump. "Now, go, before we run out of time."

She pulled up her collar and hood, tied them in place and stepped up onto the chair. Then she was crawling through on her belly, into the punishing thorns of the untamed rosebushes on the other side.

CHAPTER ELEVEN

MELINDA PUSHED HER WAY through the thorns, though they pierced straight through the clothing she had expected to protect her. It hurt to keep moving, but she realized right off that if she stopped and tried to maneuver without injury, she would be there for an hour. So she just pressed through, gritted her teeth and let the thorns do their worst. Within a minute or so, she emerged, feeling as if tiny fires had been lit all over her body where the thorns had pierced and scratched and left their itchy, burning residue behind.

She heard Matthew putting the window back in place behind her. She even looked back, but she couldn't see him.

He really cared for her. She believed that. And she cared for him. Out of all that had happened, those were the only things she knew for sure were real. That was all she needed to know right then. Whether she was a kick-ass chick or a doormat, his feelings for her—and that his life might be in her hands—would be enough to give her the strength to do what needed to be done.

And there was nothing to do right then but to move on. She ducked low, looking both ways before moving. She stayed behind the house, close to its wall, until she reached the end. Dashing to the next house, she crept along its rear wall, too.

After that, a fence separated the backyards, so she had to move around to the front. Still, she remained unseen. A dog barked, but it was far behind her, and she picked up speed, breaking into a run now that she was out of sight of the drug house. She raced back up the road, to her own place, and was just yanking open her car door and diving inside, when Annabelle stepped out onto her porch.

"Just what are you up to now, Skinny?"

She turned. "I don't have time, Annabelle."

"No? Bet it has to do with those idiots on the corner, though, doesn't it?"

"Yes." Melinda spotted the lieutenant's business card, snapped it up and then grabbed her phone from the cup holder in the center console. "They're holding Matthew hostage in their basement and they're going to kill him if I don't get help!"

"Well for the love of—"

"It's okay, Annabelle. I'm phoning the police now."

"Well, you'd best hurry it up!"

"I'm trying." But the phone rang and rang, then went to voice mail. Frowning, she flipped the card over and found a handwritten cell number on the back. Quickly, she dialed that.

A man picked up. "Conlan."

"Melinda Terwilliger," she blurted out. "Lieutenant, I know everything. Matthew is being held hostage in the basement of the drug house on the corner of Ivy and Wilson! They had me, too, but I got out to call for help. Matthew said to tell you he thinks the Big Dog is on his way and that they won't do anything to him until he gets there."

"How **did you** get out, Ms. Terwilliger?"

"What **difference** does that make? Listen, how long will it take you to get here? I don't want to leave him alone for long."

"I'm in the area, actually. Five minutes," he said.

"Meanwhile, you should get back over there and keep your eye on things. Is there any cover near the house?"

"Some bushes in the back."

"Use them. I'll be there soon."

"Good. Good, okay." She rung off and spun toward the street.

"You're *not* going back over there!" Annabelle said.

"I have to. It's okay, the cops will be here soon."

"Then stay here and let them handle it."

"I can't. They have Matthew, Annabelle. I can't risk anything happening to him."

Annabelle smiled. "You gotta love a fierce woman wanting to protect her man," she said. "I never knew you had it in you. You be careful, child."

"I will." She nodded. "You'd best stay inside. Oh, and so you know, Percy is over there, too, and he's fine. I'll bring him back with me."

Then she dashed away into the night, before Annabelle could do more than press a palm to her chest.

MELINDA NO SOONER GOT to the bushes and crouched low to crawl into them than a big meaty hand clapped onto her shoulder and pulled her upright and around. She was stunned to see the fat guy, Delaney.

"You're in a lot of trouble, sweetie pie."

She blinked, stunned. "H-how did you know?"

"A little birdie told me." He shoved his cell phone into his pocket. "Get your ass back in the house. Come on. Move."

He shoved her. She moved, her mind working overtime. Someone had phoned this thug and told him where to find her. Lieutenant Conlan had said he was only five minutes away. Why? Why was he in this neighborhood at this hour?

And who, besides him, knew *exactly* where she would be hiding?

No one.

The fat boy pushed her toward the front of the house, and as he did, Melinda spotted something she hadn't expected to see. A small, pale face, peering around the front corner of the house next door. The face of Annabelle.

She met the lady's eyes and said, "I just called a dirty cop, didn't I? The man I called for help, Lieutenant Conlan, he's actually on your side. I'm right, aren't I?"

"Shut up!"

"He's the ringleader. The man behind a dozen drug operations just like this one. Isn't he?"

He shoved her harder, and she stumbled onto the front steps.

"I should have called someone else. 911. Something."

"Yeah, you should have. And now it's too late. Your bodies will be in the river by the time they could get here. You should have minded your own business, superteacher. But no, you had to play the hero."

She looked desperately back over her shoulder, but Annabelle was no longer in sight. She wondered how much the old woman had managed to hear and hoped to God it would be enough.

THE TWO THUGS TIED HER UP again, in what might have once been a living room, but was now just a shell. A few tables lined the place, a few kitchen-style chairs. Lots of various boxes, filled with God only knew what. Matthew sat in a chair, bound at the wrists and ankles, as before. They shoved her into another chair beside him.

"Just like the Big Dog said," Delaney told the skinny one. "She was in the bushes out back."

"Right where Lieutenant Conlan told me to hide," she said softly, her eyes meeting Matthew's.

He lifted his brows.

"He's the leader," she told him. Then she shot a look at one of the thugs. "Am I right?"

"How the hell would I know? We've never met him."

"You have now." The lieutenant's voice came from the doorway, where he entered with a gun in his hand. "J, give me your gun. We have to make this look legit. I can't off these two with a police issue weapon."

"Sure, Boss." The skinny thug hustled to obey, taking the lieutenant's gun from him and trading it for his own.

The lieutenant nodded, then leveled the gun and pulled the trigger twice, so rapidly Melinda couldn't have guessed what he was going to do. The two thugs hit the floor, dead before they landed, and Melinda screamed, then bit her lip to stop herself.

"There." He wiped the gun down and walked over to the skinny thug to kick him, making sure he was dead. He checked the fat one, too, and gave a satisfied nod.

"I don't...understand," Melinda whispered.

"What's to understand?" the lieutenant asked. "Matthew here is the ringleader. He conned you into believing him, and then when you learned the truth and came charging over here to confront him, he shot you. He shot his two henchmen, too, to ensure no one who knew his true identity would live to tell the tale. I, of course, arrived just in time to make a last-ditch effort to save your life." He tipped his head to one side, seemingly making this up as he went along. "Yeah, I got here just as he was leveling his gun on you, and I shot him, but he fired at the same time. Sadly, you died." He nodded. "It's perfect."

"You've been behind this all along," Matthew accused.

"You got me to come in here undercover, just so you could set me up to take the fall as the ringleader."

"That's right. I had to do something. DEA was getting close. It was time for me to cut my losses, retire with what I've already made. But to do that, I had to make sure the case was closed, once and for all. And I'm going to get away with it, too."

"I don't think so, sonny."

Melinda gasped as the house's front door banged open. Right behind the dirty cop, there was a little old lady with a shotgun that looked as if it weighed almost as much as she did herself. And yet Annabelle held that long, heavy-looking weapon with surprising steadiness.

Lieutenant Conlan glanced over his shoulder. "Now why don't you put that down before you get hurt, ma'am. This is police business—"

"This is neighborhood business," she said. "*My* neighborhood."

"And mine," said someone else.

Annabelle stepped inside, gun leading the way, and the other neighbors poured in behind her, slowly surrounding the dangerous cop gone bad. Mr. Peabody had a baseball bat. Olive Sparks, a rolling pin. And there were others, a dozen, at least.

"Put your gun down, Officer," Annabelle said.

"Lieutenant," he corrected.

"Not for long, I'll bet," Annabelle replied. "Now put it down. I'm too old to have patience with common crooks like you."

Slowly, Conlan did. Then the others rushed forward, quickly untying Matthew and Melinda, and using the ropes to tie the cop instead.

Matthew rose and quickly picked up Conlan's gun, and

those of the thugs, as well. "Someone call nine-eleven," he said.

"Already have," Mr. Peabody replied. "The real police are on their way." Even as he said it sirens sounded in the distance.

A plaintive yowl blended with the sound, and Percy, the cat, came trotting up from the basement. Annabelle handed her shotgun to Melinda and bent to scoop up her cat. "I'm done here," she said, turning to walk out the front door.

Police cars skidded to a halt, and officers flooded into the house. Then, at long last, Matthew turned his full attention to Melinda. Smiling as he met her eyes, he said, "You did it."

"I did, didn't I?"

He wrapped his arms around her, holding her close and rocking her against him. "Don't sound so surprised. I never doubted it."

"Didn't you? I did."

He stepped back a little, stared down into her eyes. "You shouldn't have. And you shouldn't doubt this, either. I'm falling for you, Melinda. Falling hard."

She blinked up at him. "I think a kick-ass chick like me would demand you be a little more specific, Matthew."

He grinned and leaned close. "I love you. Is that specific enough for you?" Then he kissed her in a way that left no room for doubt.

Melinda had her neighborhood back. And she had a man who loved her and was going to be a part of her life for a long time to come, if she had anything to say about it. And she was pretty sure she did. Because she had something else, too. She had her true self. She'd found her, somewhere in between the shrinking violet she had been and the kick-ass chick she'd pretended to be. Melinda knew who she was now—a confident, attractive, strong woman. A good teacher, a reliable partner, a caring neighbor and, yes, just as kick-ass as she needed to be, when the situation called for it.

Warm in Matthew's adoring embrace, she didn't think she would ever lose track of who she truly was again.

* * * * *

With a special thanks to Linda Howard, who introduced me to the Smokies and has *almost* converted me entirely from a beach person to a mountain person.

RESOLUTION

USA TODAY bestselling author
Linda Winstead Jones

Dear Reader,

Now and then, a character will really speak to me. She (or he) quickly develops a unique voice; they whisper in my ear. No, I'm not crazy. At least, no more than any other writer. This voice is actually a good thing when it comes time to tell a story.

Nell Rose spoke to me. From the start, she chattered in my ear. Well, in my brain, at least. (No, I don't actually hear voices. Much.) She's the kind of person who would make a good friend. She's an ordinary woman in many ways. Imperfect, insecure, she's made mistakes. Who among us hasn't?

But even in the worst of circumstances she takes with her a glass-half-full optimism, an inborn certainty that even if her life is falling apart, tomorrow will be better. And when she finds herself snowed in with a sexy writer (who has his own issues—again, who doesn't?) she definitely makes the best of the situation. Still, she never would've thought that a winter storm could lead her to her heart's desire. If only she and Julian can survive the cold—and the person who wants one or both of them dead.

I hope you enjoy their story!

Linda

CHAPTER ONE

NELL ROSE LEANED FORWARD, gripping the steering wheel tightly as she strained to see the narrow, winding road before her. Snow fell fast and thick, obscuring what would otherwise have been a breathtaking view.

It was a conspiracy, that was it, a well-planned and widespread conspiracy to ensure that her vacation sucked in every way. The weatherman who'd predicted that the snowstorm would roll into the Smoky Mountains in the early morning hours had been off, by about twelve hours. She'd planned to be inside her rented cabin by dark, and then it could snow for the week, for all she cared. If she hadn't gone back to the office for the directions she'd printed off the day before and left sitting on her desk, she still might've beaten the weather. Who would've thought Stu Grayson—a senior partner with the law firm where Nell Rose worked as a secretary and gopher—would be working on a holiday? Naturally, Stu's "I need you for a few minutes" had turned into an hour and a half. Lawyers were such workaholics!

She never should've taken the shortcut, which according to the map she'd found online should've taken her around the main roads and saved her half an hour, or more. Instead, the winding road was too narrow, and she had to drive so slowly she was certain the "shortcut" was costing her precious time. Somehow she'd gotten herself on a mountain road with sharp drops to the left and uneven ditches to the right.

The muscles in her neck were tight. She strained forward and squinted, even though she knew the extra effort didn't help her to see any clearer or farther. Since she hadn't been able to pick up a radio station without static for the past half hour, she'd plugged in a soothing CD—before the snow had started to fall so hard. Now the occasional high notes were getting on her nerves, so she punched the eject button more fiercely than was necessary and then wallowed in the silence.

New Year's Eve. If the past week was any clue, it was going to be a sucky year. The man she'd thought might be "the one" had turned out not to be a commitmentphobe after all. He was married and had three kids. There's commitment for you! Three children, she couldn't believe it. What the hell? She had friends who had kids so she knew how time-consuming little ones could be. How had Bill found the time to try to weasel his way into her bed? Thank goodness she'd found out the truth before he'd gotten his Christmas present, which in her fantasies had included the new red teddy she'd bought herself as an early gift, a bottle of champagne, her surrender to his charms and multiple simultaneous orgasms.

To make matters worse, she'd gained ten pounds. Not since Christmas, even she couldn't manage to gain ten pounds in a week, but in the past six months the pounds had arrived, one at a time, until now her favorite pants were a bit too snug. Since the groceries she had in the backseat included chocolate in several forms—cookies, candies, hot cocoa mix, flavored coffee, which would require cream and sugar and fudge for the sundaes she planned to make once she made it to a local store and bought vanilla bean ice cream—she'd probably gain another ten before her vacation was over.

Pathetic.

Without music filling the silence, the only sounds she heard were the swish of the windshield wipers brushing away the falling snow and the whoosh of her tires rotating through the accumulating slush. They created a kind of rhythm: swish, whoosh, swish, whoosh.

Nell Rose made a commitment of her own, to the tune. No matter what a bad start she was off to, she would *not* allow this year to be a waste. She'd take control of her life, starting here and now. What better time to make a few resolutions?

First of all, no men. At all. For at least six months, and maybe the whole year—if she could stand it. She didn't enjoy being alone, didn't like to be the one who showed up at all the office parties and family gatherings solo, but obviously her radar was off where the opposite sex was concerned. Way off. She was always drawn to the wrong men. At the age of twenty-eight, you'd think she might at least have one winner in her past. But no, she let the decent ones pass her by and honed in on the overgrown children, the charmers who promised everything and delivered nothing—even a thief, once. And now, a married man. That one wasn't entirely her fault, since she hadn't known Bill was married until two weeks ago, and she'd immediately ended their relationship.

So, no more men. No casual relationships, no looking for the elusive Mr. Right. Nothing.

Second, no chocolate. How else was she going to lose the ten pounds she'd gained, and the ten she'd needed to lose before she'd gained them? Maybe she'd even start exercising. Yes, she would make herself run. On purpose. While not being chased by a wild animal or trying to beat the crowd to a shoe sale.

Third, she'd get serious about her job. For at least half

the year, she'd devote herself to her work. She'd concentrate on climbing the corporate ladder. It was a goal.

She could take night classes, work late, volunteer for the jobs no one else wanted. Stu wanted some help on a Friday night? She'd be there. New Year's Eve, Christmas, Fourth of July, she was his man—so to speak. She would devote her man-less, newly buff self to building a career. Nell Rose had never really had much in the way of career goals. She'd always imagined she'd meet a man, fall madly in love, have kids, stay at home and become a soccer mom. Maybe it wasn't an exciting dream, but it was hers. Or had been.

Fourth, and last on her list of resolutions so far, she was going to stop biting her nails when she was nervous. She suspected this last detail on the list would be the easiest resolution to keep. It wouldn't require a life change, just some of that bitter stuff to paint on her nails. Maybe it was a cheat, but—

Without warning, the car jerked to the side, as her tires lost their tenuous grip on the slushy road. She tried to get control once more, but turning the steering wheel was a waste of time. The car now had a mind of its own. It shuddered, the back tires slid wildly to the left, then to the right and back again. Though she couldn't see what was coming she felt the jerk when the car left the road, and when it plunged she felt as if the world had been snatched out from under her.

She had time to utter one last, pithy word, "Shit," before her head snapped forward and banged against the steering wheel.

Nell Rose lifted her head slowly, taking a deep breath. So, matters *could* get worse, after all. The snow continued to fall, her car sat sideways in a ditch—not the deepest she'd passed, but deep enough—and she was lost and alone.

A glow of light caught her eye. She unbuckled her seat belt and shifted to the passenger seat to glance up the steep hill. There was a house up there; her first bit of luck in the new year.

Well, her second. Things would be much worse if her car had taken a leap to the *left*.

JULIAN SAT BACK IN HIS favorite chair, a cup of steaming coffee on the table beside him, the television on with the audio muted. The picture on the screen was weather radar. The storm that was moving in, earlier than predicted, didn't concern him. He could easily get by for a month with what he had on hand. Propane for heat if the power went out. Canned goods and dried fruit, though if the power went he'd cook the fresh food first on his propane stove. He even had a camp coffeepot to use on that stove if there was no electricity, and hence no coffeemaker, because the one thing he couldn't live without was his coffee. Everything else was gravy.

For two days he'd been ignoring the stack of mail he'd picked up at his P.O. box in town, but the letters weren't going away until he dealt with them. Bills were separated and set to one side. Junk mail went straight into the garbage can that was conveniently placed behind the table where his coffee cup sat. What remained were three letters, with varying postmarks. He set the one with the Knoxville postmark and familiar handwriting aside, delaying the inevitable.

Most of his fan correspondence came via email, which suited him just fine, but a few diehards continued to send him actual letters. He'd been intending to have his webmaster remove the P.O. box address from the website and then change out his box, where he got all his mail, not just fan letters. He just hadn't done it, yet.

Dear Mr. Maddox, the first letter began formally. *I loved your latest book,* The Demon's Promise. *The hero was so real, I couldn't put the book down! I was up until three in the morning...* The letter continued, filled with praise, and ended with the inevitable. *I'm writing a horror novel myself. Would you be willing to give me your agent's name and phone number?*

The second letter had no salutation, just began with a bitter *You hack, you must've sold your soul to the devil to make the* New York Times *list with this last disgusting attempt at a novel. What drivel...* Julian read no further; the letter was dropped on top of the junk mail.

He knew what he'd find in the third letter, more or less, but he opened it anyway. A glutton for punishment, or just curious?

Dear Julian, Last night I stood outside your house and peered inside. A chill ran up his spine. *I wanted so badly to ring the doorbell and introduce myself. I'm sure we'd hit it off right away, but my shyness kept me on the porch.* Was it a lucky guess that he had a front porch, or had this nut-job actually been to the house? Most houses had some sort of front porch, so Julian was going to go with "lucky," for now. *We are connected soul-deep, I feel it when I read your books, when I dream about you. It seems you plucked this last book directly from my brain.* He'd been accused of having a disturbing brain, but that was his job. He scared people for a living; he didn't want to connect on any level with anyone whose brain worked like his did.

The letter continued, filled with lavish praise, and ended, as always, with a *See you soon. Your Number One Fan forever.*

There was never any clue in the letters as to whether the writer was a man or a woman, though the "connected soul-deep" had a definite feminine ring to it. The penmanship was neat, but not particularly swirly or austere. While the "fan"—if you could assign such a designation to the author of these particular letters—had never actually threatened harm, the letters were creepy. *See you soon.*

He was going to have to get a gun. While Julian enjoyed his privacy here in the mountains of Tennessee, he was often reminded of how isolated he was. Actually, every time he got a letter from the Knoxville fruitcake, he was reminded. Knoxville was much too close for comfort. It pissed him off that these damn letters had him thinking about buying a gun. He'd sworn years ago he would never own another one.

While he was tempted to toss the letter after the junk mail and the critique, he didn't. He slipped it into the drawer of the table at his side, on top of the last two letters from the same writer. Both his agent and the sheriff had suggested that he file them away. Just in case. Maybe they thought it would give them something to go on if he ended up dead, or missing. Maybe they were just humoring him. Neither of them took the letters seriously.

They apparently thought his imagination was running away with him. It had happened before.

When the doorbell rang, Julian nearly shot out of his chair. The radar showed an increasingly heavy snowstorm moving into the area. Who would be on his doorstep now? Wishing he'd already bought that damned gun, he settled for the next best thing, a poker sitting in a brass stand near the fireplace. An unused poker, since propane fireplaces didn't require the tools; they were just for looks, bought and placed by a decorator. He gripped the poker as the doorbell rang again, and walked to the door, peering through the narrow window beside it. Could be a neighbor, though they were few and literally far between out this way. Could be a delivery, though it was a little late in the day for UPS and FedEx always ran in the morning.

The woman standing on the front porch—bundled in a heavy coat that hid whatever shape she might have, with a colorful knitted scarf hiding her hair and framing a pretty face—was not a neighbor or a delivery person. She caught his eye, and heaven above, the look she gave him was pathetic.

"Hello," she called, loud enough to be heard through the closed door. "My car went into the ditch at the bottom of your hill." At that, she laid an easy hand over her forehead and winced.

She didn't look dangerous and he still held the poker, so he didn't hesitate to open the door.

"My cell doesn't get a signal here," she continued, looking him in the eye. Her eyes—brilliant blue, even in the unnatural front-porch light—were teary. "And I sprained my ankle walking up the hill, and I hit my head on the steering wheel when the car landed in your ditch." She moved her scarf up a bit, revealing a red spot on her forehead. She'd be bruised there by morning, he imagined. Her lower lip trembled, but she fought for control. "Can I borrow your phone to call a tow truck?"

"Sure." Julian opened the door wide and she stepped in, as cautious to be entering a stranger's house as he was to be letting a stranger in on the heels of another weird letter.

"Sorry to be a bother," she said as she limped inside, favoring her right ankle. Her eyes took in the main room of his cabin—which was in reality much too elaborate to be called a cabin. His mountain home had two stories plus an unfinished half-basement, three large bedrooms, three and a half bathrooms and a kitchen any woman would die for. If he'd built the house himself, he wouldn't have bothered with such a large, fancy kitchen, but the house had been almost finished when he'd bought it. The Herringtons, an older couple who'd lived in the area for years, had built the house, but Fred Herrington had been laid off and they'd run out of money before it was done. They'd been forced to sell and had remained in their smaller house half a mile down the road. On the few occasions he'd run into them in town, they hadn't seemed happy to see him. Especially Mary, who'd likely designed the kitchen for herself.

Not that Julian didn't cook. After the divorce he'd learned, refusing to be dependent on anyone for anything ever again. Maybe he'd learned to cook out of spite, but he *had* done it. At the moment homemade chili was simmering in a Crock-Pot in the kitchen.

The living room, where he spent most of his time, was where he—and infrequent visitors—could see his touch. Two entire walls were ceiling-to-floor bookcases, and they were filled with books of all kinds. Research, reference, fiction, history, philosophy, even cookbooks. The furnishings were dark leather and walnut, with a touch of brass and rusty-red here and there.

"Wow," she said as she hobbled into the room. "You must like to read."

"Yeah," he responded. "You?"

"Not really," she said. "I mean, I like to read but I don't have much time for it. Maybe I should make that another resolution," she said softly, as if to herself. "Number five, read more. Goodness knows I'll have the time."

If this woman was the one who'd been writing the disturbing letters, she hid her obsession well.

"My name's Nell Rose," she said, belatedly introducing herself. "I'm so sorry to intrude upon you this way. Blame the weathermen who said the snow would come in overnight," she added, a touch of bitterness in her voice. "And the online map that sent me way off the path. Though maybe I took a wrong turn… Anyway, sorry." She had a pleasant Southern accent, not too pronounced, but not without that telling lilt, either.

"I'm Julian," he said. "No need to apologize. The phone's over here." He directed her to a waist-high bookcase near the hallway that led to the kitchen and dining area. A phone sat on the top shelf; the phonebook was just below. He knew the name of the closest gas station that had a tow truck, but did not have the number memorized. He looked it up and called off the number while Nell Rose dialed.

"My car is in a ditch," she said, calmly and without preamble, and then she looked at Julian. "What's your last name?" she asked in a lowered voice.

"Maddox."

"In front of Julian Maddox's house. Do you know where that is?" Her face fell. "What do you mean you're not running? You have to be running! I'm in a freakin' ditch in the middle of nowhere!" Her composure crumbled, and for the first time, he saw real concern on her face.

"Let me," Julian said, reaching for the phone, taking it from her and holding it to his ear. "I'd be willing to pay a generous bonus—"

Before he could finish the offer, the man on the other end of the line spoke. "Mr. Maddox, I'm sorry, but there's not a thing I can do." Sam Fulton had a Southern accent, like Nell Rose, but without the pleasant lilt. He was a good ol' country boy and a bit of a grump. "There's no way we can make it up to your place."

"But—"

"Call the sheriff," Sam suggested. "He's closing roads left and right, but maybe he can get someone up there to pick up your girl before it gets too bad. I've got to get home myself," he said briskly, "before I get stuck right here. Y'all take care, now."

Julian hung up the phone, punching the off button, and then thumbed the on button to get a dial tone. The sheriff's number he *did* know by heart. He and Paul had become friends, so he didn't waste time with calling the station. He dialed the sheriff's cell number.

He explained the situation quickly, but Paul wasn't much help. The curving, hilly road that ran in front of Julian's house was being closed as they spoke. Julian did everything but beg, but there was nothing Paul could—or would—do. After a moment, Paul asked to speak to the stranded woman and Julian handed over the receiver.

"Hello?" Nell Rose said, her voice tentative. She listened for a moment, and then responded. "Nell Rose Collins, 12134 Garden Place Drive, Birmingham, Alabama." She recited a home phone number and a cell number, then gave the name of a law firm. She held the phone between her ear and her shoulder while she fumbled with her purse and answered a question while she was doing so. "I've never been to Knoxville. Why do you ask?" She looked rightfully puzzled. "No, I have no relatives in the Knoxville area, either." Eventually she pulled out her driver's license. She recited the number to Paul, and then she handed the phone back to Julian. "The sheriff wants to speak to you."

"I've got her on the computer in front of me," Paul said as Julian put the phone to his ear. "She's legit."

It wasn't enough. "You can't send a car..."

"What part of *the road is closed* don't you get? You can let her sleep in her car and deal with the bad publicity that having a woman freeze to death in your front yard brings, or you can put her up for a day or two until the roads are clear."

A day or two? Was he kidding? "But..."

"If you show up murdered, I'll arrest her myself. Promise." He could hear the smile in Paul's voice.

"Thanks for the help."

"Seriously, she checks out. And I swear, I'll get out there as soon as I can."

"Yeah, thanks."

"In the driver's license photo I pulled up on the screen she looks hot, even though it's a driver's license photo and they're never flattering." Paul's voice was much too light-hearted, given the situation. "So, am I right? Is she hot?"

Julian ignored the question. "I'll see you when I see you." He ended the call before Paul could make matters worse than they already were.

Nell Rose walked toward the fire, hands out toward the warmth. "What did he say?" she asked.

"I'm afraid you're stuck here for a day or two."

She spun around. "I can't stay here. I don't even *know* you. No offense," she added with slightly less heat.

Would the nut-job who'd been writing for the past five months look so devastated to be forced to spend the night in his home, right down the hall from his own bedroom? He thought not.

Best to be blunt. "You can stay here or you can sleep in your car."

She looked at the fire, then to the front window. It was an easy enough decision. "I won't be any trouble. I swear, you won't even know I'm here."

He very much doubted that.

"Is your car completely off the road?" he asked. Even if the road was closed, it wouldn't be a good thing for her vehicle to be jutting into the way of traffic, such as it was, when it opened again.

"Yeah. I checked before I headed up this way. Man, I don't look forward to walking down the hill again to get my stuff out of the car." She looked down and rotated her ankle, the one she'd been limping on.

"I'll take care of that."

Her head snapped up. "I didn't mean… I really wasn't trying to guilt you into fetching my bags, honestly."

"It's not a problem."

Resigned to staying with a total stranger, Nell Rose Collins removed the scarf from her head. Dark, coffee-brown hair tumbled down. She unzipped and slipped off the heavy coat, revealing a fine figure in blue jeans and a snug blue sweater. She was curvy, soft and her face, surrounded by a fall of dark hair, was classically pretty.

He supposed if he had to be stranded with someone on New Year's Eve…it could be worse.

"I have chili simmering in the Crock-Pot," he said, resigning himself to playing host, at least for the evening. "Are you hungry?"

She sighed. "Starving. Is it spicy?"

"Very."

"Good."

"Beer?"

"Oh, God, yes," she said, and then she laughed. It was a nice laugh, spontaneous and pleasant.

Julian still had good instincts when it came to people, even after a couple of years of virtual isolation. Nell Rose Collins was exactly what she appeared to be: a stranded traveler, a woman in distress.

It was her bad luck that she'd landed on his doorstep. He hadn't been a knight in shining armor for a very long time.

CHAPTER TWO

DINNER WAS VERY GOOD and warmed her insides. Nell Rose tried not to stare at her host as she ate, but hadn't been able to help herself. Julian Maddox was thirty-five or so, she'd guess, in good shape but not a gym freak. He had dark hair, cut short but not buzzed to his head, green eyes and a five o'clock shadow. He wasn't "pretty" handsome, but had pleasant, masculine features, a nicely delineated jawline and really big, long-fingered hands that were perfectly shaped, not too rough but far from soft. She was a sucker for really great hands on a man.

She couldn't stumble into an old lady's house, oh, no. This was a test, sent by the Fates to challenge her newest resolution. *No men for a year? Fine. Check this out, sister.*

Nell Rose realized that she should worry about being stranded with a stranger, but the sheriff knew where she was, and Julian didn't seem any happier to have her than she was to be here. If he'd been too thrilled or too obviously annoyed that she'd landed on his doorstep, she might be concerned, but he was appropriately resigned to the fact that she was here, and that was a normal enough response.

In a little while she'd have to call her dad and tell him where she was. She'd promised him she'd call when she got into the cabin for the night, so he wouldn't worry, but she'd delay the inevitable for a while. He'd told her not to go on vacation alone; he'd strongly suggested that she delay the trip when the weather started to look iffy. Long story short, he treated her as though she was still twelve years old, and she wasn't eager to call and basically tell him that he'd been right. Again. She loved her dad, but since her mother had passed five years earlier, he'd turned too much of his energy to protecting his only child, his little girl.

"This is a lovely house," she said, glancing across the table to her host. "Is it…just you?" She hadn't seen signs of a woman or children in the living room or the kitchen, but you never knew.

"Yes," he said. "Just me."

He didn't offer much in the way of details. She wanted to ask. Single? Divorced? Widowed? Gay? But she didn't.

"What about you?" he asked. "Were you supposed to meet someone at the cabin you rented?"

It was sad to admit that, no, she was vacationing alone, but she could answer with as few specifics as he had. "No, I'm not meeting anyone. It's…just me."

She was pretty much a failure at small talk and he wasn't helping at all, so she concentrated on finishing her chili and beer, and occasionally glancing out the kitchen window to watch the snow fall. Beyond the glass the mountain rose, and the snow made the view a postcard picture. There wasn't exactly a lot of wintry precipitation in Birmingham, Alabama, and she'd hoped to see some on vacation. But not until she got to her destination, and not so blasted much!

After dinner Julian put on a heavy coat and gloves and fetched her luggage from the car. She watched from the front window, noting how easily he walked the steep hill, the cut of his jeans, the ease with which he carried her big suitcase and the bag of food he'd grabbed from the backseat. Ah, her newly forbidden chocolate.

Once he was back inside and had shaken off the snow, Julian showed her to a very nice guest room upstairs. *Nice* was an understatement. Who was she kidding? It was decorated better than her bedroom at home, in varying shades of green that were soothing and welcoming. The whole house—what she'd seen of it—was flawlessly decorated and clean, and the guest bathroom was luxurious and large, with neutral flecked tiles and thick brown towels.

She didn't unpack, hoping that maybe in the morning the sun would come out and the snow would thaw and she'd be on her way. But she opened her suitcase and placed her bag of toiletries on the bathroom counter. She combed her hair and brushed her teeth, washed her face and changed into a clean sweater, hoping that the simple acts would make her feel better. They did, a little. She studied the red mark on her forehead and frowned as she fluffed bangs over it to hide the evidence of her accident. Thank goodness it wasn't a serious injury. What would she have done if she'd been hurt and no one could get through?

It was too early for her to retire, and since there was no television in her room, she joined Julian in watching the weather radar on the TV, like her grandparents. The radar did nothing to ease her worries. Not only was the snow moving in sooner than predicted, it was significantly heavier. A check of the local news told of roads being shut down and businesses closing for the duration. Since the past few days had been rather warm, the first of the snow had quickly turned to a sheet of ice on the roads.

Great.

Friday night and New Year's Eve to boot, and here she sat, single, unwanted and focused on the weather.

Nell Rose quickly tired of watching the Weather Channel and the unofficial weather show on the Knoxville station. The meteorologist was *so* excited, there was a moment when she thought he might have an orgasm right there, on the air, in front of all his viewers. Enough was enough. It was snowing. A lot. What else did she need to know? She left her chair and began to peruse the numerous titles on Julian's bookshelves. Surely she could find something to read. If she was sitting by the fire reading a book, she wouldn't feel awkward about not carrying on a friendly conversation. She'd always been something of a social klutz. This was not the sort of situation in which she would shine, and Julian didn't seem to be a chatterbox, either. If he was an old man, a woman, even an ordinary-looking man who didn't make her mouth water, maybe she'd be able to manage. But instead he was handsome, manly, studly—a temptation, on the heels of her resolution. At an appropriate time she'd retire for the evening, taking her book with her.

Julian had an odd collection of books. Who read about the Civil War? Mythology, legends of the werewolf, ghosts, ghost hunting, demonology? She glanced over her shoulder to study her host, who was still watching the television. Okay, he looked normal enough, but this was definitely odd. The section of financial books was a bit of a relief. They were ordinary, unalarming. She moved into a section of classic fiction, which led into a collection of more recent fiction. And then she saw them: a group of neatly arranged books, all with the same prominent name on the fat spines.

Julian Maddox.

The titles did nothing to ease her concern. *Henry's Ghost, The Demon's Promise, Wolf's Howl, Vampire's Kiss*...on and on. There were eight books in all with his name on the spine. Many of the titles seemed to be constructed of dripping blood. At least that explained away the odd volumes she'd found before heading this way. They were research.

She noticed that he was watching; felt his eyes on her even before she turned to face him. "This is you?" she asked. It was possible that he only shared a name with the author.

"Yeah," he said.

"Get out!" She slipped a book from the shelf. *Henry's Ghost,* which—judging by the title—seemed slightly less horrifying than the others. "Scary stuff?"

"Yes."

She turned the book over, and there on the back was a picture of Julian. It was a nice enough photo, but didn't do him justice.

"Do you mind if I read it?" she asked, turning the book over to study the front cover. There was no dripping blood, just an almost innocent-looking mist with what looked to be a man's form in the center.

"That's what it's for," he said.

NELL ROSE HAD SEEMED GENUINELY surprised to find his books on the shelf. If she'd asked him what he did for a living, he would've been happy to tell her, but she hadn't asked. He hadn't asked what she did, either. It wasn't like they were on a date. They were simply stranded. Together.

She'd been reading for less than forty-five minutes when she shut the book firmly, with a decided snap, and stood. "Would you mind if I borrowed your phone?"

"Of course not."

"It's long-distance. Well, naturally it's long-distance, since I don't know anyone around here. I have to call my dad. If he tries to get me on my cell and can't get through he'll worry, especially if he sees what the weather's looking like up this way."

"No problem. Talk as long as you'd like."

She carefully placed the book in her chair; she knew where the phone was and headed there with a very slight limp. To give her some privacy Julian left his seat and went to his office, where he sat at his desk to check email. But his office was right down the hall from the living room, and Nell Rose didn't make an effort to keep her voice down as she told her father what had happened, glossing over some of the details.

Nell Rose told her father she'd had car trouble, had spoken to the sheriff and a tow truck driver, and was being put up for the evening by a local resident. Apparently there were questions about the resident, until she finally admitted that yes, it was a man. Julian Maddox. No, there was no one else staying here. "You don't have to worry, Dad, Julian's a writer. He's kinda famous, I guess, and people know I'm here, so it's not like he can get away with strangling me in my sleep." Another pause. "Yes, I realize you're worried about more than the possibility of strangulation." She sounded frustrated.

"You *can't* come get me, the roads are closed. Besides, I got lost. I'm not sure I could even get you here. No way can I get you here at night, in the snow, and you can't go by the internet directions. They're all screwy." There was a long pause, while she listened, and then she said, "The sheriff's name is Paul Tielkens, he introduced himself to me when we spoke on the phone. Call him. Sheriff Tielkens and Julian are friends, and he knows I'm here. I'm perfectly safe."

As she said the words, a chill walked up Julian's spine. Who in this world was perfectly safe? No one.

She listened for a while then ended the call with a soft voice. "Love you. I'll call when I get to the cabin I rented. Maybe tomorrow!" she added with optimism.

Julian waited a few moments before he rejoined her in the living room, where she was once again reading *Henry's*

Ghost. She looked up as he entered the room, narrowing suspicious eyes.

"Did you really write this?"

"I did."

"You're sick," she said. And then, to soften the comment, she smiled. "This is really scary stuff."

"That's the point."

"I know, but…"

"You don't have to read any further," he said. "You can stop right now, put the book back, pick something else. Something not scary."

"I wouldn't want to hurt your feelings."

"You won't."

"Still…" She lifted the book again. "Darn you, I have to finish. It's too good."

He was pleased that she liked the book, that it scared her—in an entertaining way. He didn't bother to tell her that there was nothing he could write that was as horrifying as real life.

CHAPTER THREE

SHORTLY BEFORE TEN, NELL ROSE excused herself, closed herself in her bedroom and locked the door. Not that she didn't trust Julian, but…it was the smart thing to do. She wasn't sleepy, but maybe if she settled down alone she'd be able to fall asleep. Instead she put on her pajamas—red plaid flannel pants and a solid red tank top—crawled into the bed and brought *Henry's Ghost* with her. All in all, it wasn't the horrible evening she'd initially thought it would turn out to be. She was warm and well fed, and even though the wind howled outside and occasionally what sounded like sleet pelted against her window, she was comfortable.

It could be worse.

She read much longer than she should've. Julian's story was scary, but also strangely moving. Even though horror was not her genre of choice in movies or books, when she got out of here she'd find a bookstore and buy a couple of his other books. Dripping blood titles and all.

It was well past midnight—officially the New Year— when she put the book aside and turned out the light, and in spite of the scary story and the harrowing events that had brought her here, she fell asleep quickly.

When she woke, the room was completely dark. Not just a little bit dark, but pitch-black. The bedside digital clock, which had been glowing red when she'd gone to sleep, was dark. She couldn't see her hand in front of her face, even though when she'd gone to sleep a night-light had spread soft light throughout the room.

The power was out.

That meant the heater was no longer working, and soon her cozy bedroom would start cooling. She pulled her body into a tight ball beneath the covers, willing the electricity to come back on, trying to conserve her body heat beneath the covers. She lay there for a long while, unable to go back to sleep. Her body was warm enough, but all too soon her nose grew cold. Her nose, and then her toes. The cold crept, like something out of one of Julian's books.

Trying to orient herself from memory, she reached out to the bedside table, feeling around until her fingers brushed cold metal. Her cell phone. There wasn't a signal here in the boonies, which made the cell almost worthless, but she often used it as an alarm clock when she was on the road. And now, to add to the list of uses, it made a decent enough night-light.

It was 4:00 a.m., she noted as she glanced at the glowing face of the cell, so she'd slept for a little while.

She heard footsteps in the hall, caught a hint of bright light under the door. Julian with a flashlight. He stopped outside her door for a moment, but didn't say anything, didn't knock. It was still much too early for anyone in their right mind to be awake, so he probably assumed she was sleeping through the power outage. Maybe the chill had awakened him; maybe he was a *really* early riser. Eventually he continued on, down the stairs, into the living room.

Where there was a fireplace.

Nell Rose closed her cell, killing the light, and returned it to the bedside table. Since she couldn't recharge it with the power out, she might as well conserve the battery.

For a long while, too long, she lay there in the dark.

As the room—and her body—cooled, she thought about the fireplace, vividly imagining the heat from the flames. The heat would radiate from the fireplace, cutting through the cold as the fire added warmth and light to the room. Her imagination only made things worse. Thinking of the fire didn't bring the memory of heat to her skin, it actually made her cold flesh feel even colder. If this was what being a pioneer woman had been like, she never would've made it! She'd never given much thought to the inventor of central heat and air, but at the moment she was certain he needed a holiday of his own.

Finally, she gave up and threw back the covers. With the dim light of her cell phone to work by, she put socks on her feet, grabbed a cardigan from her suitcase and pulled it on and headed for the door.

It wasn't entirely dark in the hallway; a touch of light drifted up the stairs. Soft, yellow light. Firelight. She closed the cell phone, since that little bit of illumination was no longer necessary, and tiptoed down the stairs, listening— not that she expected to hear anything but the wind outside the sturdy house. When she reached the foot of the stairs and turned, she saw that Julian was sitting in his chair, wide awake, dressed in jeans and a plain gray long-sleeved Henley shirt.

"Mind if I share the fire?" she asked.

He wasn't surprised to see her. "Not at all. Did the cold wake you?"

"I guess."

"There are flashlights in all the closets. I guess I should've told you that earlier."

"My cell gave off enough light for me to see where I was going."

He looked her up and down. "How's the ankle?"

"Much better," she said, looking down and very gently

rotating the ankle in question. "There's still a little twinge, but it's not swollen like I thought it might be."

"I'm glad to hear it."

Nell Rose walked past Julian to stand near the fireplace and hold out her hands. It was an awkward moment; she didn't know what to say. She was stranded with a handsome stranger. The power was out and the house was getting colder by the minute. What if it got really cold and it became necessary to share body heat? She sighed. They were hardly cavemen. Given that he had a fireplace and they had plenty of warm clothing, it was unlikely that it would become crucial for them to huddle close to keep one another warm. Pity. Maybe it just seemed like a good idea because she'd mentally prepared herself for a week of romantic fun and decadence, but instead she was on vacation alone. Her brain had been preparing her body for weeks, and now it was feeling neglected. Why else would she fantasize about sharing body heat with a man she'd just met?

She glanced over her shoulder to find that he was staring at her. "Are you married?" she asked.

"Not anymore."

Divorced, then, which was the least horrible of the possibilities she'd considered earlier. Single might seem like the best choice, but if a man reached Julian's age and hadn't yet made that leap, it was a pretty good hint that he had serious issues. Of course, she was quickly heading into that territory herself.

The wind picked up; the house creaked, and Nell Rose flinched. She knew the building was sturdy, but after reading about ghosts for half the night, those creaks and pops sounded ominous. She should've stayed home, written off the nonrefundable deposit on the cabin and slept in her own bed with her head under the covers and her plans for the future bleak.

She turned her attention to the fire. It was gas but flames were flames, and at least they wouldn't have to worry about feeding the fire to keep it going. As long as there was plenty of gas on hand.

When Julian put his hand on her shoulder she jumped a little, even though she'd heard him coming.

"Are you all right?" he asked.

"Of course. Why do you ask?"

"You look like you've seen a ghost."

She smiled; he dropped his hand; she wanted it back again, heavy and warm, offering a connection she desperately needed. "I was reading your book before I went to sleep. I guess that's what made me a little jumpy."

"Coffee?" he asked.

She hugged the cardigan to her body. "You can make coffee?"

"I have a propane stove, as well as the propane fireplace. I also have a camp coffeepot, for occasions like this one. We're in good shape for a power outage."

"I'd love coffee," she said, following him and his flashlight to the kitchen.

IT WAS ONLY NATURAL TO BE attracted to a pretty woman under these circumstances, Julian reasoned. He'd been celibate too long; they'd been thrown together and neither of them could escape; the storm that raged on made an isolated house feel even more isolated than usual. He'd become so accustomed to being alone, the presence of this woman got under his skin.

He put coffee on, asked her if she was hungry—she wasn't—and together they watched the storm out the kitchen window while the coffee percolated. His backyard, hilly as it was, was softened with a thick fall of snow, barely lit in the presunrise light that fought through the clouds. If not for the howling wind, it would look peacefully beautiful.

While Nell Rose stared out the window, he stared at her. Fresh-faced, hair thick and mussed, obviously just out of her bed, she was tempting. Her face was classically pretty; her shape was that of a real woman. Put her in an evening gown, style her hair differently, put some red lipstick on those lips and she'd look like a movie star out of the forties. Tempting and forbidden, that's what she was. One of the things that made her so attractive was that she didn't carry herself like a woman who was aware of her beauty, the way some did.

At this moment she looked tumbled, and he wanted to tumble her again. Like that would ever happen.

He didn't care about her, didn't want to care, but as they carried tall mugs of hot coffee back into the living room, Julian found himself asking, "So what's your story?"

"What story?"

Everyone had a story. Sad, boring, terrifying or humorous—and sometimes all of those—the story was there. "Where do you work? What are your dreams? Why are you here? Is there a boyfriend?" It hadn't escaped his attention that last night she'd called her dad to tell him she was okay. No one else. Still, that didn't mean she wasn't taken. Maybe if she talked a bit more she'd reveal an unattractive part of her personality that would put to rest the impossible ideas in his head.

"Oh, *that* story." Nell Rose sat on the rug in front of the fire, closer to the heat. She wrapped both hands around the warm mug and stared into the flames. "There's really not all that much to tell."

Deciding she had a good idea, settling close to the heat,

he sat beside her. She looked surprised that he'd joined her, but didn't scoot away or tell him to back off. "Try me."

Nell Rose took a small sip of her coffee, which was too hot fresh off the stove. "I work at a lawyer's office, answering phones and helping with filing and entering data into a computer, mostly, though on occasion I run errands and make coffee and run out for doughnuts. Would you believe, my dad told me last night that one of the partners called him looking for me when he couldn't get through on my cell phone? A Friday night, and New Year's Eve, and he assumed I had nothing to do but—whatever. And, okay, he was right, but still, it's kind of insulting."

So, her story was boring. That was a shame. She deserved better.

"I'm going to go back to school," she said decisively, "later this year."

"What do you want to do?"

She hesitated, bit a fingernail, then caught herself and yanked her hand down.

"You don't want to tell me?" What could she be studying that she was embarrassed to share? Writing, maybe.

"It's not that, it's just that the answer isn't all that simple. I'll probably take paralegal classes. Actually, I've already started. I had a few classes a couple of years ago."

"There's nothing wrong with being a paralegal."

"That's what I'm *going* to do, but it's not what I *want* to do."

"And that is?"

She sighed; her chest rose and fell in an interesting way that caught his eye. Everything in him tightened, responded.

"It's kind of embarrassing," she said after a short pause, "but it's not like I'm ever going to see you again, once I get out of here. What I really want is to get married, have a couple of babies, learn to cook, make elaborate Halloween costumes and play Santa Claus, and be room mom when the kids go to school…that sort of thing. My dad says I'm a throwback to another generation."

"What's stopping you from going after that dream?" It seemed as simple as getting a paralegal degree. Simpler, even. Find a man, get knocked up and on from there.

She turned to him, her face flushed from the heat of the fire. "Men! *That's* what's stopping me. I have to have a man for my plan to work, and so far I've been a complete failure in that department."

And here was the sad part of her story.…

"I have the worst luck with men. My dad is a great guy, I work with some fabulous married guys, but the single men I meet…they never fail to disappoint."

"How so?"

She lifted one hand and began to tick off her answers. "Large child, thief who stole my grandmother's necklace, another large child, the guy who cried every time we had sex, condescending asshole—" she lifted her other hand, the one that still held the coffee, and thrust out her pinkie "—married."

Julian shook his head. "Sounds to me like you're just being picky."

For a moment Nell Rose was indignant, but then she looked him in the eye and realized that he was teasing her. She laughed; it was a very nice laugh. He had the strongest urge to lean down and kiss her. He didn't. He wasn't married, had outgrown the large child phase years ago and he certainly wasn't a thief. But he could be an asshole—and what Nell Rose wanted from life was exactly what he'd been trying to avoid.

Picket fences were not for him.

"Anyway," she continued. "This was supposed to be a romantic getaway, but a couple of weeks ago I found out Bill was married and…" She shrugged her shoulders, trying to pretend it wasn't important. "That's why I'm on vacation alone. What's your story?" she asked, before he could probe further.

"You don't want to hear it," he answered.

She sighed. "I didn't know that kind of response was an option. This is so unfair. I spilled my guts, so you should, too. It's not like we have anything else to do to pass the time."

She suddenly looked away from him, as if she'd realized how they might be passing the time, if they were better acquainted. Then again, maybe they didn't have to be all that well acquainted.…

"Were you always a writer?" she asked.

"No," he responded. "Before I was a writer, I was a cop."

SHE WAS HONESTLY SURPRISED. Julian? A cop? Maybe it wasn't so farfetched; he had the look. He was in great physical shape and had those cautious, calculating eyes. True, not every cop she ran across looked like this, but in a perfect world if she had to get a ticket the officer *would* look just like Julian. But… "How on earth did you get from cop to horror writer?"

"It's not such a stretch."

"Trust me, it is." She didn't tell him that one of the men she'd dated, a large child, had been a cop. Tim couldn't string a complete sentence together on threat of death. Then again, maybe *Tim* was the exception.…

"Surely there are better things we could be doing," Julian said.

"There's no television, and the weather is much too nasty for a hike. That leaves your life's story. Come on, Julian, I opened a vein and bled all over the living room, so to speak. You can do the same."

"I'm boring," he said. "Tell me more about you. You have terrible luck with men and you don't much like your job but you're determined to succeed anyway."

"How do you know I don't like my job?" she asked, perhaps more sharply than was necessary. It was a good job. The pay was decent. She liked the people. So what if she was crawling out of her skin by the end of the day?

"You have one of those faces that tells everything," he said, reaching out as if he planned to touch her cheek, then drawing back as if he thought better of the move. "You don't like your job," he said decisively. "What do you like to do?"

She couldn't very well tell him that she liked sex, especially after admitting that she had such bad luck with men. She couldn't tell him that she thought sex was one of nature's most exquisite pleasures, like music, or a hot shower, or a sunset that lit up the sky. Well, when it was good, it was an exquisite pleasure. When it was bad, it was the worst.

"I like to draw," she said. "And I like to bake. Unfortunately, I'm not good enough at either one to make it a career."

"You're an artist," he said, sounding intrigued.

"I doodle," she responded. Her father liked to tell her she was a great artist, but…he was her father. What choice did he have but to be unrealistically supportive?

Nell Rose repositioned herself, because sitting on the floor wasn't exactly the most comfortable position in the world. Her arm brushed Julian's, and she could swear there was a spark. A literal, heart-jolting spark. "Now, what about you? How does a man go from writing speeding tickets to writing novels about creatures that go bump in the night?"

"I don't want to talk about me."

"If you don't talk, it's going to be a very long day."

Julian set his coffee cup aside, then took hers and did the same with it. When his fingers brushed hers it was very much like when she'd swayed into him. She felt that touch in the pit of her stomach.

He took her face in his hands, looked her in the eye and said, "I'm going to kiss you, unless you tell me not to," and then he did exactly as he threatened…promised…no… threatened. *Promised*.

He kissed her, soft and complete, with firm, warm lips. She responded immediately because it was such a good kiss. Nell Rose had a theory about kissing. If a man put his mouth on yours and he tasted funny or the kiss was awkward or she couldn't wait for it to end, then the relationship had no chance. A man and a woman had a gut-deep, instinctive reaction to one another, an undeniable chemical or spiritual response that could break through any and all barriers—but could not be faked or manufactured.

Julian tasted good. His lips were soft but not mushy, not dry or sloppy, and the way he moved them, oh, it was very possibly a perfect first kiss. Her physical response grew, settling in the center of her gut, between her legs, in her knees and her toes, which curled within the warmth of her thick socks. The top of her head tingled. Outside there was wind and snow and ice, there were cars in ditches, decisions to be made and bleakness. Inside there was warmth and security and an unexpected brightness.

The world shrunk until in her mind there was nothing but the kiss, no one but her and Julian. She barely knew him, but the longer the kiss lasted, the less she cared about that small, inconsequential detail.

When he moved his mouth from hers, she sighed. "You did that just so I'd quit asking questions." Her voice was embarrassingly breathless.

"What if I did?"

Nell Rose leaned toward Julian, feeling less awkward than she had last night. "They say you should bring in the New Year with a kiss, and we missed that last night." She was normally very cautious when it came to getting intimately involved with a man, insisting on a number of dates before the big reveal—meaning her, naked—monogamy and safe sex. Always, safe sex. She'd never let a man into her bed, or made her way into his, until she knew him well and was certain that he was "the one." Mr. Perfect, the man she'd been waiting for all her life.

And look where her caution had gotten her. She was alone again, disappointed, on the verge of giving up…and Julian Maddox had been all but dumped in her lap. Well, technically, she'd been dumped onto his. Was he a test or a gift? Was he a promise that the New Year was going to be much better than she'd imagined, or a reminder that she'd never have what she most wanted, that she was destined to lose when it came to love?

Another resolution she should make, while she was at it. Now and then, she needed to think less and do more.

"Kiss me like that again and I'll probably forget that you used to be a cop, much less care how you got from there to here."

He did kiss her, and she liked it even more than before. The kiss deepened, he leaned her back until she was lying on the floor and he was above her, covering her, slipping his tongue into her mouth. Maybe they were a failure when it came to conversation, but physically they were a match. A fine match.

One side of her body, the side facing the fire, was hot. Toasty. The air on the other side was very cool. In between…in between she experienced a growing desire that had come out of nowhere. No, not nowhere. Hadn't she felt something the moment she'd looked into Julian's face?

His warm hand slipped beneath her tank top, and when his fingers touched her skin her response was extreme. Instead of screaming she deepened the kiss, parted her lips and invited more, deeper, better. She was spinning out of control and so was he, and it was exciting. Just when she'd resigned herself to an unexciting life...

She felt the ridge of his penis pressing against her hip. He didn't draw away or try to hide his response, and why should he? They were adults. She'd asked him to kiss her—the second time, at least—and had responded to that kiss and the touch of his hand in a way that had to tell him she was enjoying it. How far was she willing to go? Her body said *all the way.* Her mind said *just a little bit further.*

Had she hit her head against the steering wheel harder than she'd thought she had? What if she was still in the car at the foot of the hill, unconscious, and this was all a fantasy. She didn't really want to be pinched, but she did reach out and pinch Julian's forearm. He certainly felt real enough, warm, muscled and substantial.

Julian kissed her throat, and she liked it. The fire, the heat they generated, the sensation of surrender...what was not to like? Oh, her clothes were in the way. His were a definite impediment. She closed her eyes. Was she going to do this? Was she really going to make love to a stranger because he knew just how to touch her?

Before she could make that decision he groaned a little, removed his mouth from her throat and his hand from her side, and rose up slowly. "Breakfast," he said, his voice raspy and his eyes glazed. "What do you want?"

Nell Rose sighed. Were there any more resolutions she could break with such relish? "At this rate it might as well be chocolate, and lots of it."

CHAPTER FOUR

THE LAST THING HE NEEDED to do was to get sexually involved with a woman he barely knew, a woman who dreamed of having babies and settling down—two things Julian planned to avoid at all costs.

While he warmed the coffee and scrambled a few eggs, Nell Rose went upstairs to change clothes. Just as well. Those pajama pants with elastic in the waist and the skimpy top weren't nearly sturdy enough to keep him from stripping her naked and burying himself inside her.

It was the situation, he supposed, the isolation the storm and the place provided, that had made him momentarily lose his mind. He'd been too damn close to just going for it, but common sense had finally won out and he'd pulled back. It had been a mistake to kiss her, but the way she'd looked, sitting there lit by the fire, her face welcoming and vulnerable and so expressive...

Nell Rose entered the kitchen wearing snug jeans and a tight red sweater with a V-neck. Her hair was pulled up into a ponytail, and her face looked freshly scrubbed. Maybe cold water was her way of warding off impossible—well, improbable—thoughts.

A normal woman would've ignored the situation, but if there was one thing he knew about Nell Rose Collins, it was that she wasn't exactly normal.

"That was weird, huh?" she said as she poured another cup of coffee and headed for the sugar canister. "Just so you understand, I'm not easy, and I don't normally kiss men I just met, much less entertain thoughts... Well, anyway, I don't."

"Good," he said briskly as she loaded up her coffee with a couple of heaping teaspoons of sugar.

"Just so you know," she mumbled.

After an awkward breakfast, Julian retrieved the old-fashioned phone—one he could plug into the landline and use even if the power was out—from the hall closet and connected it into the outlet in the living room. With the fire there, and the kitchen close by, that's where they'd be spending their time until there was electricity again. He wasn't holding his breath waiting for that to happen, since it had already been out for several hours and no one would be in any hurry to get this isolated stretch of the county powered up again.

In that same closet, there was a battery-powered radio and plenty of extra batteries. He handed the radio to Nell Rose, who gratefully turned it on and searched for a station. The old radio didn't pick up anything very well out this way, but she did find a strong Knoxville station, which was broadcasting wall-to-wall weather information. The worst part of the storm was dying down, but the snow continued to fall. It would be a record breaker.

They weren't the only ones in the area without power; the outage was widespread, which meant it might be days before his electricity was restored. There had been a number of wrecks in the early morning hours—nothing serious, at least not yet—and everyone was being encouraged to stay in and wait out the storm.

Days here with Nell Rose. Could he stand it, now that he knew what she tasted like, how she responded?

"I don't suppose you have any games," she said as she

stared out the front window to the white wonderland on the other side of the glass.

"Games?"

"Monopoly, Life, Scrabble...though I suppose I would be foolish to play Scrabble with a writer," she added in a softer voice.

"No games," he said, "but I do have a deck of cards around here, somewhere."

She turned to face him, her features in shadow thanks to the brightness from the window behind her. "That'll do."

The phone rang, the jarring sound surprising him. He answered, "Hello," to dead silence. "Hello?" he tried again, and then there was a click. His wireless phones, which were useless at the moment, all had caller ID. This old phone did not, so he had no way of knowing if someone was really trying to reach him or if the lines were screwy.

"So, poker, gin rummy, war...what's your card game of choice?" Nell Rose asked.

Strip poker. "It doesn't matter." It was going to be a long day; they might end up playing every game they could think of, and then some. Strip poker would be a very bad idea.

The phone rang again, and again he answered. It was the same as before. He said hello, there was no response, and then *click,* followed by a dial tone. He fetched the cards from his office, then answered the phone once more, with the same result. Either someone was messing with him or the phone—or phone line—was on the fritz.

"We can plug the phone in if we want to try to make calls out," he said as he reached down to unplug the line from the wall. "But I'm not listening to this all day."

"I might want to call my dad later," Nell Rose said. "Just to assure him that I'm still alive." She smiled. It was a nice smile. And he wanted nothing more than to toss the cards into the fire and pick up where they'd left off, entwined on the floor in front of the fireplace.

NELL ROSE STIRRED THE FUDGE, watching it boil. If she could she'd bake Julian a cake, but since the power didn't so much as flicker, she was stuck with the propane stove. Good a baker as she was, she wasn't going to get far without an oven, and he had all the ingredients for fudge on hand. So much for her resolutions. She might as well bite off all her nails and jump Julian's bones here in the kitchen. He was standing by the table, watching her cook.

The table would do quite nicely....

She stirred faster, pursing her lips, concentrating on the task at hand. He couldn't be as perfect as she was making him out to be, in her imagination. She needed to see his flaws, to know that somehow, some way, he was no better than all the rest.

"So, how long have you been divorced?" She glanced over her shoulder to judge his reaction. He didn't reveal any; his face remained stoic.

"Seven years."

"A while, then. Was she like, you know, a real basket case? A cheater? A gold digger?" If he'd blast his ex, maybe she'd see a negative side of him that would bring her to her senses.

"No. She's a nice woman, but when I started writing we grew apart. We no longer wanted the same things from life. Simple."

"Is she pissed now that you're successful?"

"No. She's remarried, happy, has a couple of kids. I hear from her now and then."

Nell Rose turned back to the stove. Great. Julian was the only divorced man she knew who hadn't been married to evil incarnate before the bitch kicked him out, kept his dog and slept with his best friend.

The snowed-in Saturday turned into the longest day of Nell Rose's life. The fire and her sweater kept her warm enough and there was plenty of food. The wind died down, but the snow continued to fall—lightly, but still, it was snow. She and Julian played cards, and their conversation was easier, more natural than it had been the night before when she'd landed on his doorstep and he'd found himself stuck with an unwanted houseguest. She'd called her dad and informed him that she'd survived the night without harm. He'd been relieved, but still wanted to head that way to rescue her. She let him know that she didn't need to be rescued, but she appreciated the thought. When she was finished with the call, Julian unplugged the phone from the wall, not anxious for a repeat of the morning's constant ringing.

She tried not to think about it, but her mind kept going back to that morning. When a man made her feel that way, it couldn't just be undone because her rational brain knew it was a mistake. It wasn't like she could walk away, or even close herself in another room to get away from Julian. He was *right there*, real and warm and tempting. If he'd never kissed her she might be perfectly content to pass the day talking, drinking coffee and hot chocolate, playing cards and eating fudge, but she did know, and it was a bell that could not be unrung.

It was New Year's Day, and she'd already broken three of five resolutions. Chocolate, men and biting her nails. She probably would've broken the other two, but it was impossible to break a resolution to read more and go back to school later in the year when not even a full day had passed. She had lots of time to break those resolutions.

"What do you think about New Year's resolutions?" she

asked, taking a sip of hot chocolate and leaning slightly toward the fire.

Julian was staring at the flames when she looked his way. He had coffee instead of hot chocolate. She wondered if he'd sleep tonight after all the caffeine he'd consumed during the day…and she really shouldn't think about anything that put the picture of Julian in bed in her mind. Naked. All over her, hot and attentive and…good heavens, this was bad.

Underneath that shirt was he as hard and muscled as he looked? Was there a six-pack? Did he have a hairy chest?

"Resolutions are a waste of time," he said. "Why make unrealistic promises to yourself that you know you're not going to keep? If you want to change something about yourself, what's wrong with April or August?"

"So you don't make them?"

"Not anymore," he said, and she didn't press for more information. She didn't need to know more about Julian. He was a stranger. A hospitable, sexy, occasionally grumpy stranger, and once she left this house she'd never see him again.

It was almost dark when the snow stopped. They stood together at the front window and looked out on the white landscape, the snow heavy and perfect in the trees, the lump that was her car at the bottom of the hill.

"There's a lot of it, but if the sun comes out in the morning the snow will melt pretty fast," Julian said, hope in his voice.

"Anxious to get rid of me?" she teased.

He didn't answer.

WITH NO POWER, THEY BUNKED down in the living room for the night, with the fire for light and heat. Julian lit a number of candles and placed them around the room, in the darker corners. They both settled down fully dressed, with pillows and blankets. Nell Rose was on the sofa. Julian stretched out in his recliner. It wasn't as if he hadn't slept there before.

They listened to the weather on the radio before deciding to try to get to sleep. The weathermen were now predicting sun for the following morning. That was a relief. The snow would melt quickly, just as he'd promised Nell Rose it would, and he'd get her towed out of here ASAP, even if he had to pay Sam a hefty bonus to do the job personally. It wouldn't do for her to be here much longer. He wasn't all that great at denying himself what he wanted, and he wanted her.

His attraction had grown all day, thanks to close quarters and something else he could not entirely define. Since Nell Rose didn't have a thought that he couldn't see on her face, he knew his attraction wasn't one-sided. She wasn't obvious about it, but now and then he caught her looking at him, and he knew if he made a move... But he didn't.

He couldn't sleep. Neither could she, apparently. "I don't suppose it's too late to make new resolutions," she said, her voice low. "I mean, I made the others on New Year's Eve. It wasn't technically the New Year, so...I can try again. This is New Year's Day, and that's when resolutions should be made, right?"

"What kinds of resolutions?" he asked.

"No men, no chocolate, no biting my nails, school and more reading. I might even buy a few of your books, even though I don't like to be scared."

"Why no men?" He immediately regretted asking. She'd told him about her sad romantic history. "You're going to have a hard time getting what you want in life without a man."

"True, but I have bad luck where men are concerned.

Maybe it's not luck at all, maybe it's fate. Maybe I'm supposed to always want what I can't have. Or shouldn't have." She sighed, then said, "Good night, Julian. I'm going to try to get some sleep, now." She said it as if she didn't think sleep was coming, but she was going to give it a shot anyway.

Julian lay there for a while, his feet up, his eyes closed. Tonight there was no wind rattling the rafters, no sleet peppering the windows. All was silent, with the power off. There was no hum of computers or clocks, no television. Just deep, complete silence. He did fall asleep, drifting off thinking of Nell Rose, knowing what his dreams would be like.

Frustrating.

He woke with a start, as a small, soft hand grasped his shoulder and shook. "Wake up, Julian, *wake up,*" she whispered harshly.

He was instantly alert. "What is it?"

Nell Rose was well lit in firelight, thick hair mussed, lower lip caught in her teeth and then released. "I think someone's on the front porch."

NELL ROSE LOOKED DOWN at an unconcerned Julian. "I heard a creak, then footsteps. Someone's out there." She expected him to tell her she'd been dreaming—which would've been a neat trick since there was no way she could sleep while he was just a few feet away. Maybe he'd tell her that she shouldn't have read another chapter of *Henry's Ghost* before settling down to try to sleep—but he didn't. Instead he sat up and stood in one smooth motion.

"Just now?" he asked.

She nodded. "A couple of minutes ago. I tried to convince myself that it was my imagination, but then I heard another step and I thought my heart was going to come through my chest."

He put on his boots, grabbed his heavy coat from the rack by the door, then headed back to the fireplace to grab the poker, which was resting in a caddy of fireplace tools, as well as the flashlight that sat on the table by his chair.

"What are you doing?" she asked, concerned. She hadn't actually expected him to go exploring in the dark and cold, she'd just wanted not to be alone if there was a chance that someone was skulking about.

Though who would get out in this weather just to peek in the windows of Julian's house?

"Stay put," he said as he opened the front door and stepped outside, a flashlight in one hand, the poker in the other.

"Like I have anywhere to go," she said as he closed the door.

She heard his footsteps, less stealthy than the ones she'd heard moments earlier. If there was someone on the front porch who was up to no good, then Julian really shouldn't be out there at all. They could plug in the phone and call the sheriff. Maybe Sheriff Tielkens could make it up the road now to look for Peeping Toms—and rescue her.

The problem was, she didn't want to be rescued.

Julian was back in the house within a few minutes, and she was so relieved to see him she rushed to the front door, locking it as he set the flashlight and poker aside and shed his coat.

"So?" she prodded.

"There was a sign of disturbance on the west side of the house, some snow displaced, but I suspect it was an animal. Deer probably."

"Deer," she said, with a rush of relief.

"Probably. I'll check out the tracks in the morning to be sure."

This was the mountains, and there was lots of rough country around Julian's house. Deer was the least threatening of the possibilities. If he'd said bear or mountain lion, she'd probably be stuck to the ceiling. Of course, of all possibilities, "man" was the most frightening.

"I shouldn't have woken you," she said. "I'm sorry."

"No problem," he said.

"I just… I can't sleep."

"I don't think I'll be getting back to sleep for a while," he said, moving to the fireplace to warm his hands.

It was such a waste for both of them to be so stubborn in denying what they obviously felt. Someone had to give in, before it was too late. One of them had to take a leap, take a chance, make the first move. If not, she'd spend years beating herself up with "might've" and "should've."

"I'm thinking of saving my new resolutions until tomorrow," she said. After she left, after her life took a normal turn again.

"Why's that?"

Nell Rose took a deep breath and stepped toward Julian. "I don't want to give up men just yet." She wrapped her arms around him, rested her cheek against his back. "I'm not delusional. I know that after I leave here tomorrow I'll never see you again. But we have…something. It's just physical, I know, an oddity brought to life because we're trapped here, and we're both alone." She didn't want to use the word *lonely,* which was just as true, but sounded too sad and desperate. "I don't do this," she whispered. "I don't have sex with men I've just met, but this is different. You're different." When she was with him *she* felt different.

If she was wrong and he didn't want her, she'd slink back

to the couch, pretend to sleep and then get out of here in the morning, as soon as possible.

But she wasn't wrong. Julian turned, tilted her head back with one hand and kissed her, as he had that morning. He took her mouth with his, kissed her as if he were starving, as she was. His tongue speared into her mouth and she almost dropped to the ground, her body's response was so intense.

It was as if all day they'd been engaged in a subtle fore-play—and perhaps they had been. She couldn't kiss him deep enough, couldn't touch enough. Standing there, their bodies fit together as if they'd been made for this, and for what was to come.

Julian grabbed the hem of her sweater and pulled it up, over her head. He tossed it aside with one hand, kissing her throat while he unfastened her bra and slipped it off. "Are you on the pill?"

"Yes," she said, though her answer came out a barely decipherable moan as he cupped a breast in one hand and ran his thumb over the nipple.

"Good. I don't want to stop and go upstairs to search for a condom."

"No, don't stop for anything."

Just like this morning, she felt as though she was on a ride. She soared, she flew and this time she wasn't going to get off before the ride was done.

Julian unfastened her jeans and pushed them, and her panties, down. She stepped out of them and kicked them aside, which left her completely naked. Usually she was shy in front of anyone if she wasn't fully clothed, but she didn't feel shy with Julian. He looked at her as if he liked what he saw. He caressed her curves and slipped a hand between her legs, where he stroked. She was already wet, trembling, ready.

She wanted to see his body, as he was seeing hers, so she began with the shirt, pushing it up and away, tossing it aside. As she'd suspected, he had a fine, hard, well-sculpted body. There was a very nice six-pack, and a smattering of crisp, dark chest hair, as well as a dark line of hair that disappeared into his jeans. His body was perfection, except for the very nasty scar on his left side.

"Oh, my God," she whispered, laying her hand over the scar. "What on earth…"

"It doesn't matter." Julian reinforced that statement by kissing her again, driving away any thought but the most basic.

She unfastened his pants, but he had to kick off his boots in order to remove them. He did, and then there they were, naked, in front of the fire, so hot they could've stepped outside and melted the snow for miles. Who needed the sun?

They stood for several minutes, studying one another, feeling and learning each other's bodies. Julian was beautiful, scar and all. He looked the way a man was supposed to look, slightly hairy and tough and…hard. Very, very hard. She touched him, let her fingers dance up and down and up again. He quivered, and she liked it, that she could make him shake.

He laid her on the carpet in front of the fire and, looking up, she caught his eye. There was such an intensity about him, such power. No wonder she'd had such horrible luck with men in the past; she'd never known anyone like Julian. No man in the future would ever measure up to him. He was ruining her, here and now. She wanted very much to be ruined. Completely, totally ruined.

He took a nipple in his mouth and suckled there, his mouth warm and wet, his tongue thorough. He tasted her, aroused her, teased her. She was so ready for him, so anxious, so quickly and completely swept away—but he refused to rush. His mouth on her throat was almost lazy, and the touch there made her shudder and rock. Her skin against his was sensual, beautiful, and she reveled in the sensation, taking a moment to think of nothing but the way his flesh and hers met. There was a wonderful heat, a soaring need for more and a tingle of complete happiness. For now, her life was perfect.

When he parted her thighs and caressed her where she throbbed for him, she began to feel as if she were falling.

"Now, Julian," she said as his fingers teased her. "Please, *now.*"

He rose up, pushed inside her hard and fast, and it was like a relief…and also a beginning. His movements were slow at first, and so were hers. She didn't want to rush; she wanted to enjoy, to savor. She held her breath, concentrated on the exquisite sensation of Julian's body and hers coming together. He moved faster, she held on to him and met his thrusts with her own. Orgasm teased her, flitting just out of reach, there and not there, coming, coming…and then she burst, and release rushed through her body on waves that made her cry out, lurch and clutch Julian to her.

Intense, amazing, shattering…and simultaneous. Perfection.

They lay there for a moment, catching their breaths, both of them unwilling to let go. Cold? No, she wasn't at all cold. Alone? Not at the moment.

Resolutions? Maybe tomorrow.

CHAPTER FIVE

THERE WASN'T REALLY ROOM enough for both of them on the couch, but they managed. Entangled, naked, a blanket half covering them as they slept.

Well, Nell Rose slept, her back against his chest, her head in the hollow of his shoulder. Julian lay there, enjoying the feel of her skin against his, chewing on the fact that he should know better but was very glad that he'd ignored his good instincts in this case.

Nell Rose Collins, for all her talk about independence and a lack of expectations, was a woman who wanted—needed—a relationship in order to be truly happy. Julian had given up on the idea of a healthy romantic relationship long ago. He liked sex as much as the next man, and he had women who were friends. But put the two together, and it was as though every speck of common sense went out the window.

His own marriage was proof of that, as was the scar Nell Rose had asked him about earlier.

Like every other cop, Julian had hated the domestic calls. When those calls were repeatedly made to the same addresses, it was hard to continue to feel sympathy for those involved. At first, he'd tried to do everything he could to help Kaylynn Smith—a young mother of four who was very pretty if you could see past the bruises her husband made sure she wore. She'd call 911 when her life was in danger, but when push came to shove, Kaylynn always leaped to her husband's defense.

Until that night. On the night that had changed his life, Julian had walked up to the door of the Smiths' small house, stepping around the kids' toys on the porch, expecting to go through the same old routine. He'd calm everyone down, and Kaylynn would declare that she loved her husband and he was going to change. The bastard would apologize and swear it wouldn't happen again, and Julian would be ordered out of the house.

What a waste of time.

He'd heard the gunshot as he'd lifted his hand to knock on the door, had drawn his weapon as he rushed into the house to find Manny Smith lying in a puddle of his own blood and Kaylynn standing over him with a freshly blooming bruise on her face, a small revolver in her hand and a deadly gleam in her usually dull eyes. She'd looked up, caught Julian's eye and said in an emotionless voice, "I couldn't let him hit my babies."

Julian heard the little ones crying in another room, but he couldn't see them from where he stood. He certainly never saw the next move coming, as a terrified and irrational Kaylynn lifted the revolver and fired at him.

He returned fire; she dropped to the floor beside Manny, and the kids came running out of the back of the house, screaming and crying. Their parents were both dead on the floor. Julian was wounded, bleeding, calling for assistance on his radio.

And the little one, five-year-old Jacy who had blond curls and a bruise that matched her mother's, picked up the gun Kaylynn had dropped and walked over to Julian. With tears streaming down her face, she'd pointed the revolver at the man who'd shot her mother. Julian had stared down the barrel of a gun, and at the other end of that weapon stood an angelic-looking, utterly devastated child.

He'd surged up to grab the child's wrist and push the gun to the side. She tried to fight him, screamed as he easily took the weapon from her. Julian bled, his vision swam and the wail of sirens grew louder, closer. One of the older boys rushed forward to scoop Jacy up and move her out of Julian's reach, all the time glaring at the cop who'd killed their mother as if he wished with all his heart that his little sister had been able to pull the trigger.

That was horror. That was the nightmare that kept him up at night, that gave him chills—that had made him walk away from what others had told him was a "promising career."

And now he hid here, writing stories that scared other people and avoiding women like Nell Rose like the plague.

Until now.

He buried his face in her hair, closed his eyes and ran his hand down her body, breast to thigh, his fingers delving between her legs to caress. There was nothing here but sex, no deeper connection, no romance. Tomorrow she'd be gone, but that didn't mean that he couldn't enjoy tonight. Nell Rose woke slowly, her hips moving in time with his easy stroke. She sighed in contentment.

"I've never come awake like this before," she whispered. "I like it."

He moved her hair aside and kissed her neck, as his fingers moved deeper into her wetness, as he stroked her harder, faster. Her sigh turned into a gasp.

Julian didn't know what twist of fate had dumped Nell Rose on his doorstep, or what trick of chemistry attracted him to her so strongly. Maybe it didn't matter why or how.

Maybe, for the first time in years, he should just accept and enjoy.

He felt her body begin to shudder; thrust two fingers inside her heat. She came hard and fast, making a noise deep in her throat as she jerked and trembled. Her body relaxed, she unwound. Melted into him. Her gasp turned into a sigh again, and he released her.

"You're going to think I'm so easy," Nell Rose said as she turned to face him, her lips tracing a line along his throat, her hands as bold as his had been as she lifted one leg and draped it over his hip, then guided his sex to hers and gently, easily, took him into her heat. She sighed again, rocked her hips gently. "I want more," she whispered. "I want everything."

And he gave it to her.

NELL ROSE WAS SAD TO SEE the sun come out, sad to see the snow begin to melt here and there. Since the sunshine had already melted a portion of the snow by the time she and Julian awoke, it was impossible for him to tell if the disturbance beside the porch was deer tracks or not.

She no longer cared much if what she'd heard last night had been a deer or a bear or a mountain lion. To be honest, she didn't care about much at all. She couldn't remember the last time she'd been so content.

Sun or not, they still didn't have any power. It wasn't as if she was suffering from the cold anymore, and they had everything they needed. Julian had even heated water on the stove and poured it on top of cold water in the bathtub, which was heavenly. She had candlelight, warm water, soap and Julian Maddox.

Now, *this* was a vacation.

It would be silly of her to imagine that this thing with Julian was more than it was. True, she wasn't always clearheaded where men were concerned, but how could she not wonder what it would be like if she and Julian were truly together? Physically they were definitely compatible, but beyond that, did they have anything in common? Did she care if they did or not? Did he care? When he touched her this way, she thought…probably not.

She sat between his legs, his arms wound possessively around her. The water wouldn't be warm for much longer, so she savored the sensations of warm water and body heat, of one body fitting so comfortably against the other. There was such a contrast between the cold air around them and the warmth they created.

"If the sun keeps shining, I'll bet the tow truck will be able to get to my car by this afternoon," she said. Could Julian hear the regret in her voice? She didn't want to go, not yet. "Even if I can't drive to the cabin I rented, I should be able to get a ride."

"I can give you a ride," Julian said.

Her heart sank. Obviously he wasn't as happy with this arrangement as she was, though that hard length poking her in the backside kinda hinted that he was happy enough.

"Or you can stay here," he added casually.

"Can I?"

"You can."

"I don't want to impose…" she began.

Julian laughed. She hadn't heard him laugh often, and it was very nice. "Impose?" he repeated. "Is that what you think this is?"

Nell Rose didn't know what this was. She only knew she didn't want it to end.

"The water's getting cold," she said, leaning forward.

"So?" Julian reached out and grabbed her, pulling her back to him. "We can warm things up."

"Why don't we dry off and huddle under the covers on your bed for a while?" Nell Rose suggested.

"A bed sounds good to me. How about…" Julian went very still, and then he asked, "Did you hear that?"

For a moment she strained to hear sounds from afar, and just as she was about to say, "I don't hear anything," she did. A footstep. A creaking board. That was no deer—and the sound came from inside the house.

They stood together, slowly, as soundlessly as possible.

"Did you lock the door after you came in from checking the deer tracks?" Nell Rose whispered.

"I don't think so," Julian said as he stepped from the tub. Nell Rose followed, stepping onto the bath mat. Julian dried off just enough to get his jeans on, ordered her to stay put and headed for the stairs.

Stay put? Was he nuts? She dried off faster than he had and grabbed the flannel shirt Julian had set aside to put on after their bath. It was quicker than getting into her own jeans and shirt, since she only had to wear the one garment to be properly covered. She didn't want to be entirely naked if she ran into the sheriff downstairs.

Surely that was it. The sheriff and Julian were friends. Sheriff Tielkens had probably come by to check on the unwanted houseguest and see about getting the car towed. Who else could it be? They were pretty far out in the county. Maybe around here people just walked in when they dropped by. Maybe someone had realized that Julian was not alone and had sneaked right back out again, trying to avoid embarrassment.

Wearing the warm flannel shirt that fell to midthigh, Nell Rose crept halfway down the stairs, her head craning forward so she could see what was coming. As the living room came into view she saw Julian, a fireplace poker in one hand, walking from the front door toward the kitchen. He caught sight of her standing there, made a face of displeasure—either because she'd disobeyed his order or because he'd found evidence of an intruder, since he certainly didn't have anything else to be displeased about—and continued on.

JULIAN CURSED AS HE LOCKED the kitchen door. Maybe he'd left the front door unlocked, but he sure as hell hadn't left the kitchen door unlocked and *partially open*. Someone had walked in, while he and Nell Rose had been upstairs. How long had they been here? What had they taken?

He found Nell Rose sitting on the stairs, her legs bare, the too-roomy flannel shirt pooling around her. Her eyes were wide, her expression one of caution—and even fear. He barely knew her, so why did that expression get to him? Why did it grab on to his gut and hold on?

By this afternoon the roads would be clear enough to drive upon. Sam could collect her car; he could drive her to her rental cabin and drop her off there. They'd never see each other again. That was the deal, right?

"Stay," he said softly.

Nell Rose's blue eyes widened, and a new emotion blossomed there. "Here?"

"If you'd like. If you'd rather have a week of peace and quiet…"

"No." She stood slowly, bit her lower lip and then continued, "I'm not a great fan of peace and quiet." She looked toward the kitchen. "Did you find anything?"

"Both doors were unlocked. I figure one of my neighbors decided to walk through. Maybe they thought I wasn't at home and were looking for food or coffee, and when they heard us upstairs they made a hasty escape."

"That's rude," she said in a disapproving tone of voice.

"Some of the people up here…" He left it at that.

Nell Rose continued to stand in the middle of the stairs. "You look cold."

"I am."

"Lock the doors and then come to bed." She turned and walked away, her hips swaying, his plain flannel shirt the sexiest piece of clothing he had ever seen on a woman.

"Doors are locked," he said as he followed her up the stairs.

CHAPTER SIX

NELL ROSE HAD WORKED HARD to convince herself that there was no way this relationship was going anywhere. Julian was her last hurrah before giving up men for the year. He was her bag full of cheeseburgers before going on a diet. It was better to think that way than to risk wanting more or, worse, *expecting* more.

The problem was that even with her bad history, she was a world-class romantic. She'd been burned more than once, but she still got starry-eyed when she imagined the possibility of that perfect relationship dancing just out of reach. Why else would she be so content to watch Julian sleep, to wallow in the warmth and scent of the flannel shirt she wore?

He was napping, well into the afternoon, but she couldn't sleep. She didn't want to waste a moment of the little bit of time she had here. A few more days, maybe a week. She suspected a week wouldn't be nearly long enough to get everything she wanted from Julian Maddox.

Nell Rose sat in a chair by the window with her feet tucked beneath her, her drawing pad in her lap, a pencil in her hand. The natural light pouring through that window was enough for her to work by, and enough to illuminate the man on the bed. From the start she'd realized that Julian was handsome, but naked, lying across the bed that way, he was beautiful. The lines of his body, the muscles and the planes of his face, even the puckered, ugly scar on his side…they added up to perfection. She wanted a couple of drawings to remember him by, to pull out and look at when she was feeling lonely or nostalgic.

If a woman could fall in love with a picture…

Without the usual flickering that sometimes preceded the return of power, electricity returned. The clock on the bedside table began to blink; the light in the bathroom came on. The house was instantly filled with the hum of electrical appliances and computers and clocks coming to life.

In a way it was a shame. She'd rather liked the isolation the snowstorm and the loss of power had afforded them. The weekend wouldn't have happened otherwise, and she wouldn't trade this weekend for anything.

But power meant hot water, a working oven and heat well beyond the gas fireplace. Tonight, her nose and her toes would be as warm as the rest of her body. What could she make Julian for dinner? She'd raid his pantry and the freezer, which they'd kept closed while the electricity was out to preserve the food there.

Julian slept on, unaware of the return of power, unaware that she watched him. She moved the chair a few feet to the left so she had a good view from another angle. The resulting drawing revealed the power in his legs, the ripples of his torso. The scar. She wouldn't think about giving him up until she absolutely had to. Until then…cheeseburgers.

She set the pad aside when Julian began to stir, joined him in the bed as he awakened, sliding her legs along his, placing her chest against his. Oh, the way she fit here…

"How long has the power been on?" he asked as he glanced at the blinking clock.

"Long enough for there to be hot water, I'm guessing." She kissed him. Briefly and then not so briefly. It was so easy to get lost in him, to kiss until she felt as if she was falling, as if there was nothing beyond the two of them. "Join me for a shower?"

He sat up, with her in his arms. "Why not?"

Nell Rose slipped out of the bed and headed for the master bathroom, unbuttoning and dropping the flannel shirt as she went. She was not at all embarrassed to be totally naked in front of Julian; instead she felt empowered, knowing that he wanted her. As she reached the bathroom door, the phone rang.

He reached for the phone. "I'll be right there."

"Don't dillydally," she said, closing the door behind her and turning on the water.

THE CALLER ID INDICATED a Birmingham, Alabama number, but there was no name. A cell phone, most likely. "Hello?" Julian answered briskly.

"Mr. Maddox?"

"Yes."

"My name is Stu Grayson. Is Nell Rose Collins there? Please don't indicate that I've asked about her, if she's nearby," he added quickly.

"Nell Rose is here," Julian said. He didn't like the cautious tone of the man's voice. The hair on the back of his neck rose in warning. "But she's not in the room at the moment."

Grayson sighed. "I just wanted to make sure that she's okay. When her father told me where she was, I was naturally concerned. Don't get me wrong, she's a good worker, she's a valued employee, but when it comes to Julian Maddox, she's a bit of a nut."

Julian's entire body went cold. "What do you mean?"

Grayson laughed nervously. "Well, everyone in the office knows that she's your number one fan. She says she's written you a couple of times, told you that she thought you were soul mates, or some such nonsense. I just wanted to call and check on her because, lovely as she is, she can be obsessive, and I'd hate for her to get hurt."

"Obsessive how?" Julian asked tightly.

"I really shouldn't say," Grayson began cautiously, and then he continued, "but if anyone has a right to know, it's you. She recently became involved with one of our junior partners, a married man, and when he tried to break it off with her she freaked out, lost control. I think she really convinced herself that she didn't know he was married. Given that recent excitement, when her father told me she was staying at your house I was naturally concerned. It couldn't be a coincidence." Grayson cleared his throat. "Is she okay?"

Julian felt like the floor had fallen out from under him, and for a minute he couldn't catch his breath. Very quickly, his shock turned to anger. He was such an idiot! "She's fine. As a matter of fact, I'm going to take her to the cabin she rented this afternoon. The roads are clear enough for us to get out."

"Good. I hope she wasn't any trouble."

"No trouble at all."

"Um, Mr. Maddox, it might be better if you didn't tell Nell Rose that I called. She can be very sensitive when her delusions are questioned."

"Are you trying to tell me she's completely *unstable?*" Julian asked sharply.

"Good afternoon, Mr. Maddox."

Grayson ended the call, and soon Julian was listening to a dial tone. He stared at the bathroom door for a few long minutes. Was he the biggest fool in the world, or what? In the real world this sort of thing didn't happen. Pretty, lost women didn't land on a man's doorstep—and his penis— sweet and charming and ready for anything a weekend

alone might provide. He'd been such an idiot to see more
in Nell Rose than was really there. He didn't know how or
why she'd gotten those letters to Knoxville to be mailed,
or why she didn't want a Birmingham postmark on her
letters, but that was the least of his problems.

Number One Fan. Connected soul-deep. That was
enough to tell him all he needed to know.

"The hot water's not going to last forever," she called.

Julian walked into the bathroom, which was filled with
steam. Nell Rose's form was misty beyond the glass. Misty
and perfect, rounded and pale. She moved with an innate
sensuality, a sexual grace. It was all a lie, she was a lie, so
why did the sight of her make him hard?

He slid back the shower door and stepped under the
spray.

"This is the biggest shower I have ever—" Nell Rose
began.

He caught her to him, lifted her wet body. "Is this what
you want from me?" he asked, his voice raspy as he spread
her legs and pushed inside her. He hadn't touched her,
hadn't readied her, so she wasn't as slick as she'd been
before. Still, she was ready, welcoming. Without hesitation
she opened for him, took him in.

She gasped, tilted her head back, closed her eyes. "Yes,
Julian. This is what I want."

There was no kissing, no teasing, no foreplay. He just
plunged deep into her tight body, riding her hard as hot
water sprayed down upon them. There was no hint in her
soft body, her welcoming embrace, her satisfied sighs, that
she was a liar. A stalker. The Nell Rose he knew was as
much fiction as any monster he'd ever created.

She held on tight, as he backed her against the tile wall,
propped her there and slowed his movements. Nell Rose
was a lie, but damn, she felt good. Tight, hot, moving

against him in just the right rhythm as the shower sprayed over them and water ran down their joined bodies. He pounded into her, hard and fast, when slow was no longer possible for either of them. He felt her fingers in his hair, her legs around his body, but most of all he felt her where she wrapped around him, where she took him in.

Perhaps she was fiction, a real-life monster, but she came like a woman, clutching and gasping, her inner muscles spasming around him until he came with her, giving over all that he had to a lie.

She laughed as he put her back on her feet. "I didn't expect—"

He couldn't allow her to finish; he was already too caught up in the lie. "Dry off and pack your bags. I'm taking you to the cabin you rented before it turns dark and the roads refreeze."

Her face fell. Maybe Grayson hadn't been clear enough with his warning. Was Nell Rose completely delusional? Did she honestly believe everything she'd told him this weekend? Maybe she really did see herself as an ordinary woman with ordinary dreams that never seemed to work out. Had she somehow forgotten that she'd driven into the ditch at the bottom of the hill in front of his house on purpose?

"I thought…" she murmured.

"This weekend was a mistake," he said. "Fun, but definitely a mistake. I've come to my senses and it's time you did the same." He couldn't believe that he'd allowed her to get to him the way she had. She'd barreled past all his defenses with her act.

"Sure." Nell Rose turned her head, as if she couldn't bear to look at him anymore, and stepped out of the shower. "It'll just take me a few minutes to get packed."

She ran out of the bathroom, grabbing a towel as she

went. And when he was alone, Julian placed both hands against the tile and stood there in silence, letting the hot water rain down upon him.

NELL ROSE COULDN'T PACK fast enough. What had happened? One minute Julian had been fine, the next he'd been... Well, the next had been just fine, too, but after that he'd all but kicked her out of his house. There was no *all but* about it. He *had* kicked her out. Who had been on the phone?

A girlfriend! A wife! She'd done it again. Maybe whatever woman Julian had in his life was on her way, now that the roads were clearing. Naturally, he had to get his weekend fling out of the house. That's what she was, a weekend fling. An easy, willing, desperate woman who'd all but thrown herself at him. Strike the *all but*. She *had* thrown herself at him. What man wouldn't take advantage of such an offer?

Was that why he hadn't kissed her in the shower, because the call had reminded him that he wasn't free, as he'd told her he was? He always kissed her; she loved the way he kissed, but that last time had been different. It had been what she'd always said this weekend would be; just sex, with no illusion of more. Like it or not, she had begun to feel more.

No, to *imagine* more. Once again she'd ignored reality and created her own world where love at first sight was possible, and an accident could lead her to the door of the man she'd been searching for all her life.

This was it; she was done with men. Truly, this time. She didn't need a resolution to remind her that where the opposite sex was concerned, she was destined to be a failure.

Her hair was still damp—just towel dried, since she didn't even want to take the time to use her hair dryer. It wasn't smart to go out in the cold with her hair far from dry, but maybe if she was lucky she'd catch cold and die of pneumonia. She'd almost finished packing when Julian appeared in her doorway, her drawing pad hanging from one careless hand.

"I'm such an idiot," he said. "Are you really on the pill?"

It was more than she could take; with that question he pushed her past the breaking point. "Yes!" She reached for her birth control pills. The round container was tucked in a side pocket of her suitcase. Maybe she did want kids, but in her mind children were part of a package that included a husband. She was old-fashioned that way. "Check it out." She threw the pill case at him. "Count them if you like." Julian actually studied the package, as if she might be trying to pull a fast one on him. "What is it with you? The electricity comes back on and you turn into an asshole?"

"That's as good an explanation as any," he said as he passed her pills back to her.

"I won't be needing these anymore," she said as she dropped the pills into her suitcase.

"Why not?"

"Because I'm going to become a nun." Not that she was Catholic. Maybe they'd take her in out of pity, since Methodists didn't have nuns.

"I'm sure you'd make a lousy Sister Nell Rose."

"Why should I let that stop me? I'm lousy at everything else I try. Why not add chastity to the list?" Her frustration was showing, but she didn't care.

"Don't forget your souvenir." Julian tossed her drawing pad onto the bed, that last, not-quite-finished sketch on top.

She should rip up the drawings. Maybe throw them in the fireplace, for effect. But instead she dropped the pad into her suitcase and closed the lid with force. Angry as she was, she was foolishly unwilling to give up all that she had left of Julian.

NELL ROSE HADN'T BEEN as far off her route as she'd thought. The small collection of tacky rental cabins, built too close together to provide a true mountain getaway, was a little more than ten minutes from Julian's house. They made the trip in strained silence. She stared out the window. He kept his eyes on the road.

What made him the angriest was that he hadn't seen it. Hadn't even imagined that the sweet woman he'd had sex with all weekend wasn't exactly who she claimed to be. In one of his stories he'd make her a succubus or a soul-sucking vampire, but as usual, real life was much scarier than anything he could come up with. Nell Rose was the nut-job. She was the *Number One Fan* who'd purposely driven off the road and presented herself at his door as a damsel in distress.

After she collected the key from the woman at the front office, he drove her up a hill to one of the smaller rentals, a square, orangish cabin with a big deck, a long front porch, a hot tub and a decent, if not spectacular, view. It looked as if the matching cabins close by were unoccupied, though now that the roads were passable other guests might soon be arriving.

He unloaded her bags from the backseat—one heavy suitcase and a grocery sack full of chocolate—and set them on the front porch. She unlocked the door, opened it onto a rustic-looking interior.

"Thanks for the ride," she said, her voice frosty.

"No problem," he responded. "I'll call about getting your car towed in the morning, and I'll tell Sam where you're staying."

"That's very generous of you."

Watching her, he was hit with a wave of resentment that she wasn't exactly who she claimed to be. "Why didn't you just tell me the truth?"

She looked at him as if he'd lost his mind. "Excuse me?"

"Sorry. I should've kept my mouth shut."

"This doesn't make any sense. You know damn well I don't have any idea what you're talking about." Her eyes narrowed; he saw the wheels turning in that messed-up brain of hers. "I missed something," she said in a softer voice. "That phone call…I thought maybe it was a woman…"

Julian held up his hands. "It doesn't matter. All that matters is from here on out, I want you to leave me the hell alone."

Her face fell, for a moment, and then it was transformed by a rush of anger. "Gladly!" She slammed the door, and Julian couldn't get back to his car fast enough.

SHE WASN'T GOING TO CRY; she was *not* going to cry. Who cried over a cheeseburger? Julian Maddox had just been a way to pass the time, unexpected vacation entertainment.

But soon after she'd slammed the door on Julian, Nell Rose began to sob. If there was such a thing as destiny, maybe she was simply destined to always be a screwup where men were concerned. Maybe she was supposed to get her heart broken again and again. And again. How many times was she going to go through this before she just gave up? How long before it was preferable not to take the chance of getting hurt?

Maybe she was already there. Maybe this was it.

She didn't allow the tears to last long, though she continued to feel as if she'd lost something precious. Looking back she realized that she'd once again created something where there was nothing. Julian had been in it for the sex, nothing more. It wasn't like they were dating, engaged or in love. She'd become someone else for a couple of days; she'd let him believe that she was the kind of woman who spread her legs for any man with a penis and a little spare time. Like it or not, she'd felt more. Maybe he'd found the sketches and seen in them what she hadn't been able to share—that she had feelings for him. Maybe she'd been right all along and he had a woman in his life who was on her way to his house—maybe even *their* house. She didn't know; she'd never know, and that was annoying.

Her weekend with Julian should've ended better. She should have a clue as to why he'd turned so angry and hurtful.

In the cabin where she'd be spending the week, her cell got a signal, though not much of one. She called her dad and told him she was where she was supposed to be, and then, since the battery was low and she didn't want to talk to anyone anyway, she turned off the cell phone and plugged it in to charge.

She glanced around the cabin. The main room was rather plain, but the furnishings were sturdy. It was nothing like Julian's house, but then, she shouldn't expect it to be. There was a bookcase filled with paperbacks, and she spotted a familiar title. *Henry's Ghost.* She never had finished the book, since Julian had found better ways to distract her.

Her car would be drivable in a day or two, and when it was, she was out of here. But for now, her vacation could begin.

Like the New Year, her vacation was off to a horrid start.

CHAPTER SEVEN

JULIAN STARED AT THE COMPUTER screen. He might as well work, since he had nothing better to do, but he couldn't get his mind on the story he should be writing. He was still hung up on Nell Rose and what had happened with her, who she really was, how fooled he'd been by her pretty, innocent face. "Be honest," he muttered to himself. "It wasn't her *face* that robbed you of all reason."

When the phone rang, he nearly jumped out of his chair. Spotting Paul's cell number on the caller ID, he answered with a brisk, "You owe me big-time."

"You'll have to explain that later." Paul's voice sounded tired, strained. "Is Nell Rose Collins still there?"

He shouldn't be surprised that the call was about her. "No, she's not."

"Where is she?"

Julian told the sheriff where Nell Rose was staying, and then he asked, "Why? Did you find out that she's the Knoxville nut-job?"

"Huh?" Paul sounded truly confused. *Welcome to the club.*

"The letters, my *Number One Fan*. How did you figure it out?"

"Sorry, you've lost me. The Birmingham police want me to pick her up. One of the lawyers at her firm was murdered, and she was the last person known to see him alive. She's a, uh, person of interest."

Which was Paul's way of saying she was a suspect. He tried to imagine Nell Rose killing someone, anyone, and mixed up as she was—he couldn't see it. She'd lie through her teeth, paint a false picture, maybe get a little obsessive, but murder? If she was capable of killing a man, then he was blinder than he'd thought. He told Paul as much.

"Well, Stu Grayson might beg to differ. He got a bullet to the head Friday afternoon, right before Nell Rose left town."

A chill ran up Julian's spine. "Stu Grayson called here a couple of hours ago."

"Maybe in one of your books that could happen, but in real life there's no way. Grayson's body was found early this morning by a janitorial crew. He's been dead since Friday."

Julian closed his eyes, and the pieces fell into place. Nell Rose wasn't the stalker; the caller was. Somehow the freak had been watching, all this time, and he'd come up with a plan to get Nell Rose out of the house using the words he'd written in his disturbing letters to condemn her. Julian couldn't help but wonder—was he in danger? Or was *she? How the hell had his stalker known Stu Grayson's name?*

"How far are you from the cabin where Nell Rose is staying?"

"Twenty minutes."

"Ten minutes for me. I'll see you there. Hurry."

He hung up in the middle of a confused question from the sheriff. There wasn't time for explanations. If he was right, he'd all but handed Nell Rose over to an obsessed man who might be capable of anything.

NELL ROSE JUMPED OUT of her skin when someone knocked on the door. She tossed the paperback aside without marking her page. Obviously horror novels were not for her, written by Julian or not.

She walked to the door expecting to find a man about her car, or the woman who managed the cabins. It was a complete surprise to see Marcus Stillwell, a junior partner from the firm, standing there with a manila folder in his hands.

Nell Rose looked at him, then at the folder. "You have got to be kidding me," she said. "You tracked me down for *work?*" She couldn't imagine any sort of problem that someone else couldn't handle until she got back.

Marcus was as much a workaholic as Stu. In fact, she'd passed him on Friday afternoon, rushing into the office as she was rushing out.

"I'm so sorry to bother you on your vacation," he said. "Can I come in?"

"Sure." Nell Rose backed up a few steps and opened the door wide. It would soon be dark, but at the moment the evening sun lit the remaining snow and the cabins down the hill. "You could've called."

"I tried to call you on your cell, but I couldn't get through."

"Oh, yeah," she said.

Marcus was one of those upwardly mobile young guys who dated a series of beautiful women. None of his relationships lasted very long. He always led people to believe that he was the one who ended the relationships, but Nell Rose suspected that wasn't always the case. Even though he was blond and handsome—in a clean-cut, all-American way—and she had never seen him not dressed as if he'd stepped out of a magazine, he rarely looked a person in the eye, that she'd seen, and he was selfish. Everything was always about Marcus. His career, what he wanted, his schedule. Yes, he was the kind of man who would track down a woman on vacation to get what he wanted from her.

Figures.

But if she was going to concentrate on her career from here on out, and her vacation already sucked big-time, what difference did it make?

"What can I do?" she asked, reaching for the manila folder, taking it from him, opening it to look down at a small stack of blank paper. She leafed through, making sure she hadn't missed anything. "I'm confused..."

She lifted her head as Marcus pulled a gun from his spine, where it had been concealed beneath his suit jacket. He sighed as he pointed the gun at her.

"You saw me Friday afternoon."

"Yeah. So?"

"You weren't supposed to be there."

She took an instinctive step away from Marcus. "I had to go back for the directions I printed off my computer."

"Thank you for that, by the way," he said. "It was very easy to get onto your computer and find all your vacation information."

"Why would you do that?" she asked, but as she spoke her mind was spinning with possibilities. None of them were good.

"You can blow a hole in my alibi, Nell Rose," Marcus said. "I'm so sorry, but I can't allow that to happen."

AT THIS RATE, IT WOULDN'T take him a full ten minutes to get to Nell Rose, but as the day cooled, spots on the road refroze, so Julian couldn't drive as fast as he'd like.

The stalker, the nut-job, had gone to a lot of trouble to get Nell Rose out of Julian's house. Maybe he'd leave her alone, be satisfied to know that he'd accomplished what he'd set out to do in getting her out of the way, but then again…maybe not. The fact that he'd done enough research to find out the name of Nell Rose's boss—her *dead* boss—was what disturbed him the most. The stalker who had imagined a relationship with Julian might want to hurt Nell Rose, scare her…maybe even take her life. The possibilities were endless and, in the end, unimportant. All that mattered was that she was very likely in danger, and he had put her there.

He could've asked Nell Rose about that phone call, could've confronted her, but instead he'd taken the word of a stranger and kicked her out without asking for even the simplest explanation. Julian had to accept that he was so broken that he wasn't only willing but *anxious* to accept the worst about a woman who'd been nothing but open and honest with him.

He'd thrown her away. He'd ignored his gut feelings and tossed her out. Maybe he'd realized that she was getting too close, that their unexpected, powerful relationship had never been just about sex.

Maybe he'd get to Nell Rose in time. Maybe the stalker hadn't moved in yet and he could be the knight in shining armor he'd thought was long dead. Maybe she was in her cabin alone, safe and unaware, and the stalker was out there somewhere laughing at his little prank.

Julian's heart pounded; these days he didn't have a lot of faith in maybes.

NELL ROSE COULDN'T TAKE her eyes off the gun. "Alibi for what?"

"Stu caught me embezzling from a client, and he wouldn't be reasonable about the situation, wouldn't give me time to make amends. So I killed him."

Nell Rose's legs began to tremble. "You killed Stu?"

"Not half an hour after you left the office, so…" Marcus

shrugged his shoulders. "Sorry, babe, but you were in the wrong place at the wrong time."

Nell Rose licked her lips. She could hear her own heart beat; she tasted pennies—fear. "What are you going to do?"

He lifted the gun an inch or two. "This is the weapon that killed Stu. You're going to kill yourself with the same gun. I'll leave his cell phone and a couple of other effects I took from the office here, and it should be an open-and-shut case. Spurned woman kills her lover and then herself. Sad story, but common enough." He lifted the gun and put the muzzle to her forehead. "It'll make things ever so much easier if you'll write a note."

"Why should I agree to that?" she asked, taking a step back. "Why should I help you?"

"Because it'll buy you a few more minutes of life, that's why," Marcus said. When she backed up he moved with her, in an awkward kind of dance.

She didn't have much hope of rescue, but if she died immediately there was no hope at all. A few minutes might buy her the time to think, to come up with a plan to get away. If Marcus would relax enough to move that gun aside, maybe she could jump him and wrest the weapon out of his hand.

And if he did manage to kill her, maybe one last note to the world wouldn't be such a bad idea.

She sat at the table with a ballpoint pen Marcus provided and one of the sheets of paper out of his folder.

I'm so tired of being hurt, of being wrong...of falling in love too fast and having my heart broken.

"That's good," Marcus said as he read over her shoulder. The gun was still pointed at her head.

"I'm cooperating," Nell Rose said tightly. "Can you please move that gun to the side? It makes me nervous."

"I don't think so."

"You're not going to shoot me in the head with that thing, are you?" Nell Rose asked. "Women don't shoot themselves. It'll be much more believable if you use poison or a razor blade." She couldn't stop the shudder that worked through her body, as she imagined either of those possibilities. But if she could make him second-guess his plan, she'd buy a few more minutes.

"Slit wrists would be a nice touch," he said musingly. "And I wouldn't have to worry so much about gun residue and fingerprints. Keep writing," he added in a louder voice.

Sometimes I think I just have bad luck when it comes to men, but I thought this time was different. She'd thought Julian was different. And then, pen over paper, she paused. If Marcus got what he wanted, if she was found dead of an apparent suicide and this note was a part of the evidence, would Julian realize she had written about him? Would he think he was the reason she'd take her own life? As ugly as things had turned toward the end, she didn't want him to carry that burden.

The phone call.

"What did you say to Julian to turn him against me?"

"I told him you were a stalker."

"And he believed you?"

"I broke into the house yesterday. You two were upstairs, and I was trying to come up with a way to get rid of both of you without making it look like murder, because the murder of Julian Maddox would raise a few eyebrows and get the cops much too interested. I started poking around and found some letters from an obsessed fan. When I called this afternoon I used a few key phrases from those letters when I told him you'd written them, and he bought it, hook, line and sinker."

"You don't think they'll trace that phone call and figure out what happened?"

"I used Stu's cell," Marcus said, sounding pleased with himself. "That'll raise questions, maybe they'll think you had an accomplice, but…it won't lead back to me, and that's all that matters."

"You've thought of everything."

"I have, haven't I?"

Nell Rose continued writing. *None of this is your fault, so please don't blame yourself. I could've loved you. Maybe, in a strange way, I already do.*

"What's this?" Marcus grabbed the paper and read what she'd just written. "This isn't a suicide note! Stu is already dead and you're supposed to be talking about *him.*"

Nell Rose snatched the paper from him. What was he going to do, shoot her? He already planned to do that. "This is my suicide note, you nimrod. I'll say whatever the hell I want."

He grabbed her by the back of her sweater, hauled her out of the chair and ripped the paper from her hand. "Okay, we'll have to go with no note. I need to get out of here before it gets dark and the roads turn slick again." He pressed the muzzle to her temple. "I sure as hell don't have time to sit around and wait for you to bleed to death, so a shot to the head will have to do."

Nell Rose heard the revving engine that told her a car was racing up the hill. Marcus heard it, too, and his attention faltered. The gun shifted, and Nell Rose realized this was her chance. She turned, brought her knee up into Marcus's groin, and then, as he grunted and flailed, she turned and ran.

She ran for the door, which seemed horribly far away. It was like a dream where she couldn't move fast enough as she waited for a bullet to slam into her back. At least if she died this way no one would think she'd taken her own life. Not her father, not her friends…not Julian.

Marcus groaned, and a shot rang out. Nell Rose waited for the pain in her back, but it didn't come. He'd missed. She threw the door open and ran out, as Julian leaped up the steps and onto the porch.

"Are you okay?" he asked, reaching for her. She jumped; he caught her. Together they tumbled to the wooden porch as Marcus came out shooting.

JULIAN ROLLED TO THE SIDE with Nell Rose in his arms. When she was out of the direct line of fire, he released her and jumped up. He didn't have a weapon, and he was well aware that the man—the stalker?—who'd come storming out of Nell Rose's cabin could too easily shift his aim and shoot. Julian didn't like guns. He had no intention of getting shot again. But damned if he was going to cower and wait for it to happen.

Besides, he'd been shot before and had survived. No way would he roll back and wait for the man with the gun to shoot Nell Rose.

All this went through Julian's mind as he rushed the surprised gunman. He knocked the gun hand aside, wrested the weapon away and tossed it over the railing. Old training came back, and it was done in what seemed like a split second. Julian threw the gunman to the porch, pressed his knee into the man's back and twisted an arm up and back until the shooter was immobile and all but squealing for mercy.

He heard Nell Rose's step, turned his head to look at her without easing his hold. "You okay?"

She nodded, the movement quick and more hesitant than he liked.

"The sheriff's on his way."

"Good," she said softly, and then she sank down as if her legs could no longer hold her up. "Marcus was going to kill me," she said. "He…he shot one of my bosses Friday, and I saw him there, and…"

"*He* shot Stu Grayson?"

"You know about that?"

"Long story. I actually thought he was my stalker."

"The phone call," Nell Rose whispered.

"Yeah."

"He told you I was your stalker, and of course, you believed him." She was so honest, so open, he heard the raw pain in her voice. "Why shouldn't you believe him?" she added absently.

Julian felt about two inches tall at the moment. "When Paul called looking for you and told me Grayson was dead, I knew something was very wrong."

She blinked a couple of times. Her eyes, shocked and amazingly blue, widened. "You came here realizing you might run into a man with a gun? Or worse?"

"Pretty much." Julian glanced down at Marcus, who wasn't going anywhere. Marcus was a big man when he had a gun in his hand, but a coward of the first order when he was unarmed. "God, Nell Rose, I'm so sorry."

He heard the sirens approaching. It hadn't been near twenty minutes, so Paul must've dispatched a deputy who was closer to the scene.

"There's no need to apologize," Nell Rose said. "For anything. I mean, there was no reason for you not to believe Marcus when he told you I was a stalker, was there? You don't know me any better than I know you. We're strangers. You put me up for the weekend and we had a bit of fun. End of story."

"Nell Rose…"

"End of story," she whispered.

Two cruisers pulled up the hill, and the deputies were out of their cars and at a run within seconds. Nell Rose stood and moved to the stairs to meet them, though Julian noticed that she gripped the railing tightly for support.

"His name is Marcus Stillwell," she said. "He killed Stu Grayson and tried to kill me." Unable to stand she sat again, as the deputies rushed past her. Her head dropped into her hands. "God, I just want to go home. Somebody please, get me home."

CHAPTER EIGHT

NELL ROSE PUT THE FINISHING touches on the paper she'd written for her art appreciation class. She had to be at the bakery in fifteen minutes, but it was just a five-minute drive from her apartment, so she had time. Valentine's Day meant big business for Alice's Bakery, where Nell Rose worked part-time making cakes, cupcakes, muffins and decadent brownies. She wasn't earning nearly as much as she had when she'd been working at the law firm, but she had some savings to draw on, and strangely enough, she was happier than she'd been in a long time, certain parts of one particular weekend excluded.

Well, most of the time she was happy. As long as she kept herself so busy between classes and baking and drawing that she didn't think too much about Julian Maddox, she was peachy.

He should be completely out of her mind by now. After all, she was making a new life for herself, one filled with activities she loved, her friends and her father. A couple of guys from school had asked her out, and from what she could tell at first glance they weren't losers. But she wasn't interested. They were pale, not physically but in her mind's eye. None of them could hold a candle to Julian.

After the New Year's excitement, she'd gotten back to town just in time to sign up for the winter semester. She was taking a couple of art classes, as well as a history class, and she loved it. Between school and baking, her days were so full she usually fell into bed exhausted at night. There was no time for a man, and for the first time in her life, she didn't want one. No, that was wrong. The truth of the matter was, she didn't *need* a man. It didn't bother her to go to a party alone anymore. She didn't mind listening to her married friends talk about their husbands and their kids. This was her life and she was determined to make the best of it. Until she had her head on straight, how could she even think about adding a man to the mix? She was no longer willing to settle for any male who might be deemed acceptable; she was never again going to settle for anything but the best. Right now she was still convinced that Julian Maddox was the best, and until that passed…

For the first time in years, she wasn't depressed that she was single for Valentine's Day.

Nell Rose wasn't sure she'd ever again trust a man enough to really let him into her life. She was still too hurt by Julian's betrayal—which didn't make a lot of sense, since she'd known him for a much shorter time than she'd known Bill or any of the other men she'd cared for in her past. Like it or not, the man she barely knew was the one who'd hurt her the most.

He'd saved her, too, but that didn't entirely make up for believing Marcus's claim that she was a fruitcake who'd lied her way into his bed. That was just his inner cop coming out to play. Nothing more.

Maybe if she embraced her art and her baking and her single existence, she'd reach the point where she honestly, truly didn't care if she had a man or not. There was more to life; there was more to her. Maybe when she was entirely independent, her love life would miraculously fall into place.

Yeah, right.

When the doorbell rang she closed the file on her

computer and snatched up her purse on the way to the door. She had to scoot. She glanced through the peephole and saw nothing before her but a profusion of red roses.

Wrong apartment. She'd find out who the roses were for and point the poor delivery guy in the right direction. There had been a time when she might feel a bit of envy that those flowers were not for her, but that wasn't the case today.

She opened the door, the roses were lowered and there stood Julian. Nell Rose was so shocked she stutter-stepped back a bit, but her eyes never left his face. He was just as she remembered. Handsome, hard, steely-eyed and observant. And just that glance, his gaze catching hers, was enough to grab her deep down. On the heels of surprise, she felt a rush of anger. How dare he do this to her?

"I wrecked my car in your ditch," he said casually. "Can I come in?"

"I don't have a ditch, and no, you can't come in. What do you want?" she asked, sounding more shrewish than she'd intended. But honestly, how did one greet the man who'd made her fall in love, broken her heart, kicked her to the curb and then saved her life?

His eyebrows lifted slightly. "These are for you."

She didn't take the roses. "You didn't drive five hours to hand-deliver flowers."

"What if I did?"

The truth hit her. She *knew* why he was here. He was lonely; she was easy. At least, he thought that was the case. He didn't know yet that she had changed. "No thanks. I don't want flowers from you."

He didn't even look surprised. "Candy? Dinner?"

Frustration bubbled up. "Aren't there any women in Tennessee? Or have you already screwed your way through the locals and now you're forced to drive to another state looking for sex?" Belatedly, she looked down the hall for nosy, eavesdropping neighbors. Thank goodness, she didn't see any. "Well, I hate to tell you," she said in a lower voice, "but I've changed. You've wasted a trip because you're not getting anywhere near me." She didn't trust as quickly as she once had, and she sure as hell didn't trust Julian Maddox.

He remained calm. "It's more than that. Much more. The truth is, I can't get you out of my head. I've tried, but something happened between us that weekend, and I'm not ready to give you up."

"Maybe I'm ready," she whispered, sounding more vulnerable than she'd intended. "Maybe there was never anything to give up." She shook off her surprise. "Dammit, you *gave me up* when you kicked me out of your house! Look, I'm late for work. Thanks for the flowers, but…no thanks. I'm going to close the door, and when I open it again I expect you to be gone." She closed the door; she shut her eyes and took four long, deep breaths. A part of her wanted to throw open the door and chase Julian down and beg him to come back, but she didn't. She couldn't.

When she opened the door again, she was both relieved and incensed to see that Julian was *not* gone. The roses hung from his hand, no longer presented toward her. The expression in his eyes—determination, yearning, even pain—was what got to her.

He truly wanted her, or at least thought he did. She couldn't let him do this to her; couldn't allow him to make her care and then pull the rug out from under her again. How many times could she survive this kind of hurt? Julian was the one man in the world who could break her heart to the point where it would never recover.

"Give me five minutes," he said. "After that, if you still want me to go—I will."

NELL ROSE RELUCTANTLY STEPPED back and allowed Julian into her apartment. Art supplies were spread over a small dining table and schoolbooks had been set on one end of the couch. He already knew about the job change and her schooling. He also knew she wasn't seeing anyone, though she could've been out with a different man every night, if it suited her. He'd also found out that her chocolate cupcakes were a new bestseller at Alice's Bakery. So, who was the stalker now?

His own stalker had been caught—if you could call a fourteen-year-old girl with too many piercings, a black wardrobe and a vampire fetish a stalker. The poor kid had holed herself in her room every night and written letter after letter to writers, singers and actors whose work might be considered dark. She was mixed-up but harmless, and besides, her fixation with a particular actor was much more intense than her minor obsession with a writer who lived an hour or so up the road.

And now he was the one obsessed. Nell Rose was rightfully pissed with him; he could see it in her eyes and in her stance—in those protective arms crossed over her chest. But he hadn't been able to get her out of his head. He dreamed about her. The heroine in his latest novel had taken on several Nell Rose-like characteristics. No matter where he went in his house, he saw her. He felt her. He was lost without her; the house was too empty without her in it. Even though it was very possible she would reject him, he had to give it a shot.

He only had five minutes. "Paul showed me a crumpled-up piece of paper from the cabin."

Nell Rose blushed. "Marcus forced me to write a fake suicide note. I hope you didn't read too much into that note because I didn't mean a word. It was…fiction."

"You're a terrible liar."

"Well, one of us should be," she shot back, and then she glanced at her watch. "You've got three-and-a-half minutes left."

Where was the line between tenacious suitor and scary-ass dude? He wanted Nell Rose, he was willing to fight for her...but there was a line he couldn't cross. Somehow, he had to convince her to give him a chance. Now.

"I can't stop thinking about you."

"I suppose everyone needs a good laugh now and then," she responded.

Julian tossed the roses onto her couch. Playing it safe wasn't going to get him anywhere with Nell Rose. If he kept beating around the bush she was going to toss him out, close herself off...and he couldn't let that happen.

Time was running out. "I'm looking for a house in Birmingham."

Nell Rose took a step back, away from him. "Why?"

"Because you're here and I can write anywhere, and it would be difficult for me to give you everything you've ever wanted if we're not living in the same state." He didn't mean to sound testy, but chasing after a reluctant woman was new to him, and he was already frustrated.

Her eyes narrowed, and he saw something he liked there. Hope. "What are you talking about?"

"You're going to make me say it?"

She nodded.

"Fine." He closed in on her, and this time she didn't back away. "I never should've let you go. It was a mistake, the biggest I've ever made. I constantly wonder what I could've done differently, how I might've convinced you to stay. I haven't been able to think about anything else since you left."

"Not *anything* else?"

"Getting you naked has also crossed my mind a time or two."

She sighed. Her body seemed to unwind a bit. "Just a time or two?"

"I've been thinking about you and me pretty much constantly, if you must know the truth." Might as well lay it all on the line. If he lost, it wasn't going to be because he held back.

It was her hint of a smile that gave him hope of his own. That and the ease of her shoulders, the unclenching of her hands, the way she dropped her arms to her side.

"But you believed Marcus when he told you I was a stalker. How am I supposed to forget that?"

"I was an idiot. I wish I could tell you that I'll never be an idiot again, but I can't. You're just going to learn to live with it." He put his arms around Nell Rose and leaned down to kiss her. The kiss wasn't as thorough as he'd like, but it was a start. She kissed him back, and then her mouth eased away from his. Nell Rose was an open book, her face revealed everything, and he saw her uncertainty... and more.

"Look, Nell Rose, we'll take this as slow and easy as you'd like, but the truth of the matter is, I'm not going anywhere until you tell me that there's no chance for us. To be honest, you'll probably have to tell me more than once. I can be determined when I really want something, and right now what I want is you."

She tilted her head to one side; the firmness of her lips eased. "That all sounds very nice, very romantic, but I have to wonder if you really mean it." A touch of determination flickered in her eyes. "Will I scare you away if I tell you that I fell in love with you that weekend? Will you head for the hills if I tell you that l fell head over heels almost at first glance? You can't play with me, you can't say you want me and then change your mind. You broke my heart, and still, when I think about what I want from my life, I see you in it. You say you want to give me what I want, but do you know what that is? Do you really? I want a husband who'll be there every night. I want to be a mother who paints and bakes and dotes on her children. Yes, *children*. I want at least four. Maybe five. I want to take vacations to Disney World and throw elaborate birthday parties for the kids, with clowns and ponies. I want…"

"Are you trying to shock me?" Julian asked with a touch of humor.

"Yes. Is it working?" Her eyes widened slightly.

"No." He drifted closer to her, took a deep breath to take in the scent that was hers, and hers alone. He hadn't known it was possible to miss a person as much as he'd missed her. He hadn't known it was possible to love so much. "I know exactly what you want, and that's what I want, too. I want it because what scared the hell out of me in the past looks different when I imagine it through your eyes. I'll take it all, even the damn clowns. Is there anything else you'd like to add before I kiss you again?"

Nell Rose sighed and fell into Julian. He saw her surrender; he could feel to the bone that she was giving in to him, just as he had completely given in to her. "There's just one thing I'd like to add." She looked up at him and smiled. "Hang on to your hat, because slow and easy have never really been my thing."

* * * * *

To the Totton family and the warmth they share
during the Heart of Winter.

MYSTERY LOVER

USA TODAY bestselling author
Day Leclaire

Dear Reader,

There's something tough to handle about the heart of winter, those endless days and weeks that fall after all the special holidays are distant memories, when winter closes in and seems so long and endless. It often turns bitter cold, the shardlike punch of it penetrating like a fist of ice.

Darkness comes far too early and stays unreasonably late, oftentimes filling us with a longing for the joy of those sweet, shining holiday months. Or better yet, we wait for that first precious thaw that brings with it the loamy scent of an early spring.

The deepest heart of winter is that time when warmth is a precious gift. When fires are kindled and carry the embers of hope from one season into the next. There's only one thing that brightens the fire and wards off the chill. And that's love.

For Nick and Jayne, their deep abiding love begins one magical night at a masked ball and continues straight through the heart of winter. It's a love that warms the heart, fills the darkness with bright happiness and fulfills both of their hearts' desires. I hope you enjoy "Mystery Lover," and I hope it brings you a special warmth that will ward off the chill.

All the best,

Day Leclaire

CHAPTER ONE

"CONGRATULATIONS, JAYNE. You're going to the ball."

Jayne Myleston stared at Nick Fontana—her boss and head of Fontana, Inc.—in total disbelief. "I'm what?"

He offered a smile that turned his appearance from austere to an inch off stunning. "You and Jonathan Blair have worked harder for Foundation Fontana than anyone else on my staff and you deserve a reward. I'm well aware that the twenty-five-hundred-dollar price is hefty. So, as my personal thank-you for all your effort, I'm giving you each a ticket to the New Year's Eve ball."

She picked up the ticket he'd placed on her desk with due reverence. The wafer-thin metal glittered in her hand, seeming to gather every bit of light in the room and reflect it outward. The laser-etched surface read:

You are cordially invited to a Masked Ball at New York City's premier hotel, the Centoria Mark, in the Moonlight Ballroom on Friday, December 31, 8:00 p.m. Come as your favorite character, real or imaginary.

"I don't know what to say," she murmured before catching herself. Not the most professional comment to make to your boss when he'd just handed you twenty-five-hundred-dollars' worth of fun. She offered a wide smile. "Other than thank you, of course. I can't wait to attend."

"I look forward to seeing you there."

She studied Nick curiously. She'd never been able to figure him out. One minute he was the hard-driven, take-no-prisoners Boss-with-a-capital-*B*. And the next he seemed almost approachable. "Have you chosen your costume, yet?" she asked impulsively.

"I thought I'd go as Bill Gates." He combed his streaked brown hair to one side and perched a pair of half-rim tortoiseshell glasses on his nose.

Jayne struggled to keep a straight face, but couldn't contain her grin. "No way. You don't do geeky."

He whipped off the glasses and pursed his lips, pulling them down slightly at the corners. "Donald Trump?"

"Close, but you have too much hair."

"Ah. In that case, maybe I'll just go as myself."

He tucked away the glasses and ran his hands through his hair in an attempt to return it to normal. But even with the short, crisp style he favored he couldn't quite control the thick, unruly waves. She'd often thought that women around the world would have given their eyeteeth to have been born with that hair, naturally speared with shafts of sun-bleached golden-white. And here it was wasted on a clueless male. Wasn't that always the way?

"What about you?" Nick asked. "Any ideas?"

"Not a one," Jayne admitted cheerfully.

"Well, I know who I'm going as," Jonathan Blair announced from the doorway. "Zorro. Simple yet elegant, with a touch of dashing."

Jayne couldn't quite suppress a sigh. Jonathan would make a wonderful Zorro—tall and broad, with dark brown hair and bitter chocolate eyes. He was one of the handsomest men Jayne had ever met, and she'd had a major crush on him for the eighteen months she'd worked at Fontana, Inc.

Unfortunately, she wasn't alone. Women buzzed around him as if he were the most fragrant flower in the garden. In fact, the *only* flower in the garden. And good ol' Jonathan seemed all too eager to spread his pollen around. Too bad he'd never looked twice at her. Or maybe it was just as well.

"Zorro?" Nick lifted an eyebrow. "I'd have thought Don Juan."

"I considered it," Jonathan admitted. "But I like Zorro's costume better."

"Easier to get out of?"

Jonathan laughed. "Hey, I'm not that bad. I'm actually a nice guy. Plus, I'm a hard worker."

"Which is why you're on my payroll. So, I'll stop wasting your time and let you both get back to it." And with that, Nick exited Jayne's office.

Jonathan waited until they were alone before speaking. "I've never been able to get a handle on that guy," he commented, echoing her thoughts from moments before. "One minute he's friendly and easygoing and the next he's Mr. Intimidating."

"I guess he wouldn't be where he is today without having an edge." But secretly, Jayne had to agree. She'd never met anyone more adept at going from charming to steely in the blink of an eye. "It was nice of him to give us tickets to the ball, though."

Jonathan took a seat on her desk and tugged at a stray honey-blond curl that had escaped the tidy little knot at the nape of her neck. "You'll have to save me a dance once you figure out your costume."

"I'll do that." She tilted her head to one side. "Who do you suggest I go as?"

"Mary Poppins? Pollyanna?" He snapped his fingers. "I know. Hermione from *Harry Potter*."

She struggled to conceal her dismay. Was that how Jonathan really saw her? No wonder he'd never been interested in dating her. "I'll think about it," she murmured, then proved his point by tapping her pen against the file he sat on. "Now, if you don't mind?"

"Right, sorry." He winked, then slid into a fairly accurate British accent. "Remember to save me that dance, Mary."

For the rest of the week, Jayne stewed over Jonathan's comments. On Thursday, the night before the ball, she confronted her best friend and roommate, Courtney. "Is that how I come across to you?" she demanded. She held out her empty wineglass and gave it a little fill-'er-up wave. "Like some sort of intellectual do-gooder nanny?"

Courtney splashed an overly sweet Riesling into Jayne's glass, followed by her own. "Face it, girl. You go out of your way to draw attention to your brain, rather than your physical attributes. You want people to respect your intellect instead of obsessing over your figure, so you dress down." She saluted her friend with a grin. "Poor you. I wish I had that problem."

"I don't dress down. I dress…" She spared a glance at her tidy gray suit. "Okay, I dress down."

"Then why act so surprised when Jonathan buys the act?" Courtney lifted a pencil-thin eyebrow. "Or were you hoping he'd see through it? See the real you beneath the boring exterior?"

"Yes," Jayne admitted. "Is that so terrible?"

Courtney curled up on the couch beside Jayne, drawing her legs underneath her pint-sized body. "Not terrible, just unrealistic, especially when it comes to men."

"Jonathan is one of the most intelligent men I know." Jayne reconsidered. "Well, next to Nick Fontana."

"Mmm. Now there's some grade A, prime man. And he came by his money the hard way, didn't he?"

"Absolutely. He started off working for a failing company and arranged a merger with another that was also on the skids. They ended up a single successful entity." She didn't bother to disguise her admiration. "After that, he started up Fontana, Inc. and he's never looked back. He just has a knack for taking differing businesses, putting them together and making something new and successful."

"Speaking of successful mergers, I wouldn't mind checking out what he has hidden beneath that Mr. Intimidating exterior."

"I can tell you." Courtney's eyes practically popped out of her head and Jayne grinned. "A Mr. Intimidating interior. And when he's not busy intimidating people, he's all business."

Well…except for those rare occasions when he relaxed enough to be charming. Where most people saw the iconic Nick Fontana, Jayne had discovered a far different person behind the public mask. Charming. Thoughtful. Brilliant. And, from what she'd seen while working on his foundation, incredibly kind.

Courtney's expression turned mischievous. "Do you suppose he's all business in the bedroom, too?"

Jayne wrinkled her nose, then buried it in her wineglass. "Please. I don't need that image stuck in my head."

Courtney snickered. "He probably does it by the book. You know, 'Sorry, dear, but we can't deviate from the proper order of things. Tab A must go into slot B and nowhere else. We shall achieve blastoff in ten, nine, eight…'"

"Don't!" Jayne begged. "I have to work with the man. How am I supposed to face him Monday morning? Every time I look at him I'll start a mental countdown."

"Okay, okay." Courtney topped off their glasses. "I wonder what sort of woman appeals to him?"

Jayne reclined against the couch cushions and swirled her wine as she considered. "I'm trying to remember some of the women he's dated. Actually, they've all been rather stunning."

"Brainless or brilliant? His type always goes for one extreme or the other."

Jayne lifted an eyebrow and shot her roommate a teasing smile. "You seem to know a lot about Fontana's 'type.'"

"Used to date someone like him."

Jayne shook her head, adamant. "There is no one like Nick Fontana."

"Okay, fair enough. Warren's bank balance is impressive, but nowhere close to Fontana's billions. Nor was Warren particularly intimidating." Courtney grimaced. "In fact, I'd have to say he had clueless geek down pat."

"As I recall, he also preferred brainless fluff, which you certainly are not."

"No, I'm not. The awful part about the entire debacle was losing my job after my affair with the boss ended. I sure learned my lesson. Fortunately, my current job is the best one I've ever had." She waved that aside, her wine sloshing precariously close to the rim of her glass. "We've gone totally off topic here."

Jayne sighed. "I don't even remember the topic anymore."

"Jonathan—aka Zorro—and your costume for the New Year's Eve ball."

Jayne made a face. "Right. That. Maybe I won't go."

"Don't be ridiculous. Of course you'll go. And you'll stun the pants right off good ol' Jon."

Jayne straightened. "Okay. Now I'm intrigued."

Courtney tilted her head to one side in consideration. "I'm thinking we aim for totally against type."

"I have a type?"

"You do at work. So here's what I'll do for you." Her expression turned impish. "You turn thirty on New Year's Day. You know…straight into over-the-hilldom."

"Gee, thanks," Jayne said drily. "Don't forget you'll be right there with me in six more months."

"Trust me, I'm all too aware of that fact. So before you start your downward roll, my birthday present to you is a personal transformation for the ball. And just maybe that transformation will serve Jonathan up with a big black Zorro bow."

It took Jayne a moment to catch her breath enough to reply. "How are you going to pull that off?"

"Honey, when it comes to transformations, you're talking to an expert," Courtney retorted without a smidge of false modesty. "As for specifics… We'll go brunette instead of blond. Exotic instead of sweet. A siren instead of a bookworm." She leaned forward, stabbing a neon-pink fingernail in Jayne's direction. "I've decided that you're going as Cleo, queen of the whole damn Nile. And if that doesn't get Jonathan to jump you, nothing will."

THE NEXT NIGHT JAYNE STARED at herself in the mirror, not certain whether to be impressed or horrified. "You have got to be kidding me. There is no way I can pull this off."

Courtney tugged the black wig a fraction of an inch to the left and grinned. "You look incredible."

"I'm going to freeze to death."

"Very likely. But you'll die gorgeous."

Jayne's lips twitched. She would, too. The silky black wig turned her skin ivory and made a striking contrast to her light blue eyes. A gold circlet shaped like a cobra held the wig in place. Courtney had pulled out all the stops with the makeup, easy for her considering that for the past two years she'd worked as a makeup artist on a popular New York soap opera. It had also enabled her to bribe wardrobe and get her hands on a spectacular Cleopatra costume. Even better, she'd somehow managed to find that perfect line between sexy and slutty, dramatic and overdone. The end result was positively dazzling.

Jayne shook her head in disbelief. "I don't know how you do it, girl."

Courtney beamed. "Not hard when you start the process with such great material. I could tell you stories about some of the actors and actresses I've had to work with. Getting them to look even half as good as you is beyond challenging. And if I can't cover up every flaw—"

"It's all your fault?" Jayne offered knowingly.

"You got it. Doesn't matter how God made them—or more often the plastic surgeon. It's my job to create perfection. With you, I've finally achieved it." She offered Jayne a saucy wink. "So where's the venue for this pricy bash?"

"The Centoria Mark. Remember I attended the ribbon-cutting ceremony for the grand opening earlier this year?"

"Right, right. It's that one with fabulous views of the city and harbor."

"And the top floor that revolves. That's where the Moonlight Ballroom is," Jayne said. "The hotel is *the* place right now. Even if you could afford a room, you couldn't get a reservation anytime this decade."

"Unless you're Nick Fontana."

"He does have a way of turning impossible into reality," Jayne agreed. "And it doesn't hurt that he's one of the owners."

"You're kidding."

"Not even a little. Trust me, when it comes to financial acumen, that man is brilliant. He has his fingers in more pies than I can count. And all those pies are solid gold."

Courtney made a face. "Not terribly tasty, though."

Jayne grinned. "But profitable and with Fontana that's what matters most. The bottom line."

"Too bad he doesn't have a bit of swash in his buckle. But we'll see if Cleo can't snag Zorro, instead."

Jayne gave herself one final, lingering look. "I don't see how she can fail." She gave her roommate an impulsive hug. "Thanks to you."

"No, sweetie," Courtney corrected. "Every bit of what's in that costume is you. Now you just have to live the part."

"Easier said than done when you're Hermione at heart," Jayne murmured.

THE CAB DROPPED JAYNE at the sweeping entrance to the Centoria Mark. The impressive facade gave the immediate impression of grandeur combined with a snazzy avant-garde appearance. It screamed wealth. Status. Trendy. And it took every ounce of her self-possession to exit the cab, slip on the gold-and-silver sequined mask Courtney had created to match the costume and climb the marble steps to the imposing etched glass doors.

A doorman ushered her in with an easy smile. "Fontana party?" he asked.

Jayne returned his smile, relieved by his friendliness. For some reason she'd anticipated he'd be more supercil-ious. "Is it that obvious?"

"It is, Your Majesty." He offered the merest hint of a wink. "You want the central elevators. You'll need to show your ticket to access the Moonlight Ballroom. Enjoy your evening."

"Thank you."

Okay, that wasn't so bad. At least she'd made it through the front door. Tossing back a panel of the cloak covering her costume, she removed her ticket from the small pocket hidden in the ornamental girdle and joined a small group of people waiting for the elevator. Fairy princesses vied with angels. A stocky Louis XVI lavished attention on a dainty Marie Antoinette. Of more interest were Abraham Lincoln and George Washington who were in an intense discussion about whether they dared approach Fontana about an investment opportunity.

Unable to help herself, she waited until they glanced her way and shook her head pointedly. A hushed conversation followed while the two eyed her speculatively. "You sure?" one of them finally asked.

"Positive. Introduce yourselves and then ask if he'd be receptive to a meeting at a more opportune moment, but don't pitch anything tonight."

George shot her an appreciative look. "Thanks, Cleo."

The elevator arrived and they all boarded. The doors parted to reveal an elaborate foyer. On one end was a coat check. In the middle was a set of floor-to-ceiling double doors that opened to the ballroom. A pair of footmen stood on either side of the door, collecting the golden tickets.

Taking a deep breath, she checked her cloak, praying that all the various parts of her costume stayed where they belonged. Although she hadn't been part of the decoration committee for the charity event, she'd heard enough to expect to be stunned, and when she entered the ballroom she wasn't disappointed.

The decorations were all in gold, silver and scarlet. To her private amusement, her costume echoed the theme. Garlands of greenery entwined with white fairy lights adorned the railings of the staircase leading into the main ballroom and around the columns supporting the thirty-foot ceiling with its famous overhead moonlight windows. More fairy lights outlined the windows overlooking the cityscape and harbor. High overhead, globes of glittering gold and silver shot shards of sparkling color across the room. They were interspersed with huge balls of red and white roses that scented the air with their sweet perfume.

Tables laden with every imaginable food lined one section of the room. Crystal and silver sparkled, and huge red floral arrangements dotted the snowy linen tablecloth. Enthusiastic partiers swamped a champagne fountain, while molten fountains of white and dark chocolate proved equally popular with the guests. Imported fruit and squares of angel food cake filled glistening crystal bowls, ready to be dipped and consumed. And at the far end of the sweep of tables, in a place of honor, was a giant cake that recreated the New York City skyline and even had edible fireworks bursting above it.

A string quartet played nearby, while the stage awaited the band that would follow them once those in the receiving line were released from bondage. Jayne could just make out Nick's familiar profile at the head of the line. Her first order of business was to thank her boss for her ticket. Then she'd see if she could find a certain masked Zorro and discover if he found Cleopatra more interesting than plain Jayne.

It took a full thirty minutes to wend her way through the receiving line. Understandable, since most everyone attending the charity ball would probably give their bleached and/or enameled eyeteeth for a chance at some one-on-one time with the legendary Nick Fontana. It reminded her again of how fortunate she was to work for him. She couldn't help but wonder if he'd recognize her or whether she'd have to clue him in. Regardless, she looked forward to his reaction.

Or so she thought until he took her hand and gave it a quick squeeze. "Welcome, Jayne," he said with a distracted smile. "I'm glad you could attend."

"You recognized me, even with my mask and wig." The words were out before she could prevent them.

His distraction vanished and his hazel eyes honed in on her like golden lasers. "Of course I did. You're my employee. I'd recognize you anywhere."

"Oh." What could she say to that? She noticed that, unlike all the other partiers, he'd dispensed with a mask. "Love your costume, by the way."

He glanced down at his black tux. "I'm not wearing a costume."

"Sure you are." She winked. "I'll just call you Bond. James Bond."

He chuckled. "I think I'll steal your line, if you don't mind."

"Feel free, though I think I handed you more of a cliché than a line."

He lifted an eyebrow, powering up his intimidation factor to full throttle. "You think anyone's going to call me on it?"

She flashed him a swift grin. "Not a soul." She hesitated, then went for broke. "I don't suppose you've seen Jonathan?"

Nick's expression turned distracted again. "Blair? I think he came through the line a while ago."

"Zorro, right?"

"Was that who he was?"

She'd seen Nick switch off before and recognized it immediately. She was willing to bet he was busily crunching numbers or calculating the interest on his billions or figuring out which company or country to purchase next.

"Thanks for inviting me," she said politely, and moved aside to allow the next supplicant to take her spot.

Jayne spent the hour that followed wandering through the crowd, fending off potential admirers, though a few managed to persuade her onto the dance floor. To her profound relief, her gown behaved, covering all the bits and pieces it was meant to cover. The wig felt a tad warm and the mask made it difficult to see, but all in all she managed.

Other than Jonathan—assuming she could find him— she didn't know anyone else there. Most of the attendees were gathered in the small, intimate groups they'd come with. There were few, if any, singles wandering around. But then, it was New Year's Eve. Most people would have brought a date, though the price tag put that option well out of her reach and she couldn't help but wish that Nick's invitation had allowed her to bring a guest. Of course, her guest probably would have been Courtney. Just as she was ready to give up on Jonathan and call it a night, someone planted a strong hand around her waist and spun her into his arms.

"Good evening, señorita," Zorro whispered into her ear, his Spanish accent impressive. "I'm here to claim my dance. In fact, I'm here to claim *all* of your dances."

CHAPTER TWO

"Jonathan?"

Jayne gazed into Zorro's eyes, eyes partially obscured by the mask he wore. She relaxed ever so slightly when she caught sight of the familiar chocolate darkness she'd come to know so well and took a moment to examine his costume.

He was dressed all in black as befitted the legend, but he did it with style. His long-sleeved black silk shirt was fastened at his neck with a leather thong just loose enough to allow her a glimpse of the impressive breadth of his chest. With it he wore tight leather pants, a tooled leather belt and a beautifully crafted silver buckle. His features were obscured by silk, a combination mask and bandana that covered both the upper half of his face, as well as his hair, and was knotted at the nape of his neck. Knee-high black leather boots, a short-brimmed sombrero and leather gloves completed the outfit. As far as Jayne was concerned, he left Antonio Banderas in the dust.

"I am not Jonathan," he finally responded to her inquiry. He continued to maintain his impeccable Spanish accent, his voice pitched low and soft and husky…and deliciously sexy. He moved onto the floor with an elegance and grace that caught her by surprise. A calf-length silk cape flared in a dramatic circle around his muscular form as he spun her in a dizzying circle. "Tonight I am Zorro, just as you are my Cleopatra."

"Yours?" She lifted her chin. "I thought I belonged to Marc Antony."

Jonathan shook his head. "He had his chance with you. Now it's my turn to win the last and most beautiful pharaoh of Egypt."

His knowledge of history surprised her. But then, why should it? She didn't know him all that well. At least…not yet. She swirled across the floor with him. Maybe tonight would change all that. Maybe tonight she'd learn far more about the talents and abilities he'd kept hidden while at work.

He caught her off guard by wrapping her almost protectively within his arms, and she followed his lead, closing the distance between them. She reveled in the brush of hard masculine angles. His elegant business suits had only hinted at the power and strength she felt as they moved together. It was another delightful revelation.

"So, tell me, Zorro." She experimented with a flirtatious smile she'd never have attempted if it weren't for the heady camouflage of her costume. "How do you plan to win me?"

His hand slid down the length of her spine, transitioning from the filmy material of her costume to her bare back. His gloved fingertips tripped along her skin, the soft leather sending flames of desire tearing through her. "First, we will dance."

Dance? It felt more like a seduction, as though he were initiating foreplay right here in public. "I don't think a simple dance is enough to win me," she lied, avoiding his gaze.

"No, señorita, you do not strike me as the type to be won so easily." He lowered his head so that his warm breath grazed her temple. His voice dropped, filled with unmistakable urgency. "I am well aware that it will take far more than a simple dance to have what I want from you."

"What do you want from me, Jon—" She moistened her lips. "I mean, Zorro?"

"I want everything you have to give."

She almost melted onto the floor, right then and there. If he'd asked, she'd have told him she'd give him anything and everything, and then find more. That she wanted it— whatever *it* he cared to share with her—every bit as much as he did, and had for a very long time. But something held her back, a natural reticence that was such an engrained part of her personality that even buried beneath a sexy Cleopatra costume, she couldn't override it.

She forced herself to look up at him through her mask. Coolly. Calmly. "What I have to give you is a dance."

If her response disappointed him, he didn't show it. "Or maybe two?" he teased.

She couldn't help smiling. "Or maybe two."

The next hour passed with Jayne held securely within Jonathan's arms. One dance slipped into two and then a half dozen. She couldn't explain how or why she felt so comfortable within his grasp. She just did. They fit together as though they were two pieces that should have been one.

At the end of the hour, the string quartet finished their selections for the evening and the band took over. Jonathan gathered her hand in his and led her toward the buffet. "I have worked up quite an appetite." Self-deprecating humor gleamed in his eyes at the double entendre, encouraging her to laugh along. "Would you like something to eat?"

"I'm starving," she admitted.

Continuing to display Zorro-like gallantry, he selected

the choicest tidbits to fill her plate. Together, they found a table for two tucked in a small alcove beside a window that gave them a view of the slowly rotating cityscape.

"This is absolutely stunning," she murmured. "I never tire of this city. It's so magnificent."

"I agree."

He speared a sliver of duck from her plate and offered it to her. It should have struck her as practiced, but he managed to do it with such sincerity that it didn't. "You are not originally from New York, are you?"

Instead of answering his question, she eyed him curiously. "How do you do it?"

He lifted an eyebrow. "Do what?"

"Keep up the pretense with such skill? You haven't slipped with your accent even once."

"That is because I am Zorro."

"Hmm. I'm beginning to believe you are." She cupped her chin in the palm of her hand. "I couldn't begin to fake a Greek accent."

"Is that what Cleopatra spoke?"

"All the aristocracy did, though she was supposedly the first ruler to also speak Egyptian." She offered a chagrined look. "I'm terrible with accents, so I wouldn't dare attempt either Greek or Egyptian. I wouldn't even want to try Spanish, though I took it in high school."

"And where was high school for you? The Midwest, if I am not mistaken?"

"Yes." She tilted her head to one side, curious. "I don't remember ever telling you that."

He gave a graceful shrug. "You did not have to tell me. Every once in a while I hear it in your voice."

Satisfied, she nodded. "I can't deny it and wouldn't even

if I could. I was born and bred smack dab in the middle of corn country. I'm a farmer's daughter and proud of it."

"And well you should be. Yet…" She could see the questioning look in his eyes. "You left the cornfields for the allure of the big city. Why is that?"

"I wanted more. I wanted to challenge myself. Experience all the diversity our country has to offer." She gestured toward the window and the impressive sprawl of buildings and lights, bustle and commerce. "What could be more diverse than New York City?"

"I am in complete agreement with you. I love our city."

"But I remember you saying you didn't grow up here, either. Where are you originally from?"

"I grew up on a sprawling ranch outside of Los Angeles."

He'd surprised her. "Really? I didn't know that. I thought you mentioned something about upstate New York."

"California, señorita, I assure you."

Huh. She didn't often get her facts wrong. In fact, she'd been accused more than once of having an almost perfect auditory memory. But maybe he'd lived both places and neglected to mention that fact until now. "And what were you like before you hit the big city?" she probed.

He lifted a shoulder in a casual shrug, causing his cape to stir in an opulent swirl of ebony. "I was a fair gymnast."

"I guess that explains how you move so well on the dance floor."

"I am also an excellent horseman, though I do not like to brag."

A prickle of suspicion teased her and she fought back a smile. "Oh, please. Feel free to brag."

"If you insist." He fed her another morsel from her

plate before helping himself to a succulent shrimp dipped in cocktail sauce. "But I should warn you that with most people I would rather keep my true abilities a deep, dark secret. I prefer to allow those around me to think me far less than I am, since it is safer to have my competition underestimate me."

"And what are you?"

"I am a great marksman when it comes to pistols and have been acknowledged the best in the land with a rapier."

"The entire land?" Jayne marveled. "That's quite impressive."

"Indeed." He leaned in to confide, "I am forced to admit that I do suffer from an excess of compassion and a strong dislike of injustice, particularly when it comes to the underdog."

"So, you prefer to champion the underdog?"

"Always," he assured her gravely.

"Am I an underdog?"

"Only when it comes to asps, my queen." He took her hand in his and kissed her fingertips. What should have come across as corny struck her as utterly charming instead. The more she got to know Jonathan, the more he impressed her. "From those, I will protect you with great fierceness."

"You have my eternal gratitude. What can I do for you in exchange?" she dared to ask.

"Continue to share the evening with me." He glanced across the room. "I see a fountain of molten chocolate. Have you saved room for a strawberry or two? I believe there is both dark and white chocolate to dip it in."

"That sounds perfect."

"Only if we have a glass of champagne to go with it."

"Shouldn't we wait until midnight?" Even as she asked the question, she wondered if she was being presumptuous. She caught her lower lip between her teeth and waited for his response.

It came with impressive swiftness. He stood and touched the brim of his sombrero with his gloved hand. "I have something else I prefer to taste at midnight." He lowered his hand from his hat and held it out, palm up, his gaze fixed on her mouth. "I suspect it will prove far sweeter than champagne."

Without a moment's hesitation, she rose and linked her fingers with his. "I'd like that very much."

The next few hours flew by. They found endless topics to discuss, some light and casual, some more serious. Jonathan continued to impress her with the depth and scope of his knowledge. It wasn't just that he knew facts and figures, but he had insight he could offer about the various issues. Strong opinions that combined compassion with common sense.

Jayne couldn't help but be impressed by a man she had suspected was intelligent, but a bit shallow, when he proved himself to be anything but. She also realized she was in serious danger of falling for him. And falling hard. How would that affect her ability to work with him come Monday morning?

"Where did you go?" he asked, slipping his arm around her waist.

It rested comfortably there, warm and powerful. Protective. She debated whether or not to answer honestly, then went for broke. "I was thinking about Monday," she confessed.

"A mistake to worry about what will be," he said with a shake of his head. "Perhaps you should consider living in the moment."

"Worry about tomorrow, tomorrow?"

His dark eyes glittered with amusement. "Why worry at all? How will that help anything?"

Jayne hesitated, struggling to cling to the enchantment of the evening while pragmatism pounded at the door, intent on crashing the party. "Maybe I'm not as good as you are at combining fantasy with reality," she confessed. "Not in the daylight. Not in an office setting. When fantasy and reality are forced to part ways—"

"Why do they have to?"

She swiveled so that she faced him directly. He slid his other arm around her and she pressed her palms to his chest—not holding him in check, but not quite confident enough to wrap them around his neck. "Do you really think you can still be Zorro when we meet without our costumes? Because I need to warn you, I'm not Cleopatra."

"You are to me."

She shivered at the warm, tender words. "But only because I chose a character diametrically opposed to my normal personality. I mean, seriously. What costume did you suggest for me? Hermione. Mary Poppins. Pollyanna. Be honest with me, Jonathan."

"Zorro," he was swift to correct.

She relented beneath his steely insistence. "Fine, fine. *Zorro*. Would you have ever seen me as anyone other than a prim and proper librarian type or do-gooder in pigtails if I hadn't shown up here dressed as the Queen of the Nile?"

"Right now you are Cleopatra and that is all that matters." He shot her a wicked grin. "But if at some point in the future you want to try pigtails and bloomers, I would not object."

Picturing herself dressed like that swept away the gathering intensity of the moment. Jayne's mouth twitched in an answering smile and she allowed herself to slip from serious to lighthearted. Jonathan was right. Why spoil to-night's fun worrying about what would happen in the cold light of day? "And what part would you play?"

He gave it due consideration. "The schoolmaster seems too trite. I think I would choose the part of a simple farm boy wooing the schoolgirl he has had a crush on ever since he first set eyes on her cute little pigtails."

A chuckle escaped and Jayne shook her head. "You haven't met any farm boys recently, have you? Trust me, they're not simple and they don't woo. Not anymore."

"Ah, but this is my fantasy, yes?"

She conceded the point. "True."

"And right now the fantasy is Zorro and Cleopatra." He captured her chin in the leather-clad palm of his hand and tilted it upward. Though the mask shielded some of her expression, her eyes were easily read. "Shall we continue the fantasy or would you prefer to end it?"

She gave it serious consideration. If she ended things now they would return to the real world and pretend this night never happened. The possibilities would slip through her fingers and vanish with the coming of the New Year. She'd return to being plain Jayne, while Jonathan found some new flowers to pollinate.

Or she could usher in the New Year with a bang in every sense of the word. Instead of playing it safe the way she had most of her twenty-nine years, she could take a huge risk. On the dawn of her thirtieth birthday she could sample the flavor of daring. Taste the wild side of life. Drink down risk and pray for a reward unlike any she'd experienced before.

All she needed to do was say one single word.

"Fantasy." Her breath gusted out on an exhilarated laugh. "I choose fantasy."

She saw the swift approval flash across his expression, his pleasure in her decision echoed in the warmth of his dark eyes. "Fantasy it is." His mouth came to within a breath of her own, tempting her beyond reason. "And I promise, señorita, to give you a night of fantasy unlike any you have ever known. A night filled with unimaginable pleasure."

Oh, God. How was she supposed to respond to that? She'd known the pleasure of men in the past, though it had been mostly their pleasure rather than her own. But there wasn't any doubt in her mind that a night spent in Jonathan's arms—*Zorro's* arms—would be as different from those few experiences as night from day.

"Yes, please." She breathed out the words. If she just lifted up on tiptoe a scant few inches, her mouth would collide with his and she'd finally experience his kiss.

He must have read her intent because he eased back, flashing her a teasing smile. "Not until midnight, my queen."

She didn't bother to hide her disappointment. "Why wait?"

"Because a first kiss should be special. And there's nothing more special than a kiss that ends one year and begins another."

He continued to enchant her with every word he spoke and every move he made. There wasn't a doubt in her mind that by the time she turned thirty, she would experience every pleasure she'd missed out on in her twenties.

She dared to stroke his cheek, wishing she had the nerve to do more. Maybe that would come with time...and intimacy. "Then I'm content to wait until midnight."

"Come with me." He gathered her hand in his. "I want to show you something."

Jonathan led her through the crowd, giving a drunken Don Juan and the milkmaid whose tonsils he was inhaling a wide berth. He spared the couple a swift, critical look. She could understand. The charity ball was an elegant affair. Though the couples attending were flirtatious, no one other than this couple was going at each other like a pair of randy farm animals. Even Jonathan in his guise as Zorro had kept his seduction within appropriate boundaries for the venue.

He swept her through a side door leading onto a balcony that surrounded the Moonlight Ballroom. If it had been summer, the expansive area would have been crowded with people. But in December, high above the city with a blustery winter wind, they had the balcony to themselves.

Jonathan swept his cape from his shoulders and settled the flow of silk snugly around her. She felt the lingering warmth from his body and caught a hint of cedar combined with something crisp and deliciously masculine. She breathed in the scent, delighting in the tiny intimacy.

"I know it is cold," he told her. "So I promise not to keep you for long. But I think…yes, I was right."

She leaned back against him and watched the harbor rotate into view as the platform slowly spun. "About what?"

"Wait for it."

As though he'd given the heavens a signal, fat, fluffy snowflakes drifted from the sky, swirling downward in a merry dance. Jayne inhaled sharply, utterly captivated. "How beautiful," she murmured.

"Ah, but that is not the most beautiful part."

In the next instant the Statue of Liberty swung into view, majestic and brilliantly lit. For a brief moment Jayne couldn't breathe, let alone speak. She simply leaned into Jonathan and absorbed his warmth as she allowed herself to thrill at the sight.

From somewhere in the distance she heard people shouting.

Ten. Jonathan's arms tightened around her, pulling her closer still.

Nine. His hands shifted from her waist up beneath the cape she wore and along her arms.

Eight. At some point he'd removed his gloves and his fingers feathered across the curve of her shoulders to the sensitive hollow at the joining of her neck.

Seven. He turned her, ever so gently, until she faced him, his hands never leaving her shoulders.

Six. He cupped her face and tilted it upward.

Five. His fingertips painted the parts of her face bared by her mask, as though to brand each curve and angle into his memory.

Four. "Jayne," he whispered. Not Cleopatra. But plain, simple Jayne. The word came out in a soft accent, but not a Spanish one. This time his accent was one of longing.

Three. For an endless moment, he stared down at her, his eyes dark and more serious than she could ever recall seeing them before.

Two. He leaned down, the slightest of smiles tugging his mouth to one side, a mouth more tempting than any she'd ever seen.

On the count of one, he kissed her, melding fantasy with reality.

She stood on a frigid balcony, surrounded by delicious male warmth while snowflakes wept from above, glistening like diamonds against the darkness of his costume and the cape he'd draped her in. Deep thunderous booms echoed all around them signaling the start of the New Year. Her eyes fluttered closed but she could still see the flashes from the fireworks even with her lids squeezed shut.

The spectacle going on around her retreated. Nothing mattered other than that kiss and those marvelous lips working on hers. And heaven help her, could he kiss. There was a power in the taking, a sureness in the way his mouth moved on hers. A tenderness when he probed inward. The most delicious flavor when their tongues touched and mated. She could have stood there for hours, and suspected he could have, too, if the door behind them hadn't swept open. The drunken Don Juan spilled through with his milkmaid.

Jonathan whirled her in a swift, sweeping circle that had them back inside without the interlopers even noticing them. To Jayne's astonishment the overhead balls of roses were popping open, one after the other. Red and white petals filled the air, raining down on the celebrants, along with gold and silver confetti stars. The combination caught in her hair and her mask and on the lower half of her face. Jonathan was more fortunate than she. His hat kept most of the flowers and confetti out of his face.

He laughed when he caught sight of her and pulled her into his arms once again. He brushed a rose petal from her cheek. "Do you have any idea how beautiful you look?"

"What can I say? Roses and confetti must agree with me." This time she felt perfectly comfortable twining her arms around his neck. "Or maybe it's your kisses."

His laughter faded, replaced with something hard and determined. A hungry tension that caused the muscles of his face to tauten. "Spend the night with me."

"Is that a question or a demand?"

He gave it to her straight. "A demand."

"And if I refuse?"

"I will carry you off and have my wicked way with you."

She stretched upward and snatched a swift kiss. "You don't leave me any other choice, except…"

"Except?"

She offered him a smile filled with mystery and seduction. "Why, surrender, of course."

CHAPTER THREE

WHILE THE REVELERS CONTINUED to celebrate, Jonathan and Jayne slipped through the massive double doors leading to the foyer.

"Do you have a coat?" he asked.

"As a matter of fact, I do." She fumbled in the small pocket sewn into her girdle and removed the claim check. He took the ticket and in no time returned with the cloak she'd worn to the masquerade ball. "Where are we going?"

"You'll see."

He rang for the elevator and together they waited by the doors. For the first time that evening, Jayne felt intensely awkward. The few occasions she'd slept with a man had been a conscious decision, made with due diligence and forethought. She'd invite her date over for dinner, followed by a slow retreat into her bedroom. Or they'd go out on the town and return to his place for coffee, which inevitably led to the same results. That brief move from living room to bedroom had been accomplished with a minimum of wait or fuss. And a maximum of disappointment.

But this...

This felt so uncomfortable, particularly beneath the bright lights of the foyer and with the growing silence between them. Maybe she'd made a mistake. Maybe she should simply turn and thank Jonathan for a pleasant evening and suggest they not take this any further. The alternative risked making their working relationship difficult, at best, and potentially impossible.

And she loved her job. If she couldn't work alongside Jonathan because of one night of foolishness, she might feel driven to leave Fontana, Inc. How could she bear it? She'd worked so long and hard. She had goals and aspirations. She spun around to face him.

"I'm not quitting my job," she announced in a nervous rush.

Surprise held him riveted in place. "Excuse me?" All trace of his Spanish accent had vanished and his voice dipped lower than usual.

"Look. I don't date coworkers. Not ever. I mean…" It was as though every last communication skill had drained out of her. She struggled to find the right words. "I've wanted to date you for a long time, but I'm not that great when it comes to any morning-after awkwardness. If this doesn't end well or if we're not comfortable with each other after…after…well, you know, I'm not quitting my job."

"I am relieved to hear it." He'd recovered his accent and—she suspected—was quietly laughing at her. "I would not expect you to quit your job based on…well…you know."

As far as teasing went, he'd kept it very gentle. Nevertheless, she blushed. "Look, maybe nothing should happen." She pulled her cloak tight around herself. "Maybe we're making a horrible mistake."

He took a step closer, so close she could feel the warmth of his body. So close, his cape billowed and swirled with a mind of its own, enfolding her like a pair of tender wings. He cupped her face and leaned in to kiss her, holding her in place with just the power of his mouth. That's all it took. Every last doubt and worry slipped away, vanishing beneath his taking. Bit by bit, she relaxed against him, the tension seeping from her muscles.

"How do you do it?" she murmured against his mouth. "How do you manage to make everything perfect and right?"

"With you it is simple."

She stiffened, then pulled back to study him. "I'm that easy?"

"Not at all. I can make everything perfect and right because you are perfect and right. This moment is perfect and right. The two of us together are more than perfect and right."

Oh, God, his words were so beautiful that tears threatened. To her everlasting relief, the doors to the elevator opened and they stepped inside. He keyed a button on the panel for a floor a few levels down.

"You have a room here?" she asked in surprise.

"I do."

"In anticipation?" She couldn't stop the wary question.

He lifted a shoulder in a careless shrug. "I would rather not fight with the crowd over nonexistent cabs."

"I'm surprised you were able to get a room."

He shot her a swift, flashing grin. "It is amazing what you can get when you mention that you are with Fontana."

Jayne gave him a look that combined amusement with disbelief. "Does Nick know?"

"Why would he care? It is just a room at one of his hotels. As a member of the Fontana family I think I deserve the occasional perk, even if I have to help myself to it." He lifted an eyebrow. "I assume you agree?"

"No," she stated bluntly. "Not unless it's either offered or approved by Nick."

Jonathan waved that aside. "Nick gets plenty of perks. Can you really see him objecting to my finagling one small suite for a night at the Centoria Mark?"

Her breath caught. "A suite?"

He held up a hand, fingers pinched close together. "A very small suite."

"Jonathan—"

"Zorro," he stated implacably. "I insist."

She closed her eyes and took a deep breath. "Those suites go for thousands of dollars a night, especially on a holiday like New Year's Eve."

The doors parted and he stepped from the car, holding out a hand to her. "Are you coming with me?"

She blocked the doors from closing. "On one condition."

"Name it."

"That we both pay for the suite. The real price, not whatever illicit deal you were able to wrangle."

He stilled. Even his cape ceased its restless movements. His mask concealed his thoughts from her, preventing her from pinpointing his precise reaction. She couldn't even get a clear glimpse of his eyes to judge what lurked in their darkness. Then he inclined his head. "Agreed."

She smiled in relief. "In that case, it would be my pleasure to come with you," she informed him, and stepped from the car and into his arms.

The suite he'd rented was breathtaking, a romantic confection overflowing with bowls of flowers and stands of candles. He moved from section to section, lighting all the candles until the room glowed with soft light and gentle fragrance. It was a room made for seduction and though some small part of her was disappointed to realize that he'd intended all along to bring a woman here tonight, regardless of what he'd claimed, she was still happy to be that woman.

She heard the muted pop of a champagne cork, followed by the bubble and hiss as he filled a pair of crystal flutes. He approached, two drinks in hand. "A toast to ring in the New Year?" he suggested.

She accepted the glass. "What would you suggest we toast?"

"We could toast that the best of last year is the worst of this one."

"That's a lovely sentiment." She toyed with the stem of the flute. Jonathan, for all his womanizing, was dead serious when it came to his career ambitions. "Or we could toast to bigger raises and better positions within Fontana."

He shook his head. "All of your hard work will provide those without toasting to them."

"You never cease to surprise me," she marveled. "Okay. Since we're approaching the very heart of winter, why don't we toast to finding our heart's desire this year. That when the next New Year rolls around, we'll be spending it with our one true love."

She held her breath, wondering if she'd gone too far. The candlelight danced across his face as she waited, burnishing the visible portions of his face with silver while deepening the shadows that hid him from her. It was his eyes that trapped the light the most, eyes that leaped and burned with a fierce intensity. Slowly he approached and raised his glass, touching the rim of his to the rim of hers. The crystal sang, pure and brilliant, as though in joyous confirmation to her suggestion.

"To ringing in the New Year with our one true love," he murmured.

Together they drank, the effervescent wine crisp and sweet, with the perfect amount of tang. Then Jonathan took her glass and set it aside. Sweeping the sombrero from his head, he tossed it onto the nearest chair. He still wore the black bandana that masked his hair and the upper half of his face.

"Are you going to remove the mask?" she asked.

"Are you going to remove your mask and wig?"

She hesitated, feeling unusually mischievous. "I think we should leave them on. It makes it…"

"Kinky?"

"No." She moved into his arms and released her breath on a sigh. "It makes it more romantic."

"Then we stay in costume." He matched her mischievous look with one of his own. "Or we continue to wear parts of our costume."

"But not this part."

Her hands skated to the leather thong holding his black silk shirt closed. She took her time unthreading it. The minute she finished, she stripped the shirt from his shoulders, baring his chest and arms. Until that moment, she'd never seen Jonathan without a shirt. Oh, she'd suspected that he kept himself fit beneath all those fancy suits. But this exceeded her wildest expectations. She trailed her fingertips across the taut angles and into the toned valleys, anticipating the dichotomy of all that hard muscle abrading soft feminine flesh.

"And I believe we can lose this part of your costume," he informed her.

He reached behind her and released the hooks securing the ornamental girdle around her waist. The girdle secured both the upper drapes of her gown, as well as the skirt. Without it, the gold shimmering material floated around her body like a veil. She hadn't worn a bra. The costume didn't allow for one. And when he lifted the drape of bodice away, it bared her to the waist.

He looked at her, his breath escaping in a hiss. "I knew... At least, I thought I knew. But not this. Never anything as beautiful as this."

He cupped her breasts, sliding his thumbs across the peaks. She could feel her nipples harden beneath the gentle caress. He lowered his head and took one into his mouth, scraping his teeth across the rigid tip. A high, urgent cry caught in her throat, desperate for release. But she couldn't seem to move or think or speak. She could only feel. Feel the suckle and scrape and lathe as New Year's Eve fireworks exploded deep in her belly and the urgency built to a fever pitch.

Finding she could move again, she reached for his belt buckle. Fumbled it. Fumbled it again, before managing to get it open. She stripped the heavy leather strap through the belt loops. The next instant she had his trousers unzipped and slid her hands down corded abs, straight to the source of his heat.

She cupped him. Heard the swift, choked intake of his breath and the strangled word he uttered—a graphic word that for some reason made her laugh, perhaps because it was so un-Zorro-like.

"That bad or that good?" she teased.

"Good," he gritted out. "Very, very good."

"Let's see if we can make it better than good."

He caught her hands, preventing her from putting words into action. "No, my beautiful Cleo. My turn now."

In one swift move he stripped away her final veil of modesty, her pleated skirt. It left her standing in sheer, thigh-high stockings and heels and a tiny lace thong. Never taking his eyes from her, he toed off his boots and peeled off his trousers. Naked, except for his mask and bandana, he approached.

The air shuddered in and out of her lungs as she waited for his touch. When it came it felt almost reverent. Tender and appreciative. As though she were the one woman in all the world he wanted to be with. He drew her close until soft collided with firm. Curve fit to angle. Female surrendered to male.

He moved with the same grace he'd shown on the dance floor when he swept her into his arms and carried her to the huge duvet-covered bed. She sank deep into downy comfort while he blanketed her in steely heat. Then he kissed her. Ravished her mouth. Consumed her with small, hungry bites. And she let him. Even more, she gave back, dueling with the expert. Zorro. Granted, she wasn't the expert he was when it came to duels of this nature. Nor did she have his experience or moves. But she found that with him—just him—she more than held her own.

His mouth shifted from hers, skating downward to follow the length of her neck. Her head tipped backward and she moaned her encouragement. She could feel her wig slipping and shoved at it, tossing it aside while retaining her mask. Her blond hair spilled out, splashing across the red duvet in a tangled cloud. She didn't care anymore. Every ounce of focus was on Jonathan's incredible mouth and what it was busily doing to her.

He found her breasts again. And while he devoted his full attention to them, his hands discovered other employment. His thumbs slipped into the elastic band of her thong and dragged it downward. He slid farther down her body, kissing a path over the indent of her belly. He paused just

long enough to remove her heels and roll the stockings off
her legs. And then he lowered his head to kiss her once
more, this kiss the most intimate she'd ever received.

"Please," she moaned. "Please, not yet."

But it was too late. She cried out at the touch of lips
and tongue, arching beneath him as an unexpected climax
ripped through her. She gasped for air. Never. Absolutely
never had she experienced anything like that before. Tears
filled her eyes and to her utter shame, he saw them.

Instantly, he wrapped her up in his arms, tenderly
peeling off her mask and baring her expression. "What's
wrong?" he demanded in a low, gruff voice. "Did I hurt
you?"

She shook her head. "It's not that. I just… I've never…"

It took a split second for comprehension to dawn. "Not
ever?"

"No. But…I wanted it to be with you. Not…" She trailed
off, unable to continue.

His smile of reassurance was the most beautiful sight
in the world. "It will be. I promise."

She didn't doubt him. Not for a moment. Trusting him
more than she had any other man, she opened herself to
him. Her arms. Her willingness.

Her heart.

Gently, and with a mastery that stole into the heart he'd
managed to capture, he showed her how perfect it could
be between a man and a woman. He worshiped her body
with his mouth and hands. He encouraged her to explore
him just as he explored her. With every touch, every word,
he demonstrated a give-and-take that opened the door to
a world she'd never dared imagine. One where two disparate parts could unify into a perfect melding of male and
female. All through the night he took her to heights she'd
never known existed.

And with the coming of dawn, with the arrival of her thirtieth birthday, sleep claimed her. She fell with utter safety into the embrace of the New Year…and the man who'd somehow managed to fulfill her toast a whole year early.

CHAPTER FOUR

JAYNE AWOKE LATE New Year's Day to an empty bed. It took her a moment to figure out where she was and why. When her memory returned, it hit with a winter-cold slap.

What. The. *Hell*. Had. She. *Done?*

On the positive side there wasn't any awkward postcoital morning chitchat. No uncomfortable scramble from the bed, wondering how she compared in the cold light of day with his image of her from the night before. No morning breath or makeup smears. She'd also have the bathroom to herself. And best of all, she would have time to recover from the most utter and complete ravishment she'd ever experienced in her twenty-nine—*no*, thirty—years.

Unfortunately, there was a downside. She closed her eyes, her breath gusting out on a sigh. How would it have felt to awaken in Jonathan's arms? To have him sweep off his mask and bandana and look at her with those incredible dark eyes. To have them glitter with the same passion they had all through that amazing night. To let her know in some small way that what had happened between them was more than a one-night stand.

Instead, she'd have to face him Monday morning at work, with both their professional masks firmly in place, hiding their true thoughts and feelings. What would she read in his eyes then? Warmth or amusement? Hunger or triumph? Her hands balled into fists. Interest or intense indifference?

Erupting from the bed, she made a beeline for the bathroom. Guttered candles lined the swimming pool-sized jetted tub they'd shared the night before. Taking a deep, steadying breath, she paced to the shower and turned it on full blast. Instantly, she calmed. Ten minutes later and feeling more like her old self, she wrapped up in a thick, fluffy bath sheet and returned to the bedroom.

That's when it struck her. She'd have to wear her Cleopatra outfit home. Sure, she'd have her cloak to cover herself, but still… She could see the costume folded neatly on a chair, which surprised her. To the best of her recollection, it had been tossed and scattered across most of the suite. She approached and then stilled.

A stack of women's clothing rested next to her costume. Perched on top was a note on Centoria Mark stationery and a single red rose. She picked up the rose and sniffed it with a tender smile and then opened the folded note.

You were sleeping so soundly I didn't want to wake you. I also thought you might prefer returning home in street clothes. Thank you for a night of magic. Until the next fantasy.…

To her amusement, a large Z scored the bottom of the page.

Curious, she examined the clothes he'd provided. Discreet labels clung to each garment, carrying the exclusive name of one of the pricier international designers who'd been granted space in the lobby to peddle their wares. She found a cashmere sweater in deep wine-red and a pair of wool slacks in ivory. Beneath were delicate undergarments, so light they practically floated through the air like feathers.

Jayne was so happy, she could have floated, as well. With a sigh of pleasure, she dressed. It only took a few minutes to gather up the rest of her belongings and head out. She stopped by the registration desk before leaving. A woman wearing a gold name tag that read "Selene" greeted her politely and accepted the key card Jonathan had left behind.

"I believe I owe something on the suite," Jayne began.

"That's already been taken care of." Selene leaned forward with a confiding smile. "We were warned that you'd insist on paying the full, nondiscounted rate for the suite. I'm to inform you that it's been paid in full."

Jayne could feel herself light up. "He took care of it? Really?"

"Every last penny." She straightened and resumed a more professional air. "I hope everything was to your satisfaction?"

"Trust me. I was more than satisfied."

With that, Jayne swung around and left the hotel.

MONDAY MORNING ROLLED around with all the urgency of a snail. Jayne took extra pains with her outfit for the day, struggling to find something that maintained her professional image, but also revealed a feminine softness that discreetly said "Cleopatra." Since nothing in her wardrobe quite matched that criteria, she picked up a red rose on her way to work and pinned it to the lapel of her suit jacket, hoping Jonathan would read the intent behind the gesture.

The morning dragged endlessly without any word from him. Shortly before noon he waltzed into her office.

She smiled at him. Smiled? She beamed, every ounce of pleasure and hope—and hunger—bubbling out of her.

"I'm so glad you came," Jayne whispered. "Close the door."

Looking instantly intrigued, Jonathan did as she asked. "What's up? Hear some juicy gossip?" He rubbed his hands together. "Rumors from the New Year's Eve bash?"

She tilted her head to one side and wrinkled her nose, laughing. "No, silly. I just wanted to give you this…" She circled her desk and approached. She touched the soft petals of the rose decorating her lapel. "I wore this just for you."

His brows came together in a slight frown. "You did?"

Gathering her nerve—though after the incredible night they'd spent together, why be nervous?—she slid her hands up his chest and wrapped her arms around his neck. "Yes, I did. And I want to thank you for giving me one of the most amazing nights of my life…Zorro."

Then she kissed him, putting every ounce of passion she possessed into the kiss. For an instant, Jonathan didn't move. In fact, he stumbled backward a step before catching himself. She caught her name, muffled somewhere in the mess of interlocking lips before his arms came around her and he hiked her into his arms, returning the embrace with greedy pleasure. The instant he took control of their embrace, she knew—knew without the least doubt and with total and intense horror.

Jonathan wasn't Zorro.

NICK SHOVED A CONTRACT to one side, fighting for focus. Focus. Yeah, right. How the hell was he supposed to focus when all he could think about was Jayne and the night they'd spent together? He'd noticed her almost from the moment she'd come to work for Fontana, Inc., but he hadn't acted on his attraction. It didn't seem appropriate, considering he was her boss.

So he'd patiently waited for her to earn her way up the food chain to a point where his attention wouldn't cause too much gossip. The charity ball had given him the perfect opportunity to test the waters. So far, his plan had worked perfectly. One of the charity workers who Jonathan had his eye on had unwittingly assisted by urging him to change his costume to Don Juan. That had left Nick free to take on the Zorro role.

Even after two and a half days he couldn't get the image of Jayne out of his mind—his Cleopatra spread naked across the duvet, open and eager and willing. Who would have guessed so much passion seethed beneath such a calm, proficient exterior? He'd hoped. Hell, yes, he'd hoped. But, until they'd kissed, he hadn't been certain.

He'd been with passionate women before. Since he'd become an icon in the business world he'd gone from being an intelligent, fairly good-looking, ambitious man with a good sense of humor to Mr. Intimidating. Multimillionaire. Elite businessman. Women saw the public mask, not the man behind it. Playing the part of Zorro had given him the opportunity to change all that, to relate to a woman without the Nick Fontana mystique. Without all the labels.

Yet, he'd still been forced to wear a mask, hadn't he?

He capped his pen and tossed it onto his desk. This was ridiculous. Why sit here and brood? He'd already planned his next move, one that would have Jayne realizing that Zorro and Jonathan were two entirely different people. One that would reveal his true identity in a way that he hoped would help them move from delightful fantasy to delicious reality. Time to put the next step of his plan into motion.

He paused in the doorway of his strategic analyst's office

to ask how she was holding up. Her due date was fast approaching and he'd been watching her like a hawk to make certain she didn't overdo. She glanced at him, revealing a nervousness that caught him by surprise.

"What's wrong, Linda?"

"The gentleman we hired to fill in for me while I'm out on maternity leave just emailed to say that he's accepted a position in San Francisco. I called our second choice, but she's accepted a job elsewhere, as well."

Damn. "Okay. Go on to lunch and we'll take another look at the list later this afternoon. I'm sure there's someone down in the arena who can do the job. At least, that's what all their fancy diplomas say."

Choosing to take the steps rather than the elevator, Nick headed down to the twenty-fifth floor—aka "the arena"—where he stashed his clutch of MBAs. He only hired the best, and even those didn't all make the cut. He'd discovered long ago that tossing them in together on a single floor made them work harder than their competition to prove they deserved to move up the corporate ladder and onto one of the five "golden" floors above them. Some, like Jonathan and Jayne had risen to the point where they'd been awarded prime office real estate—one short step before the big leap upstairs.

He strode down a long, wide corridor studded with huge containers of live plants to a closed door one shy of a corner office. Tapping lightly on the wood panel, he didn't wait for a response, but pushed open the door.

He didn't remember moving. He sure as hell didn't remember knocking Jonathan Blair on his ass, though he sincerely wished he did. When he came to his senses, Blair was laid flat on the office carpet while Jayne struggled to wriggle off the top of her desk.

She wore a robin's egg-blue suit that perfectly matched

the color of her eyes. Her fitted skirt was hiked to her upper thighs, no doubt by Blair, and revealed a delicate ivory garter that matched the pearl-buttoned silk blouse she wore. The pale flesh of her thighs gleamed between the top of her stockings and the hem of her skirt—flesh that he'd explored in intimate detail just a few nights before.

She levered herself upward, gasping for air, her lips rosy from Blair's kisses. Her honey-blond hair, which she normally wore in a sedate knot at the nape of her neck, was loose and flowing across her shoulders, just as it had been when he'd taken her that first time on New Year's Eve.

He spared the man on the floor a single glare, one filled with rage and threat. One he feared claimed ownership to the woman Blair had dared to touch. Catching himself before he said something he'd regret, he turned his back on the two and made a point of closing the door. It gave him the precious few seconds he needed to regain his self-control. Then he faced his employees.

"I won't bother to ask what the hell is going on since that's abundantly apparent," he informed them through gritted teeth.

Jonathan sat up, rubbing his jaw. He pointed an accusing finger in Jayne's direction. "*She* came on to *me*. All I did was accept her offer."

Jayne fought to get buttons into their proper holes. Straightening her suit jacket she watched the crushed rose petals drift to the floor and winced, no doubt reacting to the symbolism.

She reluctantly glanced at Blair. "I thought you were someone else," she attempted to explain.

"You've known me for eighteen months," Jonathan snarled. "Just who the hell did you think I was?"

She couldn't meet either of their eyes. "Zorro," she whispered.

Nick kept his expression carefully blank. "I assume this has to do with New Year's Eve?"

Jayne nodded, still unable to meet his gaze. "Yes, sir."

Jonathan's eyes narrowed. "You thought I was Zorro? At the New Year's Eve party Friday night?"

"You said you were going as Zorro and to save you a dance. Then you—I mean…*Zorro* showed up and I thought… I assumed…" She trailed off, catching her lower lip between her teeth. Then she took a deep breath, squared her shoulders and faced Nick. "I'm really sorry. Jonathan's right, Mr. Fontana. This is all my fault. I thought he was someone else, and I initiated the embrace. All he did was accept the offer."

"I changed my mind about my costume at the last minute and came as Don Juan." Jonathan flashed a set of perfect white teeth, looking quite pleased with himself. "If I'd known you were interested, sweetheart, I would have stuck to my original plan."

Her cheeks warmed, almost matching the color of the rose petals scattered at her feet. Now she did look at him, her light blue eyes arctic. "Lovely," she said in a clipped voice. "Except that you've just proven that—having had Zorro—Don Juan doesn't come close to stacking up."

Nick struggled to smother his bark of laughter.

Blair wasn't slow on the uptake. He shot to his feet, anger and insult warring in his face. "Why you little—"

"That's enough." Nick stepped between them, fixing his most intimidating expression on Blair. It stopped him in his tracks. "Obviously, Ms. Myleston has made an error. She's apologized. I expect this to be the end of it. And I expect what's happened here to remain within the confines of these four walls. Am I understood?"

Reluctantly, Jonathan nodded. "Yes, sir."

Jayne didn't show the same hesitation. She nodded

with patent relief. "Thank you for understanding, Mr. Fontana."

He swept an impatient hand through the air. "It was Nick before this mess. It's still Nick now." He fixed a stern gaze on Jonathan and jerked his head toward the door. "Get moving. I'll speak with you about this tomorrow."

Aside from a single disgusted glare in Jayne's direction, Jonathan turned on his heel and exited the office. Nick folded his arms across his chest, silently swearing. This was all his fault. He'd allowed Jayne to believe that Zorro and Blair were one and the same person. He hadn't corrected that assumption in time to prevent her from ending up in the humiliating position in which she'd found herself. And worst of all, she'd been pawed by a man who'd managed to find a way beneath just about every female skirt at Fontana, Inc.

Blowing out his breath, Nick approached Jayne. She stood in the middle of the room looking utterly miserable. Without a word, he peeled back her jacket. Her eyes widened in alarm and his mouth curved to one side. "Relax, Jayne. I need you to come with me and you can't leave the office looking like you do right now."

"What...?" She glanced down and closed her eyes, turning a delicate shade of pink. "Oh."

One by one, he rebuttoned her blouse until each pearl button rested in the appropriate hole. Then, he helped her with her jacket, giving the hem a quick jerk to pull out the wrinkles. Finally, he straightened the lapel. The remains of a crushed rose dangled from a pin and something raw and painful ripped through his gut. She'd worn that for him.

No, not him. For Zorro.

"I really, truly apologize, Mr.—Nick." She stared at a spot over his left shoulder. "And I promise that nothing like this will ever happen again."

"I know."

Her gaze jerked upward to meet his. "You do?"

"You've been my employee for eighteen months, Jayne. I'm well aware of your abilities...as well as your flaws."

She winced. "Of course."

"I'm also well aware of Blair's abilities and flaws. Until today his most serious flaw has never interfered with his job performance. Nor has it adversely impacted anyone else's."

"You mean the women he's dated."

Nick's smile turned grim. "He has an uncanny knack for keeping women happy, even when he leaves them." He gave her clothing a final check. Satisfied, he indicated the door. "Come with me, please."

"Yes, sir," she murmured.

"Relax, Jayne. You're not in trouble. I have a business proposition to suggest."

He could tell he'd intrigued her. Her eyes brightened and her natural self-confidence reasserted itself. "That sounds interesting."

This time he bypassed the steps and led the way to the elevators, pressing the button. They waited for the elevator with several other employees. Each one greeted him respectfully, but the silence couldn't have been more leaden. He ignored it, accustomed to it by now. When you were known as Mr. Intimidating, it had a dampening effect in situations like this.

The doors to two cars opened almost simultaneously, one headed down, the other up. Everyone piled into the down elevator with the exception of Nick and Jayne. When they reached the thirtieth floor, the doors opened smoothly to the plush foyer of the executive level and he escorted Jayne through a pair of double doors to a private dining room off one of the smaller conference rooms. Her curiosity was almost palpable.

"I thought we could discuss my proposal over lunch," he explained.

"Oh." She blinked in surprise. "That would be lovely. Thank you."

"Don't thank me until you hear what it is. You may not be quite as appreciative."

Speculation gleamed in her eyes. "That bad?"

He lifted a shoulder in a quick shrug. "That's for you to decide."

"You definitely have me intrigued."

He held the chair at a table situated by the office windows, overlooking the hustle and bustle of the city. The view was reminiscent of the table they'd shared on New Year's Eve and, though her expression didn't offer any indication, he wondered if it roused her suspicions. They'd only just settled into their seats when a side door opened and one of the catering staff entered with a rolling cart that contained a selection of drinks.

"Lunch will be out shortly," the waiter said, once they'd made their selection. "For your starter today we have the chef's favorite, a heart of palm salad with braised radishes, pea tendrils and garnished with a delicious sesame seed puree. To follow, we are serving roasted sea scallops with green almonds and grapes, which the chef has accompanied with broccolini florettes accented with a Serrano ham vinaigrette." He nodded in Nick's direction. "I hope that will be satisfactory, sir?"

"Tell Georges it sounds perfect."

"Thank you, Mr. Fontana."

Nick caught a questioning look from Jayne and lifted an eyebrow. "Problem?"

"Not a problem, no. I'm just curious... Do you dine like this every day?"

Now that they'd gotten past the awkwardness of what had happened in her office, she relaxed. It was one of the qualities he'd always admired about her. He'd never been able to intimidate her. She just deflected it with a smile and moved on. Now if he could just get her to see the "real" him instead of the public image.

Instead of answering her question, he asked one of his own. "Would you enjoy dining like this on a regular basis?"

She flashed him a quick grin, one which gave a whimsical bent to her elegant features. "Not every day, no. It's like the New Year's Eve ball. A treat on special occasions."

"I gather you enjoyed the party?"

Her smile faded ever so slightly. "Very much. Thank you again for allowing me to attend."

"I enjoyed myself, as well." He reconsidered. "Well. I enjoyed myself once that endless receiving line broke up."

"One of the downsides of your position, I gather."

"One I can live with." He waited a moment, then dropped his next question, curious to see her reaction. He lifted his glass and swirled the ice cubes. "So I gather you rang in the New Year with Zorro?"

CHAPTER FIVE

JAYNE STARED, WIDE-EYED, while swift color mounted her cheeks. "What?"

"New Year's Eve. Zorro," Nick prompted. He shot her a look, aiming it somewhere between quizzical and innocent. He might have hit quizzical, but he could pretty much guarantee he landed wide of the mark when it came to innocent. "Zorro must have made quite an impression if you spent the entire night dancing with him."

"Dancing. Yes." She drew a deep breath, regaining a portion of her poise. "We spent the entire night dancing."

Well…maybe not the entire night, not unless he broadened his current definition of *dancing*. He eased the tension with a casual smile. "I'm glad you had fun." The waiter appeared with their appetizers, the heart of palm salad beautifully plated. The instant he left the room, Nick continued. "I gather you thought your partner was Jonathan?"

Jayne sighed. "He mentioned attending in a Zorro costume. It looked like him. He never corrected me when I called him Jonathan."

Damn it all! He sure as hell had. Nick struggled to maintain a pleasant tone when what he really wanted was to snarl in annoyance. "He didn't?" He pushed—hell, shoved. "Not once?"

A thoughtful frown touched her brow. "Now that you mention it, I guess he did. He told me he wasn't Jonathan, he was Zorro." She shook her head in dismay. "I just assumed he wanted to maintain the fantasy."

Okay. Better. "Or perhaps he was telling you something."

"I just wasn't listening." She took a bite of her salad and closed her eyes on a moan that had Nick's blood heating. "Oh, my."

"Good?"

"Outstanding." He watched the undisguised delight explode across her face. He'd seen that look before. Only the last time it had been far more intense and filled with a level of passion that mere food couldn't hope to elicit. "The puree brings it all together," she said.

"I agree."

Though in truth he didn't have a clue since he'd given his lunch scant attention. All of his senses were attuned to Jayne. He wanted her. Heaven help him, but he wanted her. It took every ounce of restraint to keep from sweeping the dishes off the table and her onto it. Only the memory of how she'd reacted with Jonathan—the panic and disbelief when she'd realized that he wasn't *her* Zorro, the confusion and revulsion at the wrongness of his touch—held Nick in place. He'd known from the start that he'd have to take this slowly. Carefully. Nothing had changed.

"Nick…" She toyed with the final few bites of her salad. "I just want to apologize again for being such an idiot."

"No need. Jonathan told you he was coming as Zorro. When Zorro approached you at the ball, you made a perfectly logical assumption. I gather you parted ways before you unmasked." To his amusement, color flowed into her face again. "And this morning, you decided to thank him for a lovely evening by giving him a kiss."

She inclined her head. "That's pretty much it."

"How did you know it wasn't him?"

Her nose wrinkled. "He didn't kiss like Zorro. He kissed like Don Juan."

"Never having kissed, either," he replied gravely, "I'm afraid I'll have to take your word for it."

His teasing caught her off guard. Then she laughed, the sound light and airy and delicate. "Trust me, there's a huge difference. Don Juan only wants one thing. Zorro, on the other hand, is all about giving to others. He's generous and strong and—" She broke off abruptly. "I'm so sorry, Mr. Fontana. This isn't the appropriate venue for this discussion. You brought me here for a business discussion and I've probably just proven that I'm the wrong person for whatever job you had in mind."

He buried a sigh. He'd hoped to lead Jayne carefully toward his revelation. Leave it to her to throw up roadblocks left, right and center. "Relax, will you? We're having a casual conversation over lunch while we get to know each other better. A short break from business isn't going to kill either one of us."

"No, sir. Of course not."

Hell. They were back to extreme formality. He leaned on the personal again, hoping to shift them back to a more intimate interaction. "So, now that you know that Jonathan isn't Zorro, what are you going to do?"

She stared in confusion. "Do?"

"Don't you want to find your Zorro?"

"Yes, absolutely."

Her response came without forethought or hesitation. It also pleased him to no end. The waiter appeared, seamlessly removed their plates and replaced them with their main course. He then opened a bottle of wine, a crisp Pinot Gris to mate with the scallops, before vanishing again.

"Do you think Zorro knew who you were?" Nick tossed out the question with a casual air.

Her head tilted to one side in consideration, her hair sweeping over her shoulder. "I hadn't thought of that," she confessed. "But, yes. He did know. At one point he called me by name."

"Interesting." He speared a roasted sea scallop and held it out for her. "You have got to try this, Jayne. I've never tasted better."

She accepted the tidbit he offered and he took an almost tender amusement in the fact that she didn't associate it with Zorro doing the exact same thing during their New Year's Eve meal together. "Oh, my," she murmured. "You're right. That's simply amazing."

"So if he called you by name," Nick persisted, "that means it's someone you worked with in connection with the foundation. Doesn't that make sense?"

The food had distracted her and it took a moment for her to switch gears. It was one of the things he appreciated learning about her, the way she gave intense focus to each and every sensation, particularly if she'd never experienced it before.

"You're right." She considered the possibilities. "Unfortunately, I worked with quite a few people."

"Maybe he'll contact you again."

Her breath caught and a look of utter delight blossomed across her face. "Do you think he might?"

He sipped his wine. "I would."

Her expression softened, edged toward endearing. "Thank you, Nick. That's very kind of you to say. As long as he doesn't work for Fontana, Inc., I'd love to pursue a relationship."

Uh-oh. "And if he does work for Fontana, Inc.?"

"Then, unfortunately, I'll have to refuse to see him again." She leaned forward, an intensity gathering in her brilliant blue eyes. "I want to make it clear to you that from this point forward I will never, ever date anyone working for your company. Not after what happened with Jonathan. I've learned my lesson. If Zorro is a Fontana, Inc. employee, I would break off the relationship rather than make the sort of mistake that could put my job at risk. You don't need to worry about my being involved in another unfortunate incident like the one you witnessed earlier."

He struggled not to smile at the way she said "unfortunate incident." "So, even if I were the one to invite you out, you'd still refuse?"

She forked up another scallop. "Especially you."

Well, hell. "Why especially me?" he demanded.

"My best friend dated the owner of the company she worked for and discovered it was a fast track toward unemployment. Let's just say that I learned from her mistake. No offense, but I'd quit sooner than make such a bad decision."

Damn it! "Jayne—"

"So, if you're Zorro, I'm sorry. It simply wouldn't work between us," she joked, then offered a teasing smile. "Not that you'd ever be interested in dating someone like me."

Double damn! "Jayne, I can't imagine any red-blooded male not wanting to date you."

She glowed with pleasure. "Thanks, Nick."

He left it at that. Time to reassess his strategy and come up with plan B. Jayne had unwittingly boxed him in and until he figured a way out of the situation, he couldn't admit to being Zorro. Throughout the remainder of lunch he kept the conversation light and casual, deliberately covering some of the ground they'd explored in their New Year's Eve guises. All the while he considered his options, not that there were many.

He waited until they'd been served coffee before broaching his business proposition. At least he could get that much sewn up. "My strategic analyst will soon be out on extended maternity leave. I need a temporary replacement who can work with me during the planning stages of the various Fontana, Inc. mergers currently on my plate." He shot her a direct look. "I want you for the job. Right now we're working on a merger between Adams and Zander."

Excitement exploded across her expression. "I've seen some of the materials on those companies. I've been curious to see how you plan to merge such a traditional firm with…" She hesitated.

"An upstart like Zander?" he suggested.

"They are two disparate concerns."

"It's definitely going to take all my patience and skill to put those two together, along with impeccable timing. And that's where you come in."

He took his time, detailing the scope of the position and stressing the endless hours, the endless meetings and the wide variety of responsibilities. "You'll have your own private secretary who can coordinate with mine on scheduling and organizing assignments so we both stay on task. And the two of us will have to work very closely over the next few months until we convince all the players to go along with my plan." He leaned back in his chair and lifted an eyebrow. "So, what do you think? Interested?"

He gave her points for maintaining a calm demeanor. But he'd been negotiating deals since his late teens and he could tell he'd staggered her with his proposition. "That's quite an offer."

"I think it will work out well for both of us. I have doubts that Linda will be returning, so there's every possibility that it will become a full-time job if you decide you like it. Or it can be a stepping-stone toward managing your own analyst team. As you know, the next step after that is a VP title. It will also put some distance between you and Blair."

He held up a hand before she could speak. "Not that you need any. But it might make you feel more comfortable in the short run and give him time to recover his pride. He's a valuable asset and I'd rather not have to fire him because he decides to cause trouble for you."

"You think he'll do that?"

"I think it's within the scope of his character," Nick said. "My hope is that he values his position here more than a small ding to his ego and will do as I ordered and keep his mouth shut. If he can't, then I can't trust him in other areas of business, either. So, he'll go. But I suspect that by removing you from the equation so you're not a constant visual reminder, this will go away a good deal quicker."

"Then, of course, I accept the position."

Nick frowned. "I don't want you accepting because of Blair."

"That's a joke, right?" She laughed in genuine amusement. "You're offering me the opportunity to work alongside the great Nick Fontana. I'll be able to watch how you conduct business and learn from a master. Do you know how many of my coworkers would toss their best friend out the nearest window for that chance?"

"Fair enough." He shoved back his chair. "Go clear out your office, Jayne. Linda will show you where to put your things. She'll also provide you with the documentation you'll need to bring you up to speed."

"Yes, sir." Her smile was absolutely breathtaking. "Thank you, Nick. I'm all yours."

He suppressed a grin. "That's what I had in mind."

Because now he had a game plan for wooing and winning Jayne Myleston. While they focused on the rather tricky upcoming merger on the work front, she'd get to know the man behind the mask. And on a separate front, he'd woo and win her on a physical, emotional and intellectual level as Zorro. Win her by proxy, as it were. She'd get to know the real man, not Mr. Intimidating or Fontana, Inc. or her boss or any of the other labels women tended to stick on him.

He'd just apply a business solution to a personal problem. Eventually, he'd find the perfect opportunity to merge the two identities. After all, mergers were his specialty. He just needed to wait for the right time and circumstances to gain the cooperation of all the parties involved. What could possibly go wrong?

FOR JAYNE, THE NEXT FEW DAYS passed with breathtaking speed. Nick kept her busier than she'd ever been before. Even better, he opened the window to a whole new world. Until then, she'd spent years with her nose pressed to the glass, longing to be part of the thrill and excitement that Nick enjoyed on a daily basis. Now, she'd have the opportunity to experience it for herself.

Not that it was easy. It wasn't. Nick proved a tough task-master. Though he never lost his temper, more than once she witnessed a dangerous edge when someone failed to complete a task on time or to the standards he set.

"If you can't do it, tell me," he informed Jayne at one point. "Be honest. Because I'm going to find out, one way or another."

"And if I can't do what you've requested?" she dared to ask.

"Then you better have a good reason why."

Something else she discovered about him was that he had a keen appreciation of the absurd. His sense of humor would show itself at the oddest times and with a few pithy words he'd have the entire room erupting with laughter. Jonathan had once commented that they laughed because Nick was the boss and they were paid to cater to the top dog. But sitting in on her very first meeting with "the big dogs," Jayne realized that wasn't it at all. Her boss was really funny.

One of the highlights of her week had been the meeting she'd been invited to attend between Nick and the directors of his charity, Foundation Fontana. It wasn't part of her day-to-day responsibilities anymore, but Nick included her because she expressed such keen interest.

In the course of the meeting, Nick was unusually vocal and passionate about how he wanted the foundation funds distributed, the bulk going to assist children with cancer. He also laid out in great detail what he hoped to accomplish over the coming years. She could tell from the general reaction that this was SOP—standard operating procedure— and part of a long-term, ongoing strategy he'd developed years before when he'd first created FF.

Best of all had been those rare moments when they were alone and Nick dropped his corporate mask. She'd always suspected he was far different from the public perception, but it came as a delightful surprise to have her suspicions confirmed. The Thursday after her temporary promotion, he stretched out on the couch in the sitting area of his office and waved her toward one of the chairs.

"Kick off your shoes and let your hair down, Jayne. We both need to decompress."

"Would you like some coffee?" she offered.

"Only if you do. Otherwise don't bother."

She crossed to the small wet bar near the sitting area and poured them both a cup of his special blend. A number of years ago he'd discovered the small coffee finca while vacationing in Costa Rica and claimed the coffee from these farms was the best he'd ever sampled. Though not an expert, Jayne had to admit it tasted absolutely delicious.

She set the cup on the table adjacent to the couch and

then retreated to her chair. "So what do you think of the job so far?" Nick asked.

"Incredible. Exhilarating. Challenging. Breathtaking," she cataloged.

"That bad, huh?"

"Mmm." She buried her nose in her cup before daring to poke the lion with a stick. "In fact, it would be the perfect job except for one minor detail."

His brows snapped together in concern. "Well, hell, Myleston. What's the one minor detail? I'll have it fixed before the end of day."

She brightened. "Great. It's my boss. If it weren't for him it would be the best job in the world."

His slow, easy grin lit a fire low in her belly. "I don't intimidate you a bit, do I? Why is that?"

"I don't know," she admitted. "It just doesn't bother me."

He lifted onto his elbows and studied her with narrowed eyes, the color settling somewhere between green and gold. "Damn it, Jayne, why not? I make grown men weep."

She lifted a shoulder. "I'm not a grown man."

"Huh. Good point." He settled down again. "To be honest, I like that I don't intimidate you. Intimidation doesn't make for a good relationship. It also prevents you from telling me what you really think."

"Do you want to know what I really think?"

His gaze grew more intense than she'd ever seen it, fixing her in place. For the first time she saw him as something more than her boss. She saw him as a man. And not just any man, but someone strong and powerful and intensely attractive.

She shook her head. Oh, no. That would never do. First Jonathan and now Nick? What in the world was wrong with her? She closed her eyes and thought about New Year's Eve and Zorro, retreating into the safety of the fantasy. Because she could never have the reality. Not that she wanted the reality. She spared Nick a final peek from beneath her lashes.

Did she?

By quitting time on Friday, she was exhausted but ecstatic. Working with the great Nick Fontana was everything she'd hoped it would be—and more. Not only had she been privy to the inner workings at Fontana, Inc., but she'd learned more in that single week than in the previous eighteen months combined. She only wished that she could keep the job on a permanent basis. But since she couldn't, Jayne intended to enjoy every last second until Linda returned.

Closing down her files, she checked her corporate email a final time in case Nick had any last requests. Sure enough, an email waited for her, though it wasn't from her employer, but from an address she didn't recognize.

Opening it up, she swiftly scanned it, feeling a sudden kick to her pulse when she saw the signature at the end—a slashing *Z*. Backing up, she read the message more carefully.

A single night with you is not enough, will never be enough. Share the fantasy if you dare. A key will be waiting for a certain Ms. L.R.R. Hood at the Centoria Mark reception desk. Mr. T.B.B. Wolf will be waiting to dine with…or on…you at our usual suite, tomorrow night at eight. Come hungry. Mask required.

She inhaled sharply, excitement thrumming through her. He'd contacted her. He'd actually contacted her. And even more intriguing, he wanted to continue the game they'd begun on New Year's Eve. It didn't take a great intellectual leap to figure out the initials for Little Red Riding Hood and The Big Bad Wolf. For endless moments, she sat and debated, struggling to be logical and cautious and practical. But all the while, excitement stirred.

This could be just what she needed to help take her mind off that odd reaction she was having to Nick. It would also offer a wonderful stress release without any of the strings normal dating created. Though it was utterly unlike her to indulge in a purely sexual relationship, New Year's Eve had been absolutely amazing. The opportunity to experience that again was simply too good to miss. She caught her lower lip between her teeth. Could she do it? Did she have the nerve?

A light tap sounded at her door. Nick stood there, leaning against the doorjamb. "It's getting late, Jayne. You've done well this week, but it's time to call it a day."

She frowned at the email. "I'm shutting down now...."

"What's wrong?"

She hesitated, aware that she was crossing the line between business and personal. Maybe it wouldn't matter since Nick already knew about her mystery man and several of their conversations this week had veered well into the personal arena. She went for broke. "Zorro emailed me. He wants to meet again."

"Great." He lifted an inquiring eyebrow. "That is great, right?"

"Yes, absolutely."

"Except?" he prompted.

She spared Nick a brief look before replying. His expression remained encouraging, so she continued. "He wants to continue with the masquerade. As in, full costume."

"Kinky."

She took instant exception. "Charming. Intriguing."

She blew out a sigh. "Okay, a tiny bit kinky, but in a good way."

"Then what's the problem?"

"I have no idea who he is."

Nick nodded in complete understanding. "Got it. In other words, what if he's a pervert…or worse."

Nick had keyed into her fears with typical precision. "Exactly."

He shrugged. "So do it in a public setting."

She allowed a hint of her exasperation to show. "In costume?"

His mouth twitched. "Good point. Okay, where does he want to meet you?"

"At the Centoria Mark."

His eyebrows shot upward. "Pricy. That suggests he has to be one of Foundation Fontana's prime donors. Not that that makes him harmless."

Jayne worried at her lip again. "What do you suggest I do?"

He walked farther into her office and paused by her desk, resting a hip on the edge. "This might be overstepping on my part, but perhaps I can ensure that you're adequately protected."

"How?"

"Since you're meeting at the Mark…" He tilted his head to one side. "In a hotel room, I assume?"

Hot color blossomed across her cheeks. "Yes," she murmured.

"I'll find out who's renting the room and make sure he's on the up-and-up."

She considered that for a moment. "You'll tell me who he is?" she asked hopefully.

"And ruin Zorro's game?" Nick shook his head, a teasing smile playing across his mouth. "No, he can keep his secret identity."

She studied him curiously. "Why, Nick? Why are you willing to go to so much trouble on my behalf?"

"Let's just say I'm a romantic at heart."

"That's not how your competitors describe you."

"How do they describe me?" When she hesitated, he pushed. "How would you describe me? Feel free to be honest. I promise I won't hold it against you."

He wanted the truth? Fine. She'd give it to him. "I think you're a confusing man," she admitted. "On one hand I think you're caring and compassionate. I've seen that aspect with your foundation work. But I also think you're strong and deliberately set out to intimidate people." Her thoughts flashed to the email and the characters Zorro had suggested for their next encounter. "Where some might play the part of a lone, corporate wolf, you actually are one. The one thing I know for certain is that I wouldn't ever want to cross you."

"Wise of you. And not a bad all-round assessment." He stood. "Time to call it a night, Jayne. I'll see you tomorrow."

"You mean Monday," she dared to correct.

He simply smiled. "Of course I did."

CHAPTER SIX

JAYNE APPROACHED THE receptionist desk at the Centoria Mark, struggling to appear calm and casual. To behave as though she belonged and not as though she were up to anything illicit.

Which she wasn't. Absolutely not.

The outfit she wore could pass as normal. She'd chosen a lovely calf-length wool skirt and silk blouse in a matching ivory. The holly berry-red of her boots and oversized bag gave the simple outfit a dramatic flair, though nothing outrageous. At least, not for New York. Her hair was tucked into a jaunty cashmere hat. The only garment that might have raised eyebrows was the ankle-length hooded cloak that perfectly matched the color of her boots and bag.

The receptionist was the same woman who'd been on duty New Year's Day and greeted Jayne with a smile of recognition. "Ms. Hood, how lovely to have you stay with us again."

Jayne struggled to keep her jaw from dropping to the stylish tips of her boots at the unexpected greeting. "Thank you—" she quickly glanced at the name tag to refresh her memory "—Selene."

"You're already checked in, though I'm afraid your usual room wasn't available this evening," Selene continued smoothly. "Our manager, Mr. Jacks, has arranged for you to stay in the Mount Olympus suite. It has two bedrooms with a connecting salon." She slid a key card across the desk. "This accesses both your bedroom as well as the salon."

Jayne hesitated. More than anything she wanted to take the key. But a two-bedroom suite? She couldn't begin to imagine what such a room must cost. "I'm not sure—" she began.

Selene offered a reassuring smile. "I understand, perfectly. It's always disappointing when your first choice of accommodation can't be met, but I promise you'll love this suite every bit as much as the other one." She gave the barest wink, a movement so quick and subtle Jayne wondered if she'd imagined it. Then she continued in a barely audible voice, "Don't worry about a thing, Ms. Hood. The account has been prepaid in full."

"That's a relief. I couldn't afford so much as a closet in this place," Jayne replied just as softly. Now that she knew her Mystery Lover wasn't Jonathan, she didn't have to worry about whether or not he was paying for the suite or using Nick's name for a special discount.

Selene resumed a normal speaking voice. "But in case you're dissatisfied with the change, Mr. Jacks will call you later this evening to make certain the accommodations meet your standards."

"I'm sure they will," Jayne said faintly.

The elevator whisked her to the upper echelons of the hotel, opening onto a plush, silent corridor with a carpet deep enough to swim in. A discreet gold placard directed her toward the harbor side of the hotel and the trio of doors that comprised the Mount Olympus suite. At a guess, the two huge double doors opened onto the salon. To her amused delight, the doorway to her bedroom was gilded in silver and designated with a moon and an image of Artemis, while the second bedroom sported gold trim, a brilliant sun and a rendition of Apollo.

The key card unlocked her door and she stepped into a fantasy that exactly mirrored the theme for the evening. The bedroom might have been a room in a small cottage in the woods except for one minor detail. Though rustic in appearance, it offered a comfort Jayne was certain the storybook Red never would have experienced. The four-poster bed sported garlands of leaves and flowers while a paper-thin cotton canopy stirred beneath the air currents in the room. Even the furniture was made from raw, un-finished wood, though it still managed to exude a certain designer chic.

Jayne shook her head in amazement. As much as she'd like to take the time to explore her surroundings, she wanted Zorro—or his latest incarnation—all the more. Exploration could come later. Much later. Glancing toward the door leading to the salon, she swiftly removed her hat and cloak. Time to put the finishing touches on her costume for their date.

At eight on the dot, she opened the door to the salon and found herself peering into the re-creation of a forest glade. And standing in the middle of the glade was a glo-riously savage, deliciously masculine wolf, complete with whiskers, bright gold eyes—no doubt courtesy of a pair of contact lenses—and a face cleverly painted to resemble a wolf. Not even Courtney could have done a better job and Jayne doubted that whoever The Big Bad really was, even his own mother wouldn't have recognized him in his current getup.

Jayne stared in amazement, seriously impressed. "My, what big *everything* you have," she marveled.

THE DOOR BETWEEN THE Artemis bedroom and the main salon opened and Nick turned. Jayne stood in the door-way, a beautiful scarlet cape adorning her from head to toe, concealing more of her than it revealed. Her elegant features were obscured by a delightfully feminine mask covered in seed pearls, white feathers and sequins.

Her breath caught sharply, and he took immense pleasure in the way she stared at him in stunned disbelief. After her humorous greeting, she stepped into the room and that's when he caught a whiff of her nervousness. Maybe it was his appearance, or perhaps his silence. But she hesitated just a few feet from the safety of her bedroom, unwittingly reenacting what must have been the real Red's response when she first came upon the wolf.

"Zorro?" she asked with an edge of anxiety.

"Once upon a time, my former Queen of the Nile." He deliberately replied with a Spanish accent in order to reassure her, then pitched his voice low and gruff. "But not tonight."

Her anxiety faded and a smile blossomed across her mouth. "You look…amazing."

Despite the mask she wore, he'd have known her anywhere—the way she stood with the carriage of a queen. The lift of her rounded chin that hinted at forced bravado flying in the face of an innate shyness. Her unique fragrance, one that the more primal aspects of his nature associated with the scent of his mate. The delicacy of her form and the fluidity of her movement as she stepped farther into the room. He knew them all. Had learned each and every one of them over the course of eighteen endless months. And now they were his.

At least, for the moment.

She halted several feet away, sweet innocence in the face of ravening threat. Then she approached and her cloak flared around her, parting briefly before rippling closed again. In that split second he caught a glimpse of a virginal white satin-and-lace bustier, complete with a tiny frilled skirt incongruously matched with a pair of thigh-high red stiletto boots.

His breath hissed from his lungs as though he'd been sucker punched. He thought he actually growled. Going by the surprise on her face, he could pretty much guarantee he growled.

Her smile grew, turned flirtatious and knowing. "My, what big eyes you have," she teased.

He almost responded in his normal voice, only remembering at the very last instant to change the intonation and diction. "All the better to see you with, my dear," he replied.

It might have been tough to maintain the voice, but it wasn't any problem at all to stay in character. He felt like a wolf, wild and savage and hot on the scent of his prey. He reached for the cloak, intent on seeing more, but she flitted out of range.

The hood fell backward and revealed her hair. She'd taken as many pains over the style as he had over his wolf guise. The honey-blond length fell past her shoulders in dozens of braids, studded with red and crystal beads, feathers to match her mask and white ribbons. Her hair moved and chattered with a life of its own. More than anything, he wanted to feel those braids and beads on his skin.

He couldn't help himself. He gave chase. She laughed in delight, her brilliant red cloak billowing behind her, revealing the pièce de résistance. She wore a thong beneath her bustier, and attached to the back, just above her pert round backside was a dainty white bow that dipped and swayed and tempted him beyond measure.

It only took two swift strides to catch her and swing her into his arms. Her laughter faded, replaced by the nervousness he'd noticed earlier. Fighting for control of his beastly side, he gently set her down, still holding her, but loosely now. Tenderly.

"I promise I won't hurt you," he said.

She studied his face. Searching. Analyzing. No doubt probing for something familiar that would give her a clue to his identity. "Who are you? I assumed you were Jonathan and you used that misunderstanding to seduce me."

"If you'll recall, I did tell you I wasn't Jonathan. I told you that the minute we met."

She didn't argue the point. Nor did she appear satisfied with his explanation. "Who are you?" she repeated.

"Does it matter?"

"Under the circumstances, I guess not."

That gave him pause. "Under the circumstances?"

"I mean since it's just…" She broke off.

"Just?" he prompted.

"Just physical," Jayne finished in an awkward little rush. She held up her hand before he could say anything. "You know, maybe this would be a good time to set up some rules."

"Rules." He didn't know whether to laugh or kiss her silent.

"I've just been offered a huge promotion at work and that has to come first."

Nick struggled for patience. "What does that have to do with us and these rules you want to discuss?"

"Well, my first rule is that we keep our meetings light and casual." She smiled encouragingly. "Since I don't have time for anything as distracting as a real relationship, this is the perfect alternative, don't you think? A purely physical connection."

"A physical connection." Son of a bitch. He felt like a damn parrot. "What does that mean, exactly?"

"Well, um. You know, a sexual relationship with no strings."

"You don't want to get to know each other better?"

She hesitated, no doubt sensing something amiss. She chose her words with care. "I can't thank you enough for everything you're doing to make our evening so fun and interesting. But I can't believe you're looking for a serious relationship, either. You can't be. I mean, if you were, you'd have told me who you are so we could get to know each other without hiding behind masks. Right?"

Son of a bitch! How did she do it? How did she keep sabotaging his plans? Every time he came up with a new plan to get closer to her, she threw up a new roadblock. Well, not this time. She might think she could hold him at an emotional distance, but she'd soon learn differently.

Winning Jayne might take a little longer than he'd initially anticipated, but one way or another he'd find a way to break through her defenses. He'd simply launch a two-pronged attack, one at work and the other on the nights they met in disguise. Eventually, one persona or the other would get through to her no matter how hard she attempted to hold him at a distance. And once that happened, he'd reveal his true identity.

He'd spent his entire career taking disparate businesses and wedding them into conformity. Merging different and unique parts into a new, stronger, more complete whole. The art of melding companies required someone capable of looking outside the box, someone with patience, someone who could get past the obstacles thrown up by hardheaded stubborn participants and encourage them to see the benefits of merging. In other words, someone like him.

Just like with Adams and Zander, Nick's two-pronged assault on Jayne's emotional defenses would require perfect timing. But eventually she'd surrender and, when she did, he'd find the perfect moment to merge his two identities. Until then...

He tightened his arms, pulling her up against his chest. He heard her sigh, felt the give of her body as it surrendered to his. "Close your eyes, sweetheart. No, don't argue. Just close your eyes."

After a momentary hesitation, she obeyed. "This is so strange," she complained.

"Maybe, but it's also right. Just let your body remember me. Remember how we were together on New Year's Eve." He waited until the last of her resistance drained away and she fully relaxed against him. "Listen to me, Red. All that matters right now is this. What we feel. How we respond to each other. The reason I suggested wearing a mask is so we can be honest with each other."

Her lips twitched and her eyes opened. "Honest?" she repeated drily. She gestured toward the wooded glen that surrounded them, then toward his getup. "This is honest?"

He chuckled. "Point taken. I guess I mean emotionally honest. You can just be yourself and play. I get the impression you don't often play."

"I did as a child." She reconsidered. Shrugged. "Growing up on a farm came with a lot of responsibilities. Those had to come before play."

"You don't have any responsibilities with me other than to have fun."

"It's not fair, you know," she complained.

"Having fun?"

"Not that." She slipped free of his arms and crossed to a table designed to look like a giant tree stump. It was set up in preparation for a late dinner. "You know who I am."

He didn't even consider lying to her. "I have from the start."

She glanced over her shoulder at him. "How is it fair that you know my identity but I don't know yours?"

"It isn't."

She turned fully around to confront him. Her braids chattered in agitation. "Care to even the scales?"

"No. But I will promise to tell you who I am." He approached and poured the wine that he'd left open to breathe. He handed her a glass before taking the other for himself, offering a wolfish smile. "Eventually."

"No matter how this ends between us?" she bargained.

"Yes."

She touched the rim of her glass to his. Just like on New Year's Eve, the crystal sang out in sweet accord and she inclined her head. "It's a deal."

He indicated the food he'd chosen for their evening together. "So, my sweet little Red. Are you hungry?"

"Starving." She took a sip of wine before carefully returning her glass to the table. Then she stepped into his embrace. "But not for food."

"I was hoping you'd say that." He swung her into his arms and carried her to his bedroom and the masculine darkness within. "Welcome to my den, Red."

FROM THAT TIME FORWARD, they met every Saturday night in the Mount Olympus suite. And each night they met offered Jayne a new theme and a suite transformed to echo their latest fantasy. She tried not to think about the time and money involved in creating the elaborate sets. But it did confirm one thing Nick had suggested.

Whoever lurked behind the disguises had to be one of the wealthier contributors to Foundation Fontana. Of course, that included most everyone she'd come into contact with during her involvement setting up the ball. And though there were times when she felt an odd familiarity about her Mystery Lover—or ML as she privately dubbed him—she couldn't quite pinpoint what it was about him that sparked the sensation. Of course, if she were brutally honest with herself, she'd admit that she didn't want to know. Knowing would spoil the fantasy and she didn't want her fantasy spoiled by reality.

Not now. Not yet.

Each passing week, Courtney assisted with her costume and oftentimes the makeup as well, transforming Jayne from pedantic to mesmerizing. And each week Jayne spent one enchanted night in the arms of Robin Hood or a sheikh or Prince Charming, or even a surprisingly sexy caveman. Only one cloud dimmed the pleasure of each of those amazing rendezvous.

Despite her having been clear that she didn't want a serious relationship, she could feel her Mystery Lover attempting to nudge them in that direction. And each time, she gently pulled back. Didn't he understand? Their time together wasn't serious. And though what they had was spectacular, it was all about sating the senses, not the mind or emotions. She had all the intellectual discourse she needed with Nick.

"Why don't you want more than just this?" ML asked her one night.

"Because what we have is enough for me," she said gently. "Why won't you tell me who you are?"

They lay on a down mattress in the captain's cabin of a pirate ship. For a change, she'd gotten to play the role of the pirate to his Admiral of Her Majesty's fleet. She'd thoroughly pillaged and ransacked the admiral. Or maybe the admiral had thoroughly pillaged and ransacked her. It was hard to tell.

"It's not time, yet." His response came in a spot-on

British accent. "Though before long you might be able to guess."

"Care to give me a clue?"

"I think that if you were willing to bend the rules, you'd discover that we're perfect for each other in all areas, not just the physical."

"That's a clue?"

He rolled over on top of her. "You want a clue? Fine. We've met without our masks…more than once."

Before she could ask anything further, he filled his hands with her breasts. He lowered his mouth to first one, then the other, giving each his undivided attention before moving on. She lost track of their conversation, her thoughts scattering before his determined seduction.

"You, Madam Pirate, are formally accused of misconduct against the Crown," he informed her. "How do you plead?"

Jayne chuckled. "Guilty. Very, very guilty."

"Very well. Prepare to be boarded and taken over."

"I believe you did that already, Admiral."

His eyes glittered through his mask, deep, navy blue eyes this time, the color intensified by his white pigtailed wig. "I've been ordered to conduct a much more thorough inspection, Lady Pirate."

She allowed the moment to pass, slipping back into her assigned role with unstinting gusto. But she filed away his clue for further consideration when she had both the occasion and the brain cells. Her Mystery Lover took her again. Ravished her again. Overwhelmed her senses with his taste. His touch. His unique scent. And as she surrendered an image popped into her head. An image of Nick, who loved and encouraged intellectual discussions, who managed to connect with her on an emotional level. Only this image had nothing to do with intellectual discussions.

Instead she pictured Nick taking her instead of ML. Nick ravishing her. Nick overwhelming every last one of her senses. She stiffened in the admiral's arms and he froze.

"What's the matter?" he demanded.

Oh, God. What was wrong with her? "Nothing. Nothing's wrong." Though whether she was attempting to convince him or herself, she couldn't say. She forced out a sultry smile. "I believe you asked me to lower my gangplank?"

But even as she fell back into character, Nick's image remained. A fantasy within a fantasy. Tantalizing. Just out of reach. A tempting, inaccessible dream. She closed her eyes, surrendering. But a final tantalizing thought remained.

If only she could find a way to merge Nick and her Mystery Lover into one, she'd have the perfect man.

CHAPTER SEVEN

NICK TOSSED THE LATEST DETAILS regarding the Adams/Zander merger onto his desk and stalked to the windows overlooking the city. "I swear, I'm going to strangle Adams before this deal is through. It's been a full month. And he's still as hidebound as ever."

"He is proving more stubborn that you anticipated," Jayne sympathized.

"If something—or someone—doesn't break soon, this merger is going to fall apart."

"I think the real problem is that Zander and Adams don't share any common ground," she offered. "If we could find some interest they both enjoy, perhaps it'll open the door to their communicating more rationally about the merger. Instead, they're both entrenched in their positions and neither is willing to budge."

Nick turned and faced her. "Well, they'd better get over it or the one thing they're guaranteed to share is bankruptcy court."

The past month had also proved frustrating when it came to his breaking through Jayne's defenses. He had assumed he'd be able to work past her intransigence about emotional intimacy during either their romantic interludes at the Centoria Mark or at the office. But each time he stripped down barriers, she busily built them up again.

"How would you handle it, Jayne?" he asked. "We have someone who would make an ideal partner. But he's taken a stand and won't back down. How do you convince him to relent? How do you erase the line he's drawn?"

Jayne frowned. "Adams is well aware of what will happen if the merger fails. It seems to me that both he and Zander are afraid to be the first to back down, as though it'll be perceived as weakness on their part." She hesitated, then offered tentatively, "Maybe if we can find a starting place for them to communicate in a nonthreatening way, they could get to know each other. I'm sure once they do they'll discover they're not as far apart as they thought."

"Excellent suggestion." And one he'd use on her. He circled the desk and approached. "Let's say you're Adams…"

She made a face. "Why do I have to be Adams?"

"Because you're more conservative than I am."

She laughed. "You wouldn't say that if you knew me," she claimed, laughter dancing in her blue eyes.

It didn't take much of a leap to guess she referred to the weekends she spent in his arms. "Maybe Adams feels the same way. Maybe he thinks Zander has made assumptions about him because he has some years under his belt. It's ticked Adams off so he figures, What the hell? You think I'm conservative? I'll show you conservative."

"Makes sense. And Zander decides to go to the other extreme. Really rub the old man's nose in how cutting edge and techy he is. Flash the body art and piercings."

Nick stepped closer, eyeing Jayne intently. "So, Mr. Adams, how do I take us from business to personal? We want to find common ground that will get you to see me as a person instead of a piece of office furniture." He allowed her to absorb the comment, before asking, "What do you do when you're not working, Jayne? What interests you outside the workplace?"

To his delight she held her ground, regarding him in

open amusement. "I love to go to museums and art galleries and plays. During the summer I like to sail. Someday I'd love to own a small sailboat."

"Really? In that case, I'll have to take you out on mine."

She regarded him eagerly. "You have one?"

"Nothing too ostentatious. A thirty-eight-foot keelboat."

"Oh, is that all."

Without her being aware of it, he guided her to the couch in the sitting area. It didn't take any effort at all to keep the conversation on sailing since they both enjoyed it so much. Better still, he could see Jayne lowering her barriers and opening up to him. When they'd exhausted the topic of sailboats, he shifted to the most recent plays she'd seen. And from there they moved on to a discussion about art and music.

Five o'clock came and went and Nick ordered take-out dinner over Jayne's halfhearted objections, using the excuse that they needed to discuss how to put Adams and Zander's relationship on a personal footing in addition to a business one. To Nick's intense pleasure, the barriers she lowered stayed down.

"Here's what I suggest," he said toward the end of the evening. "Let's do some digging and see if we can't find a few areas of mutual interest. Then we'll take the two out on some double dates."

She lifted an eyebrow. "Double dates?"

Nick grinned. "The two of us and the two of them. No business, just pleasure. Maybe we can get them out of their foxholes and talking like normal people."

"I think that's a great idea." She gathered up empty containers of Chinese and dumped them in the trash. "I'm not sure you need me for that, though."

"Don't be ridiculous. You're the linchpin to my plan."

She paused in the process of removing his coffee cup. She was so close he could catch the tantalizing scent of her perfume. See the delicious purity of her skin. More than anything he wanted to press his mouth to the delicate hollow at the base of her throat, just as he did each Saturday night. But he didn't dare. Not yet.

"I'm your linchpin?" she asked uncertainly.

"No question. I've noticed that you have a wonderful rapport with both men. You have a knack for putting them at ease. If anyone can draw them out, you can."

A soft flush swept across her cheekbones. "What a lovely compliment. Thanks, Nick."

He dared to tuck a lock of her hair behind her ear and caught a subtle shiver at his touch. "Thanks for staying late but I guess we should call it a night."

She drew back, confusion and awareness slipping across her expression. But he noticed she didn't throw up her barriers again or call him "sir" or retreat behind her corporate mask. She simply remained a woman intensely conscious of him as a man. "I enjoyed our conversation," she admitted.

"So did I. I assume I can count on you to help me entertain Adams and Zander?"

"Absolutely." She made a face. "Assuming they're not into strip clubs. Otherwise, the deal's off."

"No strip clubs," he confirmed gravely. "Good night, Jayne."

"See you tomorrow, Nick."

She smiled and he could tell he'd made a significant breakthrough, one he intended to capitalize on. The two of them had always hit it off on an intellectual level. Now, with the help of Adams and Zander, he and Jayne would connect on an emotional one. By the time he merged himself with her Zorro, he'd have created what he hoped would be an enduring connection between them—intellectually, emotionally, as well as physically.

Until then, he'd have to settle for the various pieces she gave to each identity, no matter how much he longed for an open, straightforward relationship. Patience, he reminded himself. He just had to remain patient until the perfect time.

He could only hope that would be soon.

THE WEEKS CONTINUED TO FLY BY and Jayne decided she'd discovered true Nirvana.

"I have the best of all worlds," she informed Courtney after her latest night of passion. "I work for the most brilliant man in the world. Every day at Fontana, Inc. is better than the last. I'm challenged and stimulated and can't wait to jump up in the morning and get to my desk. And once a week I'm seduced by the most exciting man in the world."

"I wouldn't call a wolf a man," Courtney pointed out.

Jayne dismissed the observation with a wave of her hand. "Details."

"What's this week's fantasy?"

"The roaring '20s."

Courtney brightened. "Oh, flappers. I can help you do flappers. And I know where I can get my hands on the perfect costume for you."

The week before that had been superhero night. The week before that had been Union soldier and Confederate Belle. There had also been vampire night, and the one that had amused her the most—come as your favorite horror movie character.

With each new fantasy came a matching decor for the suite. From antebellum mansion to gothic castle. She didn't know how her Mystery Lover pulled it off week after week. But he did. And he did it with panache. Sometimes she arrived in costume, when the fantasy for that week wasn't too outrageous—at least, by New York standards. Other times she checked in a few hours early so that she could transform herself within the privacy of the bedroom appointed to her. Fortunately, this week wouldn't require an early check-in.

"I just wish…" Jayne began, before breaking off.

"Wish what?" her friend prompted.

"That it could be real." She wrinkled her nose. "Do you know what I mean?"

Courtney snorted. "Girl, you really are asking for the world. Why crave reality when the fantasy is so fabulous? You have a great thing going here. Why ruin it?"

"Because fantasies end."

"Then take my advice. Enjoy it while you can."

Jayne smiled into her glass of wine. She intended to. She intended to savor every last moment of both her temporary job…and her temporary lover. Neither were going to last, no matter how much she might want them to. Eventually, Linda would return from maternity leave and want her job back. Seriously, who wouldn't? At which point Jayne hoped Nick would offer her a group to manage.

As for her romantic escapades, she knew that would end, too. If her Mystery Lover had wanted a real relationship with her, he'd have ditched the disguises long ago. That meant he either wasn't available or he wasn't interested in getting to know her in the real world. What she hadn't quite decided was what to do about it. Nothing for now, she decided. Instead, she'd simply enjoy what she had. But in the weeks that followed, she could feel a change coming. And she knew who was responsible.

Nick Fontana.

She couldn't say when she started to notice the shift in their relationship. A month ago? Six weeks? She struggled to pinpoint the exact time frame and realized it had actually begun that first day at lunch when he'd offered her the position. There'd been a casualness about him…and toward her. He'd been approachable. Interested in more than just her work skills. The more Jayne thought about it, the more she realized his casual attitude had continued over the weeks that followed, especially once they'd begun to entertain Adams and Zander on a social level.

Granted, except for those nights out, most of their interactions were business related. But then there were those times when they slipped from employer/employee into something else. Something more. Something that stirred her eagerness to go to work each day, as well as her excitement when he walked through the door and offered her the warm smile that transformed him from Mr. Intimidating to a one hundred percent full-blooded sexy-as-hell male.

As though her thoughts had conjured him, he stepped into her office. "I have a favor to ask that falls outside your normal work parameters," he announced. It amused her how he rarely offered a greeting when he entered a room, just cut straight to the heart of the matter. "Feel free to refuse if you have other plans."

"I'm sure I can rearrange my schedule." She hit a button on her computer to call up her calendar. "When and where?"

"This Saturday night. I've arranged with Adams and Zander to have dinner and I'm hoping to kick our negotiations into high gear. I think they're ready."

"Saturday night?" she repeated. Her Mystery Lover night?

He lifted an eyebrow. "Problem?" He gave the single word a terse, crisp edge.

Over the weeks they'd worked together, she'd learned to hold her own whenever he turned overbearing or demanding. She simply fell silent and matched him stare for stare, or like now, glare for glare. He folded his arms across his chest and blew out a sigh. It was his silent way of saying, "Okay, I'll tone it down a notch."

Burying a smile, she said, "Yes, there's a problem. I have a date that night."

"Seriously? A date?" His brows snapped together. "Wait. Are you talking about that guy from New Year's Eve? Zorro?"

"Yes, I'm talking about Zorro," she replied calmly.

"That's still going on?"

His amused disbelief annoyed her and it was her turn to answer with a single, terse word. "Yes."

He lifted a shoulder in a shrug. "In that case, it looks like you have a decision to make. Let me know by end of day."

"I don't need time to consider my decision," she found herself replying. "I'll be happy to accompany you on Saturday evening."

"Excellent. I'll pick you up at seven."

She had to give him points. He didn't reveal a hint of smugness or triumph at her capitulation. Maybe a smidge of satisfaction, but it was derived more from a sense of accomplishment at his plan coming together than because she'd chosen her job over her personal life.

She sighed in disappointment. She'd been looking forward to flapper night. Now she'd have to email ML and tell him she wouldn't be able to make it. She didn't delay sending her apologies. She did sweat the two days it took for him to get back to her. The graciousness of his reply helped ease her growing tension.

No problem, he wrote. *I understand completely. It will make our next meeting all the more special because of the delayed anticipation.*

To Jayne's surprise, she found herself looking forward to her evening with Nick every bit as much as she did her romantic encounters. It didn't make a bit of sense. She should have been irritated. Resentful. Longing for the embrace she wouldn't receive. Instead, she couldn't wait to discover what new aspect of Nick's character would be revealed. What new business maneuver he'd trot out. What new golden nugget she'd mine in regard to his personal life.

She dressed carefully, choosing the stereotypical little black dress. But it was a dress she adored. Fitted to discreetly hug her figure, it boasted long sleeves and a simple squared neckline. Her favorite part was when she turned around. A sedate slit from calf to the back of her knee was neatly pleated and accented with black satin while a whimsical flash of red lace peeked out for a wave with each step she took.

Nick showed up at seven on the dot. To her amusement, he had also chosen conservative black and also accented it with a bright red handkerchief peeking from his suit jacket pocket. He couldn't have matched her outfit any better if they'd planned it.

"You look stunning," he said.

"Thanks." She shot him a crooked smile. "So do you."

"Are you ready?"

She picked up her Red Riding Hood cape—the vibrant color perfectly matching the lace at her hemline—and swirled it around her shoulders. "All set."

He gestured toward the stairway. "After you."

There was a low, husky quality to his voice that she'd

never noticed before and the hallway lights of her apartment complex seemed to catch in his hair, picking out the gold threads that were echoed in his hazel eyes. Heaven help her, but he was a gorgeous man, even if it wasn't in the traditional sense.

His face was hewn in harder, tougher lines than Jonathan's, exuding an uncompromising masculinity versus a boyish prettiness. And as clever as Jonathan was, Nick was even more brilliant. Working side by side with him had been the most exhilarating experience of her entire career. She'd discovered that beneath his Mr. Intimidating surface lurked a personality that appealed on every level.

Generous, passionate and compassionate, curious and at times, funnier than hell. Unfortunately, he was also Untouchable with a giant, flashing, red-lettered capital *U*. Not only was he her boss, but he…well…existed in a totally different strata of the atmosphere than she did, one she couldn't reach even with a rocket booster.

"Everything okay?" he prompted as they headed downstairs to the car. "You seem distracted."

Since she couldn't explain that he distracted her, in every way imaginable, she simply shook her head. "No, I'm fine."

"If you wanted to keep your date, you should have just said so." A touch of exasperation frosted his comment. "I wouldn't have held it against you. I'm not that petty."

She paused beside the car door that Nick's driver held open. She gazed up at him, allowing her sincerity to shine through. "I wasn't distracted about that. And just so you know, if my date were more important to me, I would have kept it."

He waited until they were both in the car and maneuvering through the busy downtown traffic before speaking again. "Then why the distraction?"

"I've always admired your tenacity, Nick." She shot him an irritated look. "Until now."

If anything his focus intensified. "Answer my question, Jayne."

CHAPTER EIGHT

SUBTLE LIGHTING ILLUMINATED the back of the car, grop-
ing through the shadows. It caught in Nick's eyes and sank
into the hard, masculine angles of his face. Jayne shivered. For some reason it deepened the intimacy, turning it
from businesslike to something far more personal. Though
some of the noise and bustle from the city penetrated the
soundproofing, she could hear his steady breathing, feel
him on a purely visceral level. It unsettled her more than
she cared to admit.

Realizing he wasn't going to let the subject drop until she
answered, she reluctantly admitted, "It's your fault, Nick.
You distract me." Embarrassed, she turned her head away
to stare through the window. Instead, she found herself
watching him in the reflection of the glass. "You look different tonight."

"What's different about me?" He sounded genuinely
curious. "I'm wearing a suit and tie just like I do every day
at the office."

She shrugged, still not looking at him. "I don't know.
You're just…different."

To her surprise, he caught her chin in the palm of his
hand and turned her to face him. "If anything I should
be the one distracted. I look the same as I always do. But
you've transformed yourself."

Her eyes widened in alarm. "Should I have worn a business suit?"

"Hell, no." His gaze tracked across her face, alerting her to the fact that she'd used a bit more makeup than normal. "You usually wear your hair up."

He continued to cup her face, the texture of his hand as labor-hard and calloused as her Mystery Lover's, revealing that Nick did far more than push pencils all day. "It's more businesslike when I wear it up," she managed to say.

"I like it down." He released her chin and captured a loose curl between his fingers. He was close, oh, so close. The scent of him filled her nostrils, while the sheer strength of his character threatened to overwhelm her. "It's very '40s. Very Lauren Bacall in her heyday. You remind me of her. You share her beauty and elegance. Her intelligence."

She didn't know how to respond. "You flatter me."

He leaned closer, his mouth a breath away from her own. "It's not flattery when it's the truth."

The car pulled to a stop and Nick pulled back. What would have happened if they hadn't arrived just then? she couldn't help but wonder. If the drive had taken just a few precious moments more? Would he have kissed her? Would she have let him? And if he had...if she had, how would it have affected their work relationship?

She drew in a deep, steadying breath. There wasn't any doubt about the answer to that one. It would have ruined it. And if that happened she'd be crushed, not just because it would have an adverse impact on the work front, but because she enjoyed the casually intimate relationship she shared with him. She didn't want to do anything to rock the boat.

Climbing from the car, she donned her work mask, intent on sweeping away any lingering awareness and tension beneath a cool, friendly facade. Fortunately, she'd gotten rather good at pretending these days. Lots of practice donning the various roles she and her Mystery Lover created for their romantic escapades. She'd simply create a new role for herself—the perfect assistant.

By the end of the evening, she had fully relaxed, pleased that she managed to play her part to perfection. Somehow she succeeded in charming Adams, getting him to loosen his grasp on prim, if not on proper. And she kept Zander from pushing any of the older man's hot buttons, teasing him just enough that he was careful never to do or say anything to cause dissension. She even held Nick at a polite distance, though with some difficulty. And she thoroughly enjoyed herself the entire time.

Best of all, Nick managed to get the two men talking about the merger and discussing their differences and how they might overcome them. It was a huge breakthrough and one that promised serious movement in wedding the two enterprises. Jayne was actually sorry when the evening came to an end, and found to her utter surprise that she hadn't missed her romantic rendezvous at all. Well…hardly at all. Her brow wrinkled in bewilderment.

Why didn't it bother her to miss her usual Saturday night date?

It wasn't the passion. She definitely missed that. And it wasn't the role-playing. She thoroughly enjoyed every aspect of that. Could it be her Mystery Lover? Jayne hesitated. She still adored being with him, didn't she?

"Jayne, are you ready?"

She blinked, awareness returning. Both Adams and Zander were gone and Nick stood watching her, his eyes laser-sharp, piercing straight through her until she feared he could read her every thought and emotion. Taking her time, she drank the last of her coffee, then stood, inclining her head with a calmness she was far from feeling. "All set."

"You disappeared again," he commented.

"Yes, I did."

He retrieved her cape from the restaurant cloakroom and wrapped it around her, his hands lingering on her shoulders. "Where did you go?"

"I was thinking."

His mouth settled into a grim line. "Do I have to drag it out of you?"

"You don't have to drag anything out of me, Mr. Fontana." She deliberately retreated into formality. "The last time I checked, my thoughts were my own business."

"You were thinking about *him,* weren't you?"

She tilted her head to one side. "And if I were?"

She could practically see him running through a list of replies, sorting them one by one in the hopes of finding the perfect response. "You're on my time now. Daydream on your own."

Clever. "You're right. I apologize."

To her amusement, he swore beneath his breath. "Damn it, Jayne. You have the most annoying knack of taking the wind out of my sails."

"It is annoying, isn't it?" she sympathized. Naturally, Nick's car was waiting at the curb for them as they left the restaurant. She'd decided long ago that his driver must be a mind reader.

The minute they were ensconced inside, Nick turned to her. "Is there anything I can do to make up for stealing you away from this man you're seeing?" He grimaced. "What's his name?"

"I don't know." She attempted to keep her reply light and careless, but she doubted she'd fooled him. Nick Fontana saw entirely too much.

"Still?" She caught the hint of disapproval in the single word. "What's he hiding?"

"You should know."

He jerked in surprise. "*I* should?"

She swiveled to face him. "You know who he is. You checked into him that first night, remember?"

He dismissed her comment with an impatient wave. "I asked the manager of the Centoria Mark, Mr. Jacks, to look into your Zorro's identity. He wasn't concerned about your safety or well-being, so neither am I. You have no clue?"

She shrugged. "We don't get personal."

"Huh. What do you talk about?"

She opened her mouth and then closed it again. She couldn't believe it. Leave it to Nick. With that one simple question he nailed the source of her dissatisfaction with her romantic escapade. She and ML didn't talk. Not about things that mattered. Not like she and Nick did on those special occasions when business edged into the personal. Of course, it had been her decision to keep her relationship with ML on a purely sexual footing, but still... She and Nick had a purely business relationship. Well, for the most part. And she knew endless things about him.

She turned to Nick with sudden urgency. "I know you, don't I?"

His eyes narrowed in question. "I would hope so. After all, we've been working together for several months now."

She stabbed her finger in his direction. "Right. Exactly. Several months. The same length of time I've been seeing Zorro. For instance, I know you're a liberal. That you care passionately about the welfare of children and animals. I know you received advanced degrees from Harvard and Stanford in international business and finance. I know that when you acquire new companies your preference is to build them up rather than tear them down. You speak four languages fluently."

"Five, but who's counting," he teased. "I also speak an additional four foreign languages rather badly. Fortunately, the two categories don't overlap."

Her lips quivered into a smile, stealing away some of her intensity. "You prefer chocolate over vanilla," she continued her catalog. "You have a fondness for strawberries, but melons make your tongue itch. You like your coffee black, hot and strong, imported from a small finca in Costa Rica."

"Sounds like you've been studying me."

"That's the odd thing." She stared at him, unblinkingly. "I haven't been studying you. At least, not consciously. I've just learned all that by working with you, day in and day out."

"Okay, so what's your point?"

"This man I'm seeing—"

"The man without a name."

"Yes. It isn't just his name I don't know," she confessed. "I know nothing about him as a person. Not his likes and dislikes—other than sexual. Not whether he reads a newspaper or even knows what's going on around him. To be honest, it's my fault we haven't tried to get to know each other better, but even so…" She trailed off and shook her head.

"Sounds like a rather shallow relationship."

"Yes," she murmured. "It is."

And that was the problem. Originally, she thought she wanted a purely physical relationship, one that wouldn't distract her from work. But spending time with Nick made her long for something deeper and more meaningful.

Something with substance. Something that ran the gamut of all aspects of her personality and life, not one narrow area—even if that area was hands-down spectacular.

The worst part of it was…there was someone in her life that fit the bill perfectly. Nick. He was brilliant. He shared all parts of his life with her. He was sexy as sin. Masculine as hell. And though he'd pulled back at the last minute, she didn't doubt for a moment that had he kissed her, she'd have been a goner. Over the months she'd been with her Mystery Lover, she'd learned a lot about herself and her sexuality. The New Year's Eve fireworks display would pale in comparison to the sparks generated if she and Nick ever kissed.

Tonight had brought home one additional fact, a fact she could blame entirely on Nick. Her clandestine meetings at the Centoria Mark were no longer satisfying her. It had gotten to the point where every time she made love to her fantasy partner, she fantasized that he was Nick. What if one night she slipped up and called him by her boss's name? She closed her eyes, conceding the inevitable. The time had come to end her relationship with her Mystery Lover.

IT WAS ALMOST TIME, NICK decided, pleased. Soon he could merge his two identities and create the sort of relationship he longed to have with Jayne. He could tell from her comments that she no longer wanted to hold Zorro at a distance, that she was frustrated by the shallowness of their nights together.

Granted, the sex was off the charts. He'd never experienced such intensity and sexual intimacy with any other woman. But it lacked a matching emotional connection which left them both vaguely dissatisfied. Thank God she'd finally realized that fact.

He considered how he'd handle next weekend when she asked for more from their relationship. Should he tell her the truth then, or give her a few more weeks to get to know him in his Zorro guise? The timing was crucial. If he revealed his identity too soon, she might be offended and embarrassed by his secrecy, which had never been his intention. If he waited too long, he risked the same result.

Maybe he should wait until after the Adams/Zander merger was finalized. That way, if everything worked out the way he hoped, it wouldn't create an unwanted distraction at the office. Or if he misjudged her feelings for him, delaying the big reveal would avoid any unfortunate tension during the final merger negotiations. Delaying the truth would also have one additional benefit for Jayne. If he waited until after the Adams/Zander merger, she would know that her promotion was the result of her own hard work and not wonder if it was because of their sexual relationship.

He glanced at Jayne, tempted beyond reason to reach for her and kiss her. To say to hell with pretense and gamble on the helpless want reflected in her blue eyes. At the last instant, he shook his head. Patience, he reminded himself. Let her admit that she wanted more from her weekend rendezvous before finalizing their personal merger. Just like in all his business dealings, it would be worth it in the long run.

JAYNE SPENT THE ENTIRE WEEK before her final meeting at the Centoria Mark making preparations. First, she emailed ML and informed him that she would like to choose the theme for Saturday night and pay for the suite. He answered almost immediately, agreeing to the first and arguing over the second. But she held firm and eventually he capitulated.

Next she sent him the names of the legendary lovers she'd chosen, wondering if he'd read anything into it. She could only hope that he wouldn't take it badly when she terminated their affair. Surely he knew it would have to end at some point.

For the first time since she started working with Nick, the week dragged. Worse, he picked up on her inattentiveness. Toward the end of Friday—her boss's crunch time—it was at its worse.

"What is it with you, Myleston?" he demanded in exasperation. "Get with it, will you? I want to finish off these final few projects so they don't drag out over the weekend."

"Sorry." She rubbed her forehead, hoping to ease the tension headache rapidly gathering there. "The preliminary contract for the Adams/Zander merger, right? I've flagged the final round of changes and they should be ready to go out first thing Monday."

"Glad you've finally decided to join me." He crossed his office to the wet bar and poured two cups of his special blend coffee. "Forget the contract, Jayne. Come and sit down. Take a load off."

It wasn't a request. She joined him in the sitting area, choosing the chair across the coffee table from the sofa. She accepted the cup he offered with murmured thanks and buried her nose in the fragrant steam drifting upward from the inky surface. She glanced at him, attempting to gauge his mood. With the exception of business negotiations when he was utterly impossible to read, she'd always found him direct and straightforward about his emotions. Right now, he didn't look annoyed so much as concerned.

"What's wrong?" he asked, going straight to the heart of the matter. "You've been off all week."

"You're right." She retreated into formality. "I'm sorry, Nick. I've allowed personal distractions to interfere with my job. I promise it won't happen again."

He swore and she started in surprise, her cup chattering nervously against the saucer. His hazel eyes flashed a golden warning, one she knew from experience to heed. "I thought we knew each other well enough to be honest."

Everything inside of her melted. "I'm sorry," she repeated, though this time her apology was personal. "I've just been trying to make some decisions about my life and where I want to take it and it's split my focus. Still...I shouldn't have allowed that to intrude on my work."

Nick's brows pulled together. "You're not leaving Fontana, Inc."

She couldn't quite tell if it was a question or an order. She shot him a teasing smile. "What and give up the long hours, teetering workload, knockdown, drag-out negotiations, not to mention the pleasure of working with Mr. Intimidating, himself?"

She could tell he didn't quite know whether or not she was serious. "Right," he said. "All that."

"I'm not leaving Fontana, Inc. until you throw me out," she said gently, letting him off the hook.

He visibly relaxed. "That's fine, then."

He fell silent while he drank his coffee, though his gaze never left hers. She recognized it as one of his business tactics. With most people, that patented stare had them babbling like idiots inside a minute, confessing every real or imagined sin. During negotiations, it had his opponents caving to any and all demands. Down in the arena they referred to it as The Look. For some reason, she was immune to it, just as she was immune to his occasional attempts to overwhelm her with the strength of his personality.

She leaned back against the love seat and considered that intriguing fact. Why didn't it bother her? Could it be that she saw Nick differently from the rest of his employees and business associates? Saw past the iconic Fontana to the actual man behind the facade? It was a peculiar thought. A reassuring one, even, considering the feelings she'd developed for him.

"Son of a—"

His cup and saucer hit the coffee table with enough force to shatter the delicate porcelain. Fortunately, it didn't. He climbed to his feet and came for her. She had just enough time to put her own cup and saucer on the coffee table before he hauled her to her feet.

"How do you do it?" he demanded, glaring down at her.

She shook her head in bewilderment. "Do what?"

"You're not the least intimidated by me, are you? You never have been. Whatever I do rolls off of you like frigging raindrops off an oblivious mallard."

She glared at him. "Are you calling me a duck?"

"Yes. A duck. An effing duck." Only he didn't say *effing*.

Maybe if she hadn't been so tired and distracted. Or maybe if they hadn't spent last Saturday night together, she could have responded appropriately, even if he was deliberately pushing her buttons. But how could she when he appealed to her in every possible way?

He was also touching her, his hands warm and firm through her blouse. And he stood so close, the deliciously masculine scent of him flooding her senses. His voice rumbled with power…and something more. A hint of passion. It was just enough to tip her from prudence into foolishness.

"You intimidate me, Nick," she admitted. "But not as my employer."

"Then how?" he demanded.

"As a man."

She slid her arms up his chest and cupped that strong, rugged face in her palms. Lifting onto tiptoe she kissed him, putting every ounce of passion into the taking. He froze…not a good sign. His lips molded briefly to hers and her thoughts flashed to her Mystery Lover and the first kiss they'd shared as one year ended and another began. With a soft cry of utter disbelief, she ripped free. How could she keep kissing one man while longing for the other? It was crazy.

"I'm sorry," she whispered, utterly horrified by what she'd done. "I'm so sorry." She spun on her heel and ran from his office.

"Jayne, wait—"

She ignored him. Dashing to her office, she snatched up her coat and purse. He'd expect her to head for the elevators and would no doubt intercept her there. She made a beeline for the stairs. One floor down she caught an empty elevator headed down. The instant the doors parted on the lobby level, she darted from the building into a wintry snarl of rush-hour traffic.

She was crying uncontrollably by the time she arrived at her apartment building. Instead of going to her room, she banged on Courtney's door, practically falling into her friend's arms when it swung open. Two shots of whiskey later, she stopped crying and stared at her friend through bleary, reddened eyes.

"What is wrong with me?" she demanded. "Tomorrow I plan to end my relationship with ML because whenever we're together all I can think about is Nick. And the first time I kiss Nick—a colossal mistake, by the way—who do I think about?"

Courtney took a wild stab in the dark. "ML?"

Jayne thrust a finger in her friend's direction. "Exactly. Sick. I'm sick. It's the only explanation."

"Hmm." Courtney poured them another round of drinks, looking annoyingly unconcerned. "If you say so."

"What else could it be? I'm falling in love with my boss while having a torrid affair with a man who's name and face I don't even know. You tell me. Is that normal?"

Courtney grinned, toasting Jayne with her shot glass. "Not for the average person, no. But it sure sounds like fun."

Jayne blew out a sigh and stretched out on the couch, hooking her arm across her eyes. "I've come to the conclusion that I'm just not made for fun. It's not in my nature to be outrageous. I'm not Cleopatra or a Southern belle or Dracula's mate or Maid Marian."

"Sure you are. At least, part of you is." Courtney tugged at Jayne's arm, forcing her to sit up again. "Sweetie, a few months ago you were buried beneath a plain Jayne facade. Now look at you. You're vibrant and colorful and dynamic. And it's all because of your Mystery Lover. He released the woman in you. He freed you to be who you really are."

Jayne frowned. "Then you think I should stay with him?"

"Not if you think your feelings for Nick are serious, no." Courtney shrugged. "Only you can make that decision, though I'm a textbook example for why women should never date their boss."

Jayne nodded with a bittersweet smile. "I wish I could

have both. But since I can't, I've already made my decision. Even if Nick fires me or gives me hell for crossing the line with that kiss, I still choose reality over the fantasy."

Courtney shrugged. "If that's what you want." Her expression turned mischievous. "But something tells me come tomorrow night you're going to change your mind."

CHAPTER NINE

SATURDAY EVENING, JAYNE entered the Centoria Mark for the last time. She chatted briefly with Selene, who handed over the key to the Mount Olympus suite. Then Jayne headed for the elevator. She'd decided to give herself this one final night of fantasy and passion. But when morning dawned she planned to say a final farewell to her Mystery Lover and end their affair.

How would he take it when she told him? Would he accept it philosophically and move on to another woman and another series of fantasies? Or would he be disappointed? Would he try and talk her out of her decision? Not that he could.

She entered the Artemis bedroom and paused, her breath catching. The decor topped anything she'd seen to date. She wasn't quite certain it fit the theme she'd suggested for their final rendezvous, but she didn't care. The room had been transformed into a bridal suite. Lace, tulle, pearl-beaded ribbons and pure white teacup roses twined around the posts of the bed and canopied the mattress. A silk virgin-white duvet edged in delicate lace covered the bed, while pure-white tower candles threw a soft glow over the room. The only color in the room came from the rose petals scattered across the duvet, the colors ranging from the palest blush to the deepest ruby-red. Bowls and vases of flowers were everywhere, filling the room with their heady scent.

Slowly she undressed. Tonight she'd be wearing a Renaissance-era gown. She only hoped she wouldn't have any trouble getting into it. But when she opened the large box Courtney had stored it in, Jayne discovered a far different gown. It was utterly beautiful, but not something Juliet would have worn for Romeo.

The dress was made of chiffon, sheer and featherlight, the color variegated like the rose petals on the bed in every shade from sunrise-pink to deepest rose. It boasted an empire waist while two spaghetti straps held the bodice in place. The chiffon was tightly ruched across her breasts, practically serving them up on a platter. And the dress even had a train, the airy material flowing and rippling behind her with each step she took.

Deep inside the folds of tissue she discovered a necklace, a simple silver chain with a huge teardrop diamond set in delicate filigree threads of silver. No doubt it was one of the props from Courtney's soap opera, but it was a beautiful piece and looked surprisingly real. Once Jane had secured the diamond around her neck, she checked the mirror. She'd decided to leave her hair down in the style Nick had admired the week before. It suited both the gown and her mood, if not the role of Juliet.

She knocked softly on the door between her bedroom and the salon before entering. To her surprise the salon was also decorated like a bridal suite with more candles, these in a deep shade of ruby. In addition to the candles, floral arrangements decorated every surface. Romeo stood in the shadows at one end of the room and she hesitated, suddenly realizing he wasn't dressed in character, either. Instead he wore a black tux, a gray-and-white-striped cummerbund, gray gloves and a dashing black mask.

For the first time since he'd seduced her, Jayne felt an

odd hesitation. "This doesn't look like *Romeo and Juliet*," she offered by way of greeting.

"No, *signorina*. I am not a fan of that particular play."

She relaxed. She knew that soft, husky voice, pitched whisper-soft and hungry with passion. "Your Italian accent is even better than your Spanish."

"There is a reason for that."

"Are you Italian?" she asked lightly.

He inclined his head. "My family came from Italy, though it was many generations ago." He escaped the shadows and approached. "I'm glad you've finally asked me a personal question. I was hoping you would eventually."

She frowned. "And why is that?"

"Because I've discovered that a purely sexual relationship isn't enough for me. I want more."

Jayne was so taken aback she didn't know what to say. He reached her side and cupped her face, lifting her for his kiss. Gently, oh so gently, he nibbled a path across her lips before sinking in, deepening the embrace. For a few precious seconds she melted against him. One last night, she reminded herself. One final night of passion. His arms tightened, sealing her against him, allowing her to feel his hunger.

"I missed you last week."

"I—" She started to say, "I missed you, too," but something stopped her. The truth. The truth stopped her. She allowed him to kiss her once again, then carefully eased back, slipping free of his grasp. "I didn't miss you," she confessed. "Not the way I thought I would."

He froze. "Not at all?"

She studied his eyes through the slits of the mask. He'd chosen to use the bitter chocolate contacts from their first meeting and she found it annoying that she didn't know the true color of his eyes. Even that was a fantasy. A lie. "I missed...pretending. I missed the fun we have." She forced herself to admit the painful truth. "I missed the sex. You are truly amazing in bed."

"We," he corrected. "We are truly amazing in bed."

It was hard to read his expression, much harder than reading Nick's, probably because of the mask ML hid behind. "I thought I could handle one last night with you," she murmured.

"But you can't." When she didn't reply, he inclined his head. "I wondered when you said the theme would be *Romeo and Juliet* if you were sending me a subtle hint."

"You're right. I was."

He waited, much as Nick waited when he wanted her to break the silence. When she didn't, he said, "So did you come to say goodbye or are you here for one last night in my arms?"

"I thought I came for both." She offered a self-deprecating smile. "I didn't realize that I couldn't spend another night with you."

"Why?" He bit the question out, hard and sharp.

"Honestly?"

"At the risk of completely destroying the fantasy... yes."

"Considering the time we've spent together, it's only fair." She took a deep breath and confessed, "There's some-one else."

"Ah." For some reason her admission caused him to relax. "And this man...he feels the same way about you?"

"No," she admitted. "But that doesn't really matter. I have feelings for him and because I do, it makes it impossible for me to be with another man. Can you understand that?"

"Yes, as a matter of fact, I can."

As difficult as it was, she offered him the only gift she had left to give. "I won't ask your identity. Maybe it's best if you don't tell me. And I'm sorry I couldn't give you the sort of relationship you were obviously hoping for." Weariness settled over her like a heavy blanket and she felt precariously close to tears. "If you don't mind, I'd like to go home." She didn't wait for his response, but turned toward the door to her suite.

"Jayne."

That one single word stopped her dead in her tracks. He'd dropped the accent. Tossed off the low, husky whisper. Her name resonated with power and strength and a familiarity she couldn't ignore. She knew that voice. Knew it intimately. Worked with it every single day. His mask came spinning over her shoulder, hitting the ground directly in front of her.

She shook her head. "No."

"Jayne," Nick repeated.

She whirled around, facing her boss, fury and anger vying for control. "No! How could you? How dare you?"

"Because I wanted you and couldn't think of any other way to have you without causing serious complications at work."

The blunt truth struck her like a blow. "*You* wanted. *You* took." She fought to catch her breath. She was simply an object to him, a toy to be picked up and played with until he became bored. "You son of a bitch! You didn't give a damn about how I might feel."

He managed to look utterly bewildered. "Your feelings matter to me above everything else. Why else would I have gone to this much trouble?"

"You played me, Nick. You played me for an utter fool." She rushed toward him, pulling up short just before she reached him. Hauling back her arm, she slapped him, putting every ounce of strength into the blow. "Consider that my resignation."

"Jayne, wait! Please, let me explain."

But she didn't wait. Couldn't wait. She darted across the salon to the Artemis bedroom. Slamming the door closed behind her, she threw the dead bolt between the two rooms. It only took a few minutes to strip off her gown and change into her street clothes. To her profound relief, Nick was nowhere to be seen when she exited the suite. If he had been, she suspected she'd have said something unforgivable. Done something unforgivable.

Tears blurred her vision. Instead, she'd return home and have the entire weekend to wallow in her humiliation.

NICK SWORE BENEATH HIS BREATH.

He'd screwed up royally. All he'd wanted from the start was to protect Jayne. Protect her from office gossip. Protect her from any discomfort she might feel if he'd originally approached her as her boss. Protect her from feeling obligated to leave Fontana, Inc. if their relationship didn't work out.

Instead, he'd made her feel like a fool. He ripped off his tux jacket and slung it over a nearby chair. He couldn't remember a time when he'd screwed up a merger this badly. Maybe if he'd been attempting a business deal the end result would have been different. But Jayne wasn't a business and couldn't be treated like one.

Hell, he should have realized that. But he'd been so blinded by his eagerness to finally forge a relationship with her, he hadn't been able to consider all the possible angles. He was too close to the situation to weigh his options rationally.

He heard the outer door to Jayne's bedroom slam shut. He was tempted to go after her, but knew better. She needed time to cool off. Like maybe a year or two. Damn it all! How did he explain to her that he wanted her from the moment he'd first set eyes on her? That he'd had any number of affairs go south because the women he'd dated only saw the Fontana name, never the actual man? That he'd hoped when he approached her at the New Year's Eve ball he could seduce her and then reveal the truth in such a way that she'd be open to having a relationship with him. A real relationship.

She'd never give him the chance now. Nor could he come up with an alternate plan. He stared at the locked door to the Artemis suite. Probably just as well since his plans and Jayne seemed to be diametrically opposed.

JAYNE PACED THE TINY apartment. "The simple truth is, he played me, Courtney."

"I suppose you're right," her friend replied, but doubt wove through her voice.

"What other explanation is there? He knew I didn't want to get involved with someone at work, so this was his clever way around it."

"How did he know?" Courtney asked diffidently.

Jayne frowned. "What?"

"How did Nick know that you didn't want to get involved with a coworker?"

"Well, I…I told him, of course."

"When?" Courtney tilted her head to one side, her bright red hair a brilliant contrast to her neon purple T-shirt. "Before or after the charity ball?"

"It was—" Jayne's frown deepened. "Okay, it was after. But, still. Why did he seduce me at the ball while pretending to be Jonathan?"

"I don't know. What did he have to say for himself?"

Jayne sank onto the couch. "To be honest, after I slapped him, he didn't say much of anything."

Courtney's eyes bugged out. "You slapped Nick Fontana?" she asked in awe.

"Oh, God. I did, didn't I?" Jayne fought to keep from hyperventilating. "But he deserved it. What he did was wrong on so many levels."

"Jayne, I've listened to you talk endlessly about Nick ever since New Year's. Even before New Year's. Not once has he given you the impression that he's a user or intent on getting beneath the skirt of every woman he meets. Jonathan, yes. But not Nick. You need to talk to the man and find out why he tricked you the way he did. You deserve to know and he should be forced to explain himself."

"I don't know…"

"You still have to clean out your desk, don't you?"

"Yes." Jayne closed her eyes, wanting to weep. Her job. She loved her job. Loved working for Nick. Or she had. "I don't want to see him again. It's too embarrassing knowing what we—" She broke off with a groan as a series of images flashed through her mind, images of the two of them together in their various sexual disguises.

Courtney wrinkled her nose, picking up on the cause of Jayne's distress. "Yeah, that's harsh. All this time he knew it was you. Saw you naked. And all the while you were totally clueless."

Jayne flinched. "Courtney, please."

"Sorry." She curled up next to Jayne and gave her a swift hug. "So, go talk to him. At the very least you can give him another slap, right?"

"Right."

But for some reason Jayne didn't want to, not now that the first flash of anger had faded. She simply wanted to curl up in a miserable little ball and make the events of the past several months disappear. But Courtney was right. Jayne needed to face him. It took her the entire day Sunday and several hours Monday morning to gather the nerve to go into work. The instant she approached the desk of Nick's PA, she was waved straight through.

"Go right in. He's been expecting you, Ms. Myleston."

Jayne found her boss—her *ex*-boss—standing at the bank of windows, resting his forearm against the glass while he stared broodingly out at the cityscape. "Nick."

He stiffened, turned, his expression one of intense relief. "You came to work. I wasn't sure you would."

"Only to clear out my desk, and—"

"And?" he prompted.

She steeled herself. "And to demand an explanation."

He fixed her with a wary gaze. "I tried to explain on Saturday."

"I wasn't ready to hear what you had to say on Saturday." She folded her arms across her chest. "I am now."

He chose his words with care. "You want to know why I went to the extreme measure of approaching you at the New Year's Eve ball in disguise instead of inviting you out on a normal date?"

Jayne nodded. "That would be a good place to start, yes."

"I couldn't approach you in the real world," he stated simply. "I'm your boss."

"So you disguised yourself as Jonathan—"

"As Zorro," he cut in.

She wouldn't let him get away with the distinction. "Knowing I'd assume you were Jonathan. Knowing I *did* assume you were Jonathan."

The muscles along his jaw tightened. "I told you any number of times that I wasn't."

She ignored that. "All so you could get me into bed."

"I never thought the night would go that far."

"Then why the suite?" she shot back. "You had the room all primed for seduction."

The muscles along his jawline flexed and tightened. "Okay, fine. I hoped. Hoped we'd end the night there."

"Hoped I wouldn't trip to the fact that you weren't Jonathan. You even wore contacts that matched Jonathan's eye color."

Nick ran a hand through his hair and blew out a sigh. He spun to face her. "Fine. I knew you'd think I was Jonathan, though I hoped you'd realize I was someone different before we went to the suite. Someone better. Do you have any idea how difficult it is for me to get to know a woman without the Fontana trappings?" he asked in a low, harsh voice.

She refused to cut him any slack. "Poor you."

"Damn it, Jayne! That ball finally gave me the opportunity to meet a woman on an even footing, a woman I'd wanted to get to know better for eighteen endless months," he persisted. "Until that night, all the women in my life only ever saw the Fontana name and fortune. They could give two damns about whether or not I have the personality of a kumquat."

Despite herself, Jayne felt her lips twitch and clamped down on her amusement with ruthless self-control. "That's very sad, Nick."

"It is." He paced in front of her like a caged lion. "Especially when I finally meet a woman who appeals on every possible level. Unfortunately, she works for me and I can't lay a finger on her because it could open me up to a sexual harassment lawsuit. So, I watch from the sidelines for all those endless months while she moons over that oblivious ass, Blair, and pray that he won't notice her. That he won't take her and use her and dump her like he has every other woman."

Bright color lit Jayne's cheeks. "Would you have stopped him?" The question escaped before she could prevent it.

He approached. "Hell, yes, I would have stopped him. Somehow. Some way. But I didn't have to, did I? Because the perfect opportunity finally presented itself."

She lifted her chin and glared. "All because you wanted to sleep with me before Jonathan did?"

"No. All because I wanted to sleep with you first, last and forever. Because I wanted to find a way to seduce you—not just in the bedroom, but on all possible fronts. After we spent the night together I was going to admit the truth."

"I don't believe you." Didn't dare believe him.

"Why the hell would I lie now?" His hands fisted. "I was going to tell you at lunch the Monday after the charity ball. But right before the big reveal, you informed me that after what happened with Jonathan—when I found you together in your office—you'd never date a coworker. That you particularly wouldn't date me."

Jayne froze. She had, hadn't she? She remembered the conversation almost word for word. "You should have told me anyway."

"Looking back, you're right. But you were so earnest. So determined to win my respect and move ahead in the company. So an alternate solution occurred to me. I could continue the masquerade. I'd attempt to seduce you as your Zorro. That once our relationship deepened I'd tell you who I really was. But I miscalculated. Badly."

Jayne struggled to keep his words from affecting her, but there was such raw passion and sincerity in what he said that it was a struggle to hang on to her anger. "You, the great Nick Fontana, miscalculated?"

A mocking smile touched his mouth, a mouth she'd spent endless nights kissing. It still came as a shock to know that the man she'd been making love to for the past several months was actually Nick. She found it unsettling. Embarrassing. And oddly exciting.

"You informed me, in my Mystery Lover guise, that you only wanted sex. So now I was really stuck. How was I supposed to create a relationship with a woman who insisted on holding me at an emotional distance?"

"What did you decide?" She realized something the instant she asked the question. She believed him. There was no mistaking the rawness of his honesty or the pain in his voice and attitude. "What was your next plan of action?"

"To attempt a business solution to a personal problem. I decided to seduce you on both fronts and then merge the two identities." He grimaced. "You see how well that worked."

"I can't help but wonder if on some level I didn't know you were my Mystery Lover," she admitted. "Maybe I was deliberately overlooking all the clues—like how you managed to email me through my company address. Your ability to rent such an expensive suite week after week. How you knew what Jonathan intended to wear to the ball. Maybe I was afraid to question it too closely in case I figured it out."

"And was forced to act on your newfound knowledge?"

"Yes." She closed her eyes. "But after a while I couldn't let the affair continue."

"Because you fell for Nick. Me." He shook his head. "Hell, you know what I mean. You fell for the real man, not the fantasy."

"I thought I did."

Passion exploded in his gaze. "You know you did. I may have handled this badly but that doesn't change our feelings for each other. Maybe it would have been simpler if you'd fallen for Zorro or Robin Hood or Blackbeard."

He'd lost her. "I don't understand," she said. "Why would that have made things simpler?"

"Because it would have given us more time, time for our relationship to deepen and develop."

"And now?" She couldn't help asking the question.

His jaw set. "I won't give you up." Before she could stop him, he gathered her in his arms. "Whether it's as Nick and Jayne, or Zorro and Cleopatra, or any of the other characters we've played, one simple fact hasn't changed. We belong together. Please, Jayne. I love you. Give us a chance."

Everything within her melted. How could she refuse when he offered exactly what she wanted? When every emotion he expressed mirrored her own. "I...I'd like that," she confessed.

He kissed her then, a kiss filled with fantasy and romance...and a delicious reality. She fought for reason. Fought to retain her sanity. But sanity vanished beneath the onslaught of his mouth. The familiar sweep of his hands. The distinctive press of his body. She could feel her anger and distrust fade, replaced by a need and a joy and a love that transcended everything else.

He released her long enough to snatch up the phone. "Hold all calls," he instructed his PA. "I don't want to be interrupted for any reason."

Then he swept her into his arms. He paused by the door to the outer office and locked it, then carried her to the couch in the sitting room. Slowly he undressed her, then himself. For the first time, Jayne felt a touch of self-consciousness which made her laugh.

"How many times have we done this?" she marveled. "And yet, I'm actually feeling shy."

"I think I can fix that." He wrapped his arms around her. "Close your eyes."

"Nick—"

"Shh. Just do it. Close them." He cupped her face and feathered a soft kiss across her mouth. "Now feel and remember."

The minute she did as he asked everything snapped back into place. She knew this man, adored him, was intimately familiar with his shape and size and weight. With the way he kissed and the tenor of his touch. She relaxed into the embrace.

"I love you, Nick. I can't believe I'm saying that," she marveled. "This is the best fantasy, yet."

"Maybe because it isn't a fantasy. It's reality."

He took it slow, acting as though it were their first time together, which in a way it was. She wanted this moment to last while he built sensation upon sensation. She whispered his name—his real name—and felt his shudder, knew that he'd been longing for her, just once, to make love to him, to Nick, instead of a mysterious fantasy man. And so she called to him, swept him off to a place where reality and fantasy met and melded.

To Jayne's delight, that day proved more spectacular than any night that had gone before. And she knew why. She'd finally gotten her wish, had been given the best of both worlds. She'd found a man who made reality a fantasy and who had turned her every fantasy into reality.

Eighteen months later...

JAYNE APPROACHED THE registration desk at the Centoria Mark and greeted Selene with a broad smile. "Good evening. I believe you have a reservation for me?"

"Why, yes, Mrs. Fon—" She broke off with a chagrined

laugh. "Sorry, I mean, Ms. Angel. I have your key right here. Your usual room is ready for you."

"Would you happen to know if Mr. Lucifer has checked in yet?"

"He has. He checked in a half hour ago." Selene leaned forward. "He mentioned something about a little surprise."

"Did he?" Jayne grinned. "I do believe he's in for a little surprise of his own."

"I hope you have a lovely evening," Selene said with a wistful sigh. "But then, I guess you always do."

How could Jayne deny it when it was the truth? With a quick wave, she headed for the elevators and then on to her suite. She opened the Artemis door and stepped into heaven. To her amusement, cherubs looked on while angelic hosts sang through speakers concealed around the room.

She couldn't wait to see what Nick—er, Lucifer—had done with his bedroom. She looked forward to sampling all that heaven offered, as well as the sinfully delicious Underworld. After donning her costume and checking to make sure she looked suitably angelic, she headed for the salon and her Lover from Down Under. He was waiting for her, wearing a lot of red body paint, horns and little else.

"G'day, mate," he greeted her with a broad grin.

She burst out laughing at his Aussie accent. "Brilliant. Absolutely brilliant." She approached her husband. "I have it on excellent authority that you have a surprise for me."

He opened the champagne and poured the wine into two crystal flutes. He handed her one of the glasses, along with a small box. "Happy anniversary, darling. It doesn't matter whether we're in heaven or hell, so long as we're there together."

She deliberately set down the flute—no alcohol for her—and opened the box. Inside were a pair of earrings that matched the diamond necklace he'd given her the night she'd discovered his true identity. A diamond necklace that hadn't been a prop or fantasy, but the real thing.

"They're beautiful," she told him, wrapping her arms around his neck. "Thank you."

"You're welcome." He glanced down at her white gown. "I'm afraid some of this body paint may be rubbing off on your dress."

"That's what I get for giving in to temptation," she teased. She lifted for his kiss, slowed it down, then deepened it. How was it possible that it only got better? "Are you ready for your gift?"

He shook his head. "I think you already gave it to me."

"Not yet. Not for about seven more months."

It took a split second before he understood. He grinned broadly. "Son of a— You're pregnant?"

"I am. And there's only one question." She snuggled close. "Am I expecting an angel…or a devil?"

"It doesn't matter." He slipped a hand and rested it low on his wife's abdomen. "Angel or imp, this is one reality that beats the hell out of every other fantasy."

* * * * *

Try these Healthy and Delicious Spring Rolls!

INGREDIENTS

2 packages rice-paper spring roll wrappers (20 wrappers)

1 cup grated carrot

¼ cup bean sprouts

1 cucumber, julienned

1 red bell pepper, without stem and seeds, julienned

4 green onions finely chopped— use only the green part

DIRECTIONS

1. Soak one rice-paper wrapper in a large bowl of hot water until softened.

2. Place a pinch each of carrots, sprouts, cucumber, bell pepper and green onion on the wrapper toward the bottom third of the rice paper.

3. Fold ends in and roll tightly to enclose filling.

4. Repeat with remaining wrappers. Chill before serving.

Find this and many more delectable recipes including the perfect dipping sauce in

YOUR BEST BODY NOW

by

TOSCA RENO

WITH STACY BAKER

Bestselling Author of
THE EAT-CLEAN DIET®

Available wherever books are sold!

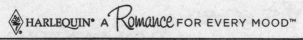

HARLEQUIN® A *Romance* FOR EVERY MOOD™

SUSPENSE & PARANORMAL

Heartstopping stories of intrigue and mystery—
where true love always triumphs.

Harlequin Intrigue®
Breathtaking romantic suspense. Crime stories that will keep you on the edge of your seat.

Silhouette® Romantic Suspense
Heart-racing sensuality and the promise of a sweeping romance set against the backdrop of suspense.

Harlequin® Nocturne™
Dark and sensual paranormal romance reads that stretch the boundaries of conflict and desire, life and death.

Look for these and many other Harlequin and Silhouette romance books wherever books are sold, including most bookstores, supermarkets, drugstores and discount stores.

SUSCAT

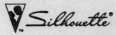

ROMANTIC

SUSPENSE

Sparked by Danger, Fueled by Passion.

CARLA CASSIDY

Special Agent's Surrender

There's a killer on the loose in Black Rock,
and former FBI agent Jacob Grayson isn't about
to let Layla West become the next victim.

While she's hiding at the family ranch under Jacob's
protection, the desire between them burns hot.
But when the investigation turns personal,
their love and Layla's life are put on the line,
and the stakes have never been higher.

A brand-new tale of the

LAWMEN of BLACK ROCK

Available in March wherever books are sold!

Visit Silhouette Books at www.eHarlequin.com

SRS27718

REQUEST YOUR FREE BOOKS!
2 FREE NOVELS PLUS 2
FREE GIFTS!

HARLEQUIN *Romance*.

From the Heart, For the Heart

HR10R2